By

Tom Barber

*****

The Getaway
Copyright: Tom Barber
Published: 29th June 2012

The right of Tom Barber to be identified as author of
this Work has been asserted by he in accordance with
sections 77 and 78 of the Copyright, Designs and
Patents Act 1988.

This book is a work of fiction and, except in the case
of historical fact, any resemblance to actual persons,
living or dead, is purely coincidental.

The Sam Archer thriller series
by
Tom Barber

NINE LIVES

26 year old Sam Archer has just been selected to join
a new counter-terrorist squad, the Armed Response
Unit. And they have their first case. A team of suicide
bombers are planning to attack London on New
Year's Eve. The problem?
No one knows where any of them are.

THE GETAWAY

Archer is in New York City for a funeral. After the
service, an old familiar face approaches him with a
proposition. A team of bank robbers are tearing the
city apart, robbing it for millions.
The FBI agent needs Archer to go undercover and try
to stop them.

BLACKOUT

Three men have been killed in the UK and USA in
one morning. The deaths take place thousands of
miles apart, yet are connected by an event fifteen
years ago. Before long, Archer and the ARU are
drawn into the violent fray. And there's a problem.
One of their own men is on the extermination list.

SILENT NIGHT

A dead body is found in Central Park, a man who was killed by a deadly virus. Someone out there has more of the substance and is planning to use it. Archer must find where this virus came from and secure it before any more is released.

But he is already too late.

ONE WAY

On his way home, Archer saves a team of US Marshals and a child they are protecting from a violent ambush in the middle of the Upper West Side. The group are forced to take cover in a tenement block in Harlem, their ambushers locking them in and sealing off the only way in or out of the building.

And there are more killers on the way to finish the job.

RETURN FIRE

Four months after they first encountered one another, Sam Archer and Alice Vargas are both working in the NYPD Counter-Terrorism Bureau and also living together. But a week after Vargas leaves for a trip to Europe, Archer gets a knock on his front door.

Apparently Vargas has completely disappeared.

And it appears she's been abducted.

GREEN LIGHT

A nineteen year old woman is gunned down in a Queens car park, the latest victim in a brutal gang turf war that goes back almost a century. Suspended from duty, his badge and gun confiscated, Archer is nevertheless drawn into the fray as he seeks justice for the girl. People are going missing, all over New York.

And soon, so does he.

Also:

CONDITION BLACK (A novella)

In the year 2113, a US 101st Airborne soldier wakes up after crash landing on a moon somewhere in space. All but two of his squad are dead. He has no idea where he is, or who shot him down.

But he quickly learns that some nightmares don't stop when you wake up.

To all my friends in Astoria and at the Esper Studio.

ONE

They were in and out of the bank in three minutes.

It was late summer, a beautiful August morning in New York City, and the heat and humidity were at just the right level, pleasantly warm yet not stifling or uncomfortable. Above Manhattan, the sun beat down from the cloudless sky on the sea of tall buildings and skyscrapers scattered all over the island below. It had been a scorcher of a summer, the daily temperature consistently in the high 80s, but today was slightly cooler and brought much welcome relief for the eight million people living in the city area.

It was just past 9 am, Monday. As a consequence the streets were flooded with people making their way to work, sipping coffees, talking into phones or just striding on, head down, ready to get to the office and get started. The sidewalks and subway were crowded, but the slight drop on the thermostat meant that tempers were under control, making the journey into work a little more pleasant than it had been earlier in the summer.

One particular business opening its doors for service that Monday morning was a Chase Manhattan Bank. It was located on 2nd Avenue between 62nd and 63rd Streets, towards the southern tip of the Upper East Side, a neighbourhood running up the right side of Central Park that was renowned all over the world for its affluence and wealth. Chase had thirty banks in various locations all over Manhattan and this was one of the best placed of them all.

Across the United States, Chase as a financial institution enjoyed a staggering amount of daily custom and had amounts of cash in their reserves that could cure a third-world country's deficit. With a company ATM inside the hundreds of Duane Reade drug stores in the city and immaculately clean and professional branch headquarters set up in locations such as this, it came as no surprise that Chase was one of the founding pillars of

8

The Big Four, the four banks that held 39 % of every customer deposit across the United States. As a business, Chase had earned all those dollars and custom with the convenience of their branch locations and their excellent quality of service. They were renowned as one of the most reliable and dependable banks out there and it was a reputation they had worked hard to earn.

On that summer day it was also the last Monday of the month, August, and that meant something else to this particular bank.

Delivery day.

To keep the branch fully supplied with dollar currency, two men and a thick white armoured truck arrived at 9 am sharp every second Monday, never early, never late. One of the two men would step outside, unload a considerable amount of money from a hatch on the side of the vehicle and then take it into the bank, headed straight to the vault. It was an awkward yet vital part of running a financial institution: no bank can operate without money inside. Most modern banks around the world were built like military bunkers, the kind of places to give bank robbers nightmares. But for those twenty minutes or so each month whenever cash was delivered the bank was momentarily vulnerable, their collective managers secretly on edge despite their pretending to the contrary.

On the other side of the deal, anyone who decided to take a job inside the armoured truck was made well aware of the risks that came with that line of work before they signed on the dotted line. With the second highest mortality rate amongst all security roles in the United States, anyone inside one of these vehicles knew three undeniable facts.

One.

There were people out there who had a great interest in killing you.

Two.

doctors' overcoats, the kind a GP or a chemist would wear in a lab, also fresh from the packets. The driver wasn't wearing one; he was staying in the car and wouldn't need it.

The outfits were crisp and clean, covering every possible source of trace evidence, not a speck or stain on any part or any piece of the white fabric. If anyone studied them, the outfits would seem absurd; the three passengers were wearing a medic and a doctor's uniform combined, something that never happened at the hospital or in the O.R. But to a casual observer, the clothing wouldn't cast suspicion. There were much stranger and wackier outfits being worn across the city at that very moment, outfits far more peculiar than these.

Beside the driver, the guy in the front passenger seat checked his watch.

9:04 am.

He glanced up at the front door of the Chase branch.

No sign of the guard returning yet.

Inside the bank, the time lock on the vault would be off for another six minutes.

The world-wide back and forth battle between banks and thieves throughout history had seen modern vaults become close to impenetrable from the outside. The latest designs were cased with thick, steel-reinforced concrete, rendering the vaults themselves stronger than most nuclear bomb shelters. There was a famous story from the past of how four Japanese bank vaults in Hiroshima had survived the Atomic bomb of 1945. When survivors and rescue aid had eventually worked their way through the ruins of the city, they'd discovered the steel vaults fully intact. And when they got each one open, they also found that all the money inside was unharmed while everything else around each vault had been completely levelled by the devastating nuclear blast and subsequent fallout. The designs in those Teikoku banks that day were now over sixty years old. Bank

12

vaults were amazingly resilient back then, able to withstand nuclear weapons, but now they were as close to impenetrable as was humanly possible to design.

The model in this particular Chase bank could definitely survive the same kind of destruction and punishment. It was a rock-solid piece. Two layers, an outer steel and concrete shell controlled by a spinlock code leading into a second vault, which was opened by simple lock-and-key and only by the bank manager himself. Once closed, it was pretty much impossible to open. Explosives would be useless. Anyone who tried to use them to open it would bring the building down before they made a scratch on the surface. And even if the correct combination was entered on the outer spinlock dial, the vault still wouldn't open outside this fortnightly ten-minute window.

But despite those factors and the seemingly insurmountable odds, the four thieves inside the taxi were cool, calm and confident.

Because they knew one unalterable fact.

No matter how strong any bank vault was, at some point it had to be opened.

The man in the front seat checked his watch again. 9:05 am. He looked over at the bank, lit up in the morning sunlight. Still no sign of the tubby guard. He hadn't come back out yet.

Any major drop-off, deposit or withdrawal from the vault itself had to happen every fourteen days in those two ten-minute periods. The manager had to plan all those things far in advance and operate fast from the moment the big hand on the clock ticked to 9am, working through a spread-sheet of planned transactions and satisfying every business and customer on the sheet. Hundreds of thousands of dollars were delivered from the truck, topping up the branch's supply from the banking organisation itself, and equal amounts were often withdrawn. But outside that ten minute window

13

every fortnight, the electronic lock would stay shut and the vault wouldn't open, even if the correct code was entered.

An extra security measure was also to have an alarm code. If under duress or with a gun to their head, a manager or teller could pretend to enter the code to the vault and instead enter a six-digit code that triggered a silent alarm. The thieves would be standing there, waiting for the steel vault to open and suddenly find an entire police ESU team bursting in through the front doors behind them. Banks and their security divisions were constantly having to come up with new ways to foil any attempted bank robbery, methods and tricks the thieves didn't yet know about; the silent alarm dial code was one of the latest and favourite measures at their disposal.

The man checked his watch again.

9:06 am.

Four minutes to go.

He didn't panic. He'd observed the last four drop-offs. The guards in the truck, despite both being out of shape and relatively slow, always worked to a clock and the fat guy inside would be out in the next minute, giving them three left to work with.

One hundred and eighty seconds.

Plenty of time.

And just then, right on cue, the front door of the bank swung open. The guard reappeared, walking to the truck, and tapped the passenger door three times with his fist, waiting for his partner inside to put down his newspaper and unlock it.

'Mark,' said the man inside the taxi.

He watched the guard pull open the door and step inside the truck. At the same time, all four of the thieves in the taxi looked down and clicked a black digital Casio stopwatch wrapped around their wrists. The clock was ticking.

14

They had three minutes and counting.

The next instant, the guy behind the wheel took off the handbrake. Above them, the light flicked to green, perfect timing, and the driver moved the taxi forward, parking outside the bank like he was dropping off a customer. As the armoured truck drove off ahead of them and turned the corner, disappearing out of sight, the guy in the front passenger seat of the taxi grabbed the receiver to the vehicle radio off its handle. It had been retuned from the taxi dispatch depot to the NYPD frequency. He gripped it in his gloved hand and pushed down the buttons either side.

'Officer down, I repeat, Officer down!' he yelled into the handle. *'I'm on East 95th and 1st! I need back-up, goddammit!'*

As he spoke, the man and woman in the back seat lifted white surgical masks over the lower half of their faces, right up to their eyes, and pulled scrub hats over the top, concealing the upper half of their heads. All four of them were already wearing large aviator sunglasses, covering their eyes, the defining characteristic that would leave them identifiable to a witness and CCTV. Not wasting a second, the three thieves pushed open the doors and moved swiftly out of the car, the driver remaining behind the wheel, checking his watch.

From his seat he watched the rear-view mirror and saw a commotion in the traffic behind them, right on cue.

Police cars were streaming into the street from a building four blocks north, speeding east and north, their lights flashing, responding to the distress call. He smiled.

The NYPD's 19th Precinct, New York City's finest.

Every car and officer heading the opposite way.

And at that same moment, the three thieves entered the bank.

The second they passed through the front doors, the trio moved fast. The first task was to subdue everyone inside, most importantly the two guards. That had to happen before anything else. The man and woman from the back seat each pulled out a weapon hanging from a black strap looped around their right shoulders, hidden under the doctor's coats. They were two Ithaca 37 12-gauge shotguns, police issue, the stocks sawn off so the weapons could be concealed under the coats. Clyde Barrow of *Bonnie and Clyde* fame had come up with the idea of removing the stock and hiding a shotgun under a coat when pulling a heist. The weapons possessed brutal power and with the stocks gone they were a cinch to conceal, unlike machine guns which were too bulky and wide to hide effectively. Clyde had called the sawn-off shotgun a *whippit*. The Sicilians, who were fond of the weapon themselves, called it a *lupara*. With seven shells locked and loaded inside the weapons, the three thieves robbing this bank called it instant crowd control.

They ran forward, each racking a shell by pulling the brown slide on the barrel of the weapon back and forth with their left hand, the weapons crunching as a shell was loaded into each chamber. Across the bank floor, customers turned and saw the sudden commotion. It took a split second for what they were seeing to fully register in their brains.

Then they reacted, some of them covering their mouths as others started to scream.

There were two guards in the bank, Walter Pick and Peter Willis, both retired NYPD, both sporting a paunch that middle age and the promise of an imminent pension brought. Both men also had a Glock 17 on their hip, like the two guys in the truck, but neither had a moment to reach for it as the three thieves ran forward, two of them brandishing the sawn-off shotguns, shoving them in people's faces.

'Down! Everybody down! Down!' they shouted.

Meanwhile, the big guy who'd been in the front passenger seat of the taxi had already vaulted the counter. He was the point man, the guy who would control the room, but his first job was to get to the tellers. He knew the button for the silent alarm and the direct line to the 19th Precinct four blocks away was by the third teller's foot. Before the woman had time to react and push it with her toe, he was already too close, pulling his own shotgun from under his coat, racking a round and pointing the weapon an inch from her face.

'Up! Get up!' he shouted. *'UP!'*

He grabbed the woman by her hair and hauled her from her seat, dragging her around the counter and throwing her to the floor to join the others. He turned, the shotgun aimed at the other tellers, and they all rose and rushed out to the main bank floor quickly, joining everyone else face down on the polished marble, trembling.

The point man grabbed a civilian who was cowering on the floor, pulling him to his feet. The guy was young, in his late twenties and dressed for the summer in t-shirt and shorts, sunglasses and a backwards cap on his head. The point man took his shotgun and put it against the man's jaw, who started shaking with fear in the man's grip as the barrel of the weapon nestled in under his chin.

'If anyone makes a sound, tries to do something stupid, I blow this guy's head off!' the man shouted. *'I want this place as quiet as a church! Clear?'*

No one replied. Everyone was face down on the marble, no one daring to speak or move.

'Everybody, get your phones out,' the point man shouted, quickly. *'Out! Slide them across the floor. If any of you don't and I find out, this guy's brains will be sprayed in the air like confetti!'*

The people on the floor all complied and the sound of scores of cell phones sliding across the floor echoed off the silent bank's walls. Across the room, the other two thieves finished plasti-cuffing the two guards, pushing them face-down to the marble floor, each guard landing with an *oomph* as the air was knocked out of them. The

17

bank robbers reached over and pulled each guard's Glock pistol from their holsters and threw them over the teller counter, out of reach, the guns clattering against the wood and marble as they hit the floor.

That done, the pair ran forward to their next tasks. The man vaulted the counter and slammed open the door to the security room, rushing inside. A series of monitors were in the room, the place humming, each small screen showing a different view inside the bank and on the street. He yanked out a small white bag from the inside pocket of his doctor's coat and started pulling out all the tapes from the monitors, dumping them in the bag one-by-one, checking the time on his wrist-watch as he did so.

Fifty seconds down.

2:10 to go.

Back inside the main floor, the woman spotted the manager cowering on the floor across the room. She moved towards him swiftly, the shotgun aimed at his head, her gloved hands around the sawn-off pistol grip.

'Up,' she ordered, standing over him.

He hesitated then rose, unsure.

He had good reason to be. In the same moment, she smashed the barrel of the shotgun into his face hard, breaking his nose. People started to scream, shocked at the violence.

'*Shut up! Shut the hell up*' the point man shouted, his shotgun against the hostage's neck. '*Or I'll kill this man and you can decide who takes his place!*'

That got them quiet. The manager had fallen to the floor, moaning and gasping with pain, blood pouring from his nose, leaking all over the clean white marble. The woman grabbed him and pulled him back to his feet with brutal strength for her size. She dragged him around the counter and towards the vault as he clutched his face, blood staining his hands and fingers and slammed him against the steel with a *thud*.

18

She put the shotgun against his groin, her finger on the trigger, her face hidden behind the surgical masks and sunglasses.

'Open it,' she ordered.

Two words. One shotgun.

All she needed.

Without a moment's hesitation, the man reached for the lock with his right hand, clutching his smashed nose with his left, blood pouring out and staining the sleeve of his white shirt. He twisted the dial, trying to keep his shaking hand steady, and paused three times on the combination then paused again. It clicked. He had a key looped on a chain attached to his top pocket. She grabbed it and yanked it off violently, then hit him in the face again with the Ithaca, dropping him like a stone. He fell to the ground, covering his nose, whimpering from the second blow. He wasn't going to be any trouble.

The woman grabbed the handle on the vault, twisted it, and pulled open the steel door. It led into a room holding a second vault, but this one had no spin-dial, just a normal lock. Rushing forward, she pushed the key inside the lock and twisted. It clicked, and she pulled the handle, opening the door to the second vault.

Inside were a series of metallic shelves, like four large filing cabinets pushed against the walls. Each shelf was packed with stacks of hundred dollar bills, bricked and banded.

She moved inside quickly. Dropping the shotgun and letting it swing back under her coat on its strap, she unzipped the front of her medic's overalls and pulled out two large empty black bags.

Back outside on the bank floor, the point man tilted his wrist so the shotgun nestled against the hostage's neck, and checked his watch.

'*Forty seconds*!' he called.

Inside the vault, the woman worked fast. She swept the bill stacks from the shelves straight into the bags. Once

19

loaded, she zipped them both shut. The third man had just finished taking the tapes in the security room and rushed inside to join her, taking one of the bags and looping it over his shoulder, keeping his shotgun in his right hand and the white bag of security tapes in the other. She took the other bag and followed him, and they moved outside, pulling the vault doors shut behind them, twisting the handles, then heading towards the front door.

They paused by the exit, tucking their shotguns away under the coats, then pushing their way through the doors, left the building.

The point man checked his watch and started backing away to the door, dragging the terrified hostage with him, his gun still jammed in the guy's neck.

'This guy is coming with us,' he shouted. 'If any of you move, or we see anyone on the street in the next two minutes, he dies. *DO NOT MOVE!*'

He turned his back and shouldered his way through the doors, taking the hostage with him.

And suddenly, the bank was eerily quiet.

They were gone.

In the silence, everyone stayed face down, too terrified to look up or even speak. The large hand on a large clock mounted on the wall ticked forward.

9:10 am.

And across the bank, the lock on the vault clicked shut.

*

Three hours later, a small cluster of detectives and a handful of vehicles had gathered in an almost empty parking lot across the East River in Queens. Police tape had been pulled up and around some knee-high traffic cones, cordoning off the scene, and beyond them were four blue wooden road blocks, *Police, Do Not Cross* printed on each in faded white lettering.

In the rough square the tape and wooden roadblocks created, several experts from Forensics out of the FBI's

Violent Crimes team were examining the burnt-out wreck of what used to be an NYC taxi cab. The carcass of the vehicle smouldered and smoked in the midday sun, the once-yellow exterior blackened and burnt, the interior melted down by the fire that had engulfed it. Fifteen yards from the car, two officers from the NYPD stood near the tape, ready to keep back any civilians who might decide to approach and take a closer look.

The officers had been the ones who'd discovered the wreckage, driving their beat in their squad car nearby and noticing fire coming from the taxi parked across the lot. They'd called it in, reporting the plates while they approached the vehicle and put out the flames with two fire extinguishers. To their surprise, the FBI had turned up and immediately taken over. Apparently the vehicle was linked to an on-going investigation of theirs and they wanted sole control of the crime-scene.

A black Mercedes pulled into the parking lot and drove up towards the people gathered there, coming to a halt and parking beside the NYPD squad car. The driver killed the engine and stepped out, closing the door behind him and smoothing down his tie.

His name was Todd Gerrard and he was a Supervisory Special Agent with the FBI. Gerrard was a few years past fifty but fit for his age, a benefit of his constantly hectic lifestyle, a seasoned veteran in every sense of the word. He'd been around for a long time, and had arrived at hundreds of crime-scenes like this during his long career. He was tall and well-built, six two and a hair over a hundred and ninety pounds. Although he'd only arrived in New York from D.C. last summer, he'd started out in this city, literally from the first moment of his life, born and raised in Brooklyn. He'd joined the NYPD as a rookie in the early 80s, and had stayed with the department for eleven years. After the bombing at the World Trade Center in '93, he'd then applied and been accepted into the FBI and had been with them ever since.

But lately everything had gone wrong. Trouble with his superiors, his marriage on the rocks and a recent demotion had meant Gerrard's career would now never hit the heights of many of the guys he'd started out with, and he was still battling his anger about it. He'd been shifted from Washington to New York City last summer, down-graded and put in charge of a six-man Violent Crimes Unit specialising in bank robbery in the city, known simply as the Bank Robbery Task Force. He was still smarting from the humiliation. He'd been well on his way to maybe an Assistant Director or Executive Assistant Director position, but then had been busted back down to a Supervisory Special Agent, back among the bright-eyed kids in their twenties and thirties. The only way he was getting out of here was by breaking a major case and he knew it.

And judging from events of the past few months, that didn't look as if it was going to happen any time soon.

Standing alone, Gerrard slid a pair of sunglasses over his nose and looked at the parking lot around him. It was pretty much empty, only a handful of cars parked in odd spaces, and it was hot, the merciless sun beating down on the tarmac as it had done all summer. He looked to his right and saw the Manhattan skyline across the East River, sunlight reflecting off the glass windows of the buildings. They were near the water, the Queensborough Bridge looming a hundred yards over and behind them. He could hear car horns and distant shouts, the constant soundtrack of the city, but the parking lot itself was quiet. The only physical activity in the area was the small gathering by the burnt-out taxi. His gaze settled on the charred ruins of the vehicle, and from his position across the tarmac he examined it.

The taxi had been torched from the inside, the interior blackened and destroyed from the blaze. There were several detectives from Forensics examining the wreckage and an FBI agent from his team was standing

22

alongside talking with them, all of them wearing white latex gloves. He sniffed and smelt something in the air and instinctively covered his nose. There was no mistaking what it was. It was slightly sweet yet sickening and unforgettable. He'd smelt it once before, when he was still a cop and had been down at the World Trade Center after the bomb went off in '93.

Burnt human flesh.

Trying to adjust to the smell Gerrard walked forward, stepping past the blue wooden NYPD roadblock and pulling his badge from his pocket. One of the NYPD officers at the tape saw him approaching, badge-in-hand, and nodded, letting the FBI agent pass as he stepped over the taped cordon.

A woman in a dark work suit standing near the vehicle also saw him coming and turned to meet him. Her name was Special Agent Mina Katic, one of the five agents under his command in the detail. She was a slim, dark-haired woman in her late twenties, competent, determined and quick. She was athletically built, as if she played in some kind of sports league on the weekends or had maybe just been blessed with great genetics, but Gerrard knew that she burned off most of those calories just with her day-to-day activities working for the Bureau, much like himself. She was a single mother but was far too proud to live on maternity grants, and he knew she was determined to prove people wrong and maintain and build a successful career, all while raising a nine year-old girl.

He saw her walking towards him, a file in her hand, and thought about her situation. Despite the monthly pay-checks and the impressive poker face that she wore at work, Gerrard knew that she was struggling to make ends meet. She'd had the kid and married young, but her husband had died prematurely from cancer the year before, leaving her to fend for herself and the child alone.

He would never tell her but she was the best agent on his team, professional and intelligent. But for some reason Gerrard didn't warm to her. He saw something in her eyes every time she looked at him, almost as if she was mad at him or just didn't want him around. He figured she was probably pissed that he'd been placed as head of the Bank Robbery Task Force and not her.

She was one of the three originals who were on the team before Gerrard arrived with the other two newly-assigned agents. He knew all three of them had been gunning for the promotion, especially considering the great work they'd done in lowering the heist-rate across the city in the last couple of years. They'd been instrumental in that process and they knew it, and they'd also managed to develop a solid working relationship with the NYPD, which in itself was pretty damn rare for any Federal office. He figured she was angry at being ignored for the post, or just angry at the shitty cards life had dealt her following the death of her husband. She was the only woman on his Task Force and had clearly learned to fight her corner in a male-dominated organisation. Gerrard watched her walk towards him. Despite being her boss, that constant look of distrust in her eye suggested that she considered him another opponent across the ring.

She had a latex glove on her right hand and was cradling an open yellow folder in the crook of her left arm, containing some kind of report. Pulling off the glove she stood beside Gerrard, who was surveying the scene through his sunglasses. Neither bothered with greetings.

'They strike again,' he said.

She nodded. 'Did you come from the bank?'

'I was downtown. Fill me in.'

'The bank was a Chase, Upper East Side,' Katic said, reading from the file in her hand. '2nd Avenue, between 62nd and 63rd. Today was delivery day, so they got the vault when the time-lock was off. Cleaned house. Did a fake-hostage routine and left. In-and-out in three minutes and got away clean.'

'Anyone inside get an I.D?'

She shook her head.

'They were fully disguised,' she said. 'Full medical gear, surgical masks, aviator sunglasses and latex gloves. No DNA, no fingerprints, no traces, no luck. Everything was fresh out the packet. Doesn't matter anyway. They left it all on the back seat to be burned. There's hardly any of it left.'

'The hostage?'

'Parker and Siletti are over at the bank interviewing witnesses,' she said. 'Most of them were staring at the floor, too scared to look up. One lady, a teller, said the guy was wearing sunglasses and a cap, but that was about all she could tell us. Nothing that would hold up in a perp walk.'

'Clever,' Gerrard said. 'They put one of their own team in the bank. He's disguised to the point that people would struggle to place him in a line-up, yet not enough to demonstrate that he's a part of the job. They put an empty gun to his head and say if anyone leaves the bank or alerts the cops, they blow his brains out. The moment they walk outside, they take the gun off him and he gets in the car alongside them. They drive off, and everyone's a winner.'

'Buys them instant co-operation inside the bank and saves having to get rid of a real hostage who may act unpredictably,' Katic added.

Gerrard nodded. 'OK. What else?'

'Security tapes were taken, so checking them isn't an option. They're on the back seat of the car beside the remains of the disguises, all melted up. The bank was on 62nd and 2nd so they were near the Bridge. They could have gotten over within sixty seconds if traffic was light.'

She turned from the folder and pointed at the car.

'And the rest is clear. They parked here, unloaded the cash into a switch car, poured petrol into the cab then tossed a match and left.'

Gerrard glanced around the parking lot again.

'Any witnesses? Homeless guys, or kids?'

'None. The vehicle wouldn't have attracted attention. They weren't being pursued or breaking the speed limit, and their disguises would be easy to remove. And a taxi-cab in Long Island City is just about as invisible as a vehicle can get.'

Gerrard nodded, looking back over his shoulder towards the Bridge. Just a few blocks away on Vernon Boulevard was the central taxi depot for the entire area. Thousands of the yellow vehicles, all in a tight radius, hundreds of them moving around, coming to and from the depot. The thieves who pulled this job were intelligent. Even if they were being pursued, once they made it over the Bridge and turned down the side streets they'd soon have become invisible, especially if they moved anywhere near the depot itself.

He turned back to Katic.

'How about tracers in the bank? Or should I even bother to ask?'

She shook her head. 'No luck. They left the registers. They knew where the dye packs and bait money were. They went straight for the vault. The bank manager is over at Lenox Hill getting his nose fixed. They busted him up pretty bad. He took a shotgun barrel to the bridge of his nose twice.'

'What was the take?'

'Just over five hundred thousand. Half a million.'

Gerrard shook his head and swore, long and hard.

'Shit.'

'Like I said, it was delivery day. The vault was fully stocked up. They cleaned house.' She looked back down at the report in the folder. 'A silent alarm they didn't

26

know about was tripped, but it didn't matter. Every cop in the area was uptown. Judging from the timings, it looks like they called in a fake emergency on the police frequency and it emptied the entire 19th Precinct as they headed in the opposite direction, responding to the call.'

Gerrard closed his eyes, processing everything she'd just told him, picturing the entire heist in his head from start to finish. There were a few moments of silence as he mentally ran through the job, seeing it unfold in his mind.

Then he opened his eyes and looked back at the torched getaway car.

'These people have done their homework,' he said. Katic nodded in agreement as he started walking towards the burnt-out wreck. 'And they've got some serious nerve. It takes a lot of balls to hold up a bank four blocks from a police station.'

He paused, ten yards from the taxi.

'But this doesn't make sense,' he said, pointing at the cab. 'All that proficiency yet this? Five armoured trucks, four banks, and this is the first getaway car they've ever burned. In fact, this is the first one they've even left for us to find. Why?'

Katic didn't reply.

She just pointed to the rear of the car.

The trunk was popped open, one of the Forensics detectives peering inside. Gerrard walked forward and that sickeningly sweet smell of burnt flesh grew stronger. He grabbed the end of his tie and covering his nose and mouth, took a look inside.

A body was in there, a man. His skin and hair had been burned away, and he was red raw where his skin had scorched, stained with black, his flesh and remaining skin smouldering. A terrible and agonising death, cooking like meat in an oven. No escape, just frenzy and desperation as the flames ate up the car as he tried to thrash, kick and claw his way out. Gerrard saw the

27

stringy remains of binds around his hands and ankles and a gag tied around his head and in his mouth.

'Jesus,' he muttered, his tie still to his nose.

'The driver of the cab,' Katic said. 'He was gagged and bound after they lifted the taxi. When they lit the interior, he couldn't get out.'

Gerrard glanced at what was left of the man's hands. The fingernails were mostly still intact and he saw black fabric and blood there from where he had scrabbled at the interior, trying to claw his way out. He'd ripped off a few of them in his desperation.

Having seen enough Gerrard stepped back, turning and taking a deep breath to clear his airways of the awful smell, releasing his tie and letting it drop back down to his shirt.

'Now we're getting somewhere. They screwed up,' he told Katic, who joined him. 'The ball's in our court. This is a homicide charge.'

'Double,' Katic corrected. Gerrard looked at her and she nodded with her head towards the front seat of the taxi.

He stepped forward and walked around the car. A female detective from Forensics was peering inside. Gerrard tapped her on the shoulder and she turned and nodded, moving to one side to let him see for himself.

A second dead body was in the front seat, behind the wheel. His torso, arms and legs had been torched by the flames, but his head was the worst mess of all. Half of it was missing. Ahead of him, some of the front windshield was smashed out, blood spattered amongst the black char.

'Someone shot him up close, from the back seat,' Katic said. 'Shotgun, point-blank. One shell. No cartridge left behind.'

Gerrard looked closer at the corpse. He saw the remains of white clothing clinging to his burnt flesh, patches of it on his legs, torso and arms. Katic had said that all the thieves had been wearing white, save for the hostage.

So this guy was one of the four.

'No prizes for guessing who it is,' Katic added.

'Oh shit,' Gerrard said, realising who the dead man was. 'Oh shit, shit, shit.'

He stepped back, turning and cursing, walking away from the carcass of the vehicle and kicking over a traffic cone in frustration.

'Great. There goes our inside man,' he said.

Katic nodded, walking with him across the tarmac.

'But we're making progress,' she said. 'Our first getaway car. Two homicides. They're getting sloppy and careless. And now we know one thing for sure about them.'

Gerrard looked at her, his eyes narrow behind his sunglasses. 'And what's that?'

'They're going to need a new driver.'

TWO

The pub was called McCann's. It was an Irish joint on Ditmars Boulevard, a long stretch of road which ran through the north-west Greek neighbourhood of Astoria, Queens, the last stop on the N train from Manhattan and Brooklyn. For a Monday night, the place was filling up fast. The two guys behind the bar were hard at work, serving customers, pouring draughts and shots and working the till, while a handful of waitresses moved out into the seating area ahead of the bar, taking orders from customers and earning their tips.

The crowd inside were a real blend. Half of them were office workers, the men still in shirt and tie having come straight from the office to the bar, the other half sports fans who were avidly watching television screens mounted in various positions around the room. There was some kind of big baseball game going on, the Yankees versus the Red Sox, and fans in navy blue Yankees gear were transfixed by the action on the screens. In most cities and towns around the world, different sports teams carried the hopes and dreams of the neighbourhoods they represented and Astoria was no different. Around these parts, the Yankees were like a religion. They were the most famous and successful baseball team in the world and their fans liked to let everyone know it.

Amongst the busy throng of people, a man sat alone towards the back of the pub, his forearms resting on the table in front of him, not interested in the baseball but watching the screen anyway. Dressed in a t-shirt and jeans, he was in his mid-twenties, handsome, blond hair and blue eyes, healthy and in the prime of his physical life.

He picked up a bottle of Budweiser from the table beside his forearm and took a long pull. The bottle was frosty and cool and he felt the beer slide down the back of his throat, the liquid ice cold. The air conditioning in the pub was working flat out despite the slight drop in heat, but it was still hot and humid. He took another pull from the beer, enjoying it, glancing at the bottle in his hand. A droplet of water slid down the bottle and over the logo above his thumb.

King of Beers, the label told him. With a taste that good, he didn't doubt it.

Shifting his gaze from the television, he glanced at the interior of the bar around him. It was a welcoming place. Sports memorabilia and signed jerseys were mounted on the walls around Irish flags and three-leaf clovers, typical decorations, designed to bring out patriotism and pride of heritage and make customers nostalgic enough to want to go buy a beer. It was a typical local bar, familiar and constant, like an old friend who would always be there for you no matter what kind of day you'd had. He figured pretty much everyone in here was a local, judging by the way different groups greeted and interacted with each other. He was the only outsider.

There was a sudden crack on the TV, and people around the bar started yelling and shouting excitedly at the screen. The blond man glanced up at the action and saw a player running base-to-base. He was a big guy but he hustled forward as fast as he could and the bar was filled with the sound of cheering from the stadium over the sound-system as the commentators called the play over the action. The Red Sox team in the field worked quickly though, as an outfielder scooped up the ball with his glove then threw it hard with impressive speed to a team-mate standing on one of the bases. The batter only made it to second. If he was thirty pounds lighter, he probably could have made third.

Watching the action, the blond man drinking the Budweiser was baffled. Baseball seemed like the most confusing game on the planet. The scoring system, the way the pitcher worked, the batting rules. The only thing

31

he'd ever learned about baseball was three strikes and you're out, but then again everyone and their grandmother knew that one. It went both ways though. He'd tried explaining cricket to an American once but it had been as if he was speaking a foreign language, judging from the blank stare on the guy's face as he laid out the rules. Both sports had a bat and a ball, but he guessed understanding how the hell to play each one depended on which side of the Atlantic you were brought up.

Taking another pull from the cold beer the man glanced around the bar again, but at the people this time, not the furnishings. He was surprised at how busy the place was for a Monday, but then again, he'd been to the city enough times to know the rules were different in the New York summer. The days were longer and the nights seemed even more so, and people made the most of every single one, no matter what day of the week it was.

To his left by the bar, a group of four were sitting on stools, each hitting a shot and wincing from the taste as they proceeded to suck on a lemon slice. Two men, two women, all still in work-clothes but all having a good time. He watched them laughing and enjoying each other's company, much the same as everyone else around them. He figured the bar would be something for them to look forward to, a treat for getting through the first working day of the week, the carrot at the end of the stick. If he worked in an office, he'd probably be doing the exact same thing.

But there was one group who weren't interacting with anyone else. They were sitting ahead of the blond man at a table near the door, up against the window with the bar's name and an Irish flag painted on the glass. They were talking in low voices, keeping to themselves, private and quiet, casting occasional glances at the baseball on the screens.

32

There were three men and a woman, all four of them dressed in a mixed combination of jeans and tracksuit tops, sportswear and casual. Two of the men had short, buzz-cut hair and thick tattooed forearms. They both looked tough, guys who worked in construction or who did something physical for a job. The third man had slightly longer hair and was skinnier, but he shared the same grim expression and disinterest in the rest of the bar around him. They had a half-filled pitcher of beer going in the middle of the table alongside a series of empty shot glasses. Plenty of drinks but seemingly not much pleasure.

Shifting his gaze to the right of the table, the man glanced at the fourth member of the group. The woman. Her three companions looked pretty tough but she was the most menacing of the bunch by far. She was Hispanic, Dominican or Mexican maybe, and was wearing a tight grey t-shirt that revealed brown sinewy arms. She reached forward for a cell phone resting on the table and he saw the muscles and tendons in her forearm work, contracting and flexing as she moved her fingers and picked up the phone. There wasn't a single ounce of body fat on her entire frame. Her dark hair was braided into tight corn-rows lining her head, her face unusually hard for a woman, unemotional, a solid jaw-line, not feminine or delicate. He also noticed that while the three guys were drinking the beer and shots, she was nursing a small bottle of water. *Some kind of athlete*, he thought, as he watched her. Whatever her sport, he figured it would involve some kind of confrontation. She looked the epitome of a woman that you did not want to mess with.

He took another pull from his beer, and observed the foursome over the bottle, curious. Suddenly, the woman rose from her seat and started walking down the bar, headed straight towards him. He'd shifted his attention, looking up at the television again, but for a split-second he thought she was coming over to confront him. He couldn't resist flicking his eyes to her face and they made eye contact as she approached.

Her gaze burned into his, no emotion, brown eyes that were cold and hard, accustomed to staring people down.

He looked straight back as she passed him and he heard a door behind him swing open as she entered the restroom.

A waitress from the bar approached him from the left, the polar opposite of the Hispanic woman. She was young, early twenties and smiled a customary smile, her face and demeanour innocent, her features soft.

'One more, hun?' she asked, seeing his beer was almost gone.

The blond man nodded. 'Thanks.'

She stood for a moment as if she was about to speak again, then changed her mind and left. He watched her go and drained his first beer. Considering the heat, the final pull tasted just as good as the first. Across the pub, it seemed on the television that the baseball game was reaching a climax. Fans around the bar were sitting forward in their seats as a Yankee batter stepped up to the plate, the noise quietening as people watched. The guy swung and connected first time, but he didn't catch the ball cleanly and only made it to first.

Suddenly, he felt someone grab his right arm. He also felt something pressed into his back. It was metal and cool, the shape unmistakeable.

The barrel of a pistol.

'Outside,' a voice said. Female. He didn't need to turn to see who it was.

But he didn't move.

'Outside, *pendejo*,' she said again.

'I've got another beer coming. Give me ten minutes,' he told her.

She didn't respond, grunting with indignation instead and pulled him from the stool with surprising strength.

She pushed him forward, keeping herself tight behind him, concealing the gun she'd jammed into his back. Around them, no-one was paying any attention. They were too wrapped up in the game or in their own private conversations.

As she pushed him through the bar, he glanced at his arm and saw her fingers curled tight around his right bicep, gripping him firmly. Up ahead, the three guys she'd been sitting with watched the pair walk by as they headed for the exit, and he saw them rise as they passed, preparing to follow them outside.

Shit.

There was a big white guy by the entrance, the doorman, but he didn't react when he saw the pair, watching them pass. The blond man saw the bouncer nod to the woman as they moved through the doors, a silent code. Whatever trouble she had, he'd turn a blind eye as long as she took it outside. In other places, a guy in such a position might have intervened or separated them. But in a joint like this, there was an unspoken trust that the blond man understood.

The foursome and the doorman were locals.

He wasn't.

And that meant they called the shots.

Outside on the street the woman turned left and pushed him towards the glass window of the bar, tucking the pistol into the rear waistband of her sweatpants. He turned around after she shoved him, just as her three companions appeared beside them from the exit. He had his back to the glass window, and was trapped, the four of them positioning in a semi-circle to close off any potential escape.

One of the two shaved-headed guys, the biggest one of the group, spoke. He was standing directly in front of the blond man, the woman to his right, the two other guys either side of them.

The leader.

'So who the hell are you?' the big guy said, a deep New York accent.

'What?' the blond man said.

The guy stepped forward. 'I said who the hell are you? I've seen you staring. You seem awful interested in our table, asshole.'

The woman passed him the blond man's wallet. She'd lifted it from his pocket as she pushed him outside. He flipped it open and pulled out a driving licence.

'Sam Archer,' he said, reading the card. 'You a cop?'

'No. Why should I be?'

'You look like a cop.'

'Well I'm not.'

Looking down, the guy checked the licence in his hands again.

'From England, huh? So what the hell are you doing here? How come we've never seen you before?'

'I'm visiting.'

'Who?'

'No one in particular. The city.'

'You alone?'

'Yeah. Didn't realise that was a crime. Is this how you treat every guy who walks into the bar to grab a beer?'

The guy looked at him. He was about to speak, but the other man with the shaved head behind him spoke, an edge of concern in his voice.

'Sean.'

The big guy turned as his friend beckoned to their right with his head. Archer looked in the same direction.

And saw six men walking straight towards them from up the street.

Every one of them was over six feet tall and thickly built, guys who were naturally strong and who'd hit the weights to increase that strength even more. They'd appeared out of nowhere. They took up the whole sidewalk as they approached in a line and came to a halt in front of the foursome from the bar.

The leader of the second group was staring straight at the guy called Sean opposite him, his eyes narrowed, his face tense. They'd walked down the street with purpose, not casually, almost as if they'd been waiting for the foursome to leave the bar. One thing was for sure, these weren't just pedestrians or a gang of American football players out on the town.

These guys oozed aggression and impending violence.

The way the two groups lined up, it was six-on-four. Archer glanced to his right and saw the woman still had the pistol jammed in the back of her waistband. That could be a game-changer if she decided to pull it. If she did, the difference in numbers would mean shit. But to his surprise she made no effort to reach for it, her hands staying by her side. She was just staring at the guy across from her, not a glimmer of intimidation in her body language, front-on, staring him down. She looked almost like she was relishing it, swaying side-to-side slowly, savouring the confrontation.

'Keep walking,' Sean told the other group. 'Save yourself some trouble.'

The leader on their side didn't move. He just smiled.

'And why should I do that, Farrell?' the man said in a thick Irish accent. 'This is our pub. My family owns this bar. And to be honest, we've had enough of you and your wetback bitch hanging out here. You're bringing us a shitload of trouble we don't want.'

As he spoke, Archer suddenly realised he was standing in line with Farrell and the three who'd pulled him from the bar.

Which meant one of the six guys opposite was staring straight down at him.

Archer cursed inwardly. *Shit. He thinks I'm part of their group*, he thought.

And his recent luck dictated that he was facing the biggest one of them all.

The guy was six three and over two-twenty easily, probably a line-backer in his high-school days or a wrestler, a guy used to getting his hands on someone and slamming them around. He looked down at the smaller man, an arrogant and self-satisfied sneer on his face; he'd probably never lost a fight in his life, being the size that he was. And from the look on his face, he figured he was going to stomp this little guy across from him just as if he was squashing a bug.

He was wrong.

The leader of the other gang, the Irish guy, threw the first punch. It was a wild right hook, the shot that had started pretty much every street fight in history. That or the head-butt. The guy pushed his considerable bodyweight and muscle-mass behind it and swung with all his strength, trying to take Farrell's head off. No technique, just pure, brutal power, a haymaker, swinging for the fences. If it connected, it would have done some considerable damage.

But Farrell saw it coming. It was so telegraphed, he probably could have spotted it from New Jersey. He swayed to the side and threw a cover hand up, blocking the punch. He propelled his bodyweight forward in the next instant, firing back his own overhand right that hammered into the other man's jaw. The punch mashed the Irish guy's lips into his teeth and he staggered back from the blow as Farrell followed it up with a left hook that also connected, sending him back. That lit the dynamite, and beside them everyone else started brawling.

The guy across from Archer suddenly snapped his big hand forward and grabbed the smaller man's collar with his right hand, gripping it tight. Archer knew what the guy was planning. He would hold him with one hand and beat his face relentlessly with the other, like a club, using his strength to his advantage. Pound on him until he decided to let go, until Archer's face was a pulpy, bloody mess or when he was unconscious. Probably both. No need for technique. Sheer power would be enough.

But the guy had made a mistake. He'd extended his arm.

Check.

Archer reacted fast. He slammed the guy's arm up hard with his left palm, hard enough to get out of his grip. In the same moment, he threw his body forward, wrapping his right arm around the guy's neck, tight under his chin. The big guy had the power, but Archer had the speed. He ducked his head under the guy's shoulder in the same motion and locked the fingers of his right hand on his left bicep. He put his left arm to the guy's forehead and started to squeeze, his grip as tight as a vice, strangling the guy's neck like there was a snake wrapped around it going for the kill. A front-on choke, an arm-triangle, applied in less than a second.

Checkmate.

He'd taken the big guy by surprise, who started trying to fight his way out of it. He was as strong as an ox, but it wasn't happening. He wasn't getting out. Now his strength advantage meant shit. Archer was strong for his size, and he cinched tighter, squeezing his arms, his grip locked up and secure. He heard the guy gargling as the choke-hold took away his oxygen, thrashing and scrabbling as he tried to escape. He was going out. Archer tightened the choke.

As he squeezed his arms as hard as he could and kept his head to the guy's massive shoulder, Archer saw Farrell and the two other guys had knocked their opponents down, continuing to beat on them on the sidewalk. Across the street he heard people shouting, calling from them to break it up, some of them probably calling the cops.

39

But he ignored them all and glanced over at the woman.

He couldn't believe it.

Two of the guys had gone for her. Two-on-one, and the one was a woman. But she hadn't opted to use the gun in her waistband. Instead, Archer saw that one of them was out cold, face down in the gutter, motionless. He wasn't even twitching. He watched her block a punch from the other guy and moved in close, clasping her hands behind his neck in a clinch. She pulled his head down and then started firing hard and vicious knees into his chin, one after the other, the guy's face taking each one like a sledge-hammer, smashing his nose and cheekbones as he tried to fight his way out of it. She was relentless, a perfect balance of ferocity and technique. He took about nine or ten of her knees then collapsed out of her grip to the pavement, his face a bloody mess, his eyes rolled back in his head.

At that same moment, Archer felt the big guy in his choke give a final thrash and gargle, then he sagged and a shitload of slack bodyweight suddenly weighed down his arms. He wasn't faking it. The big guy was out. Archer eased him to the concrete, which was no easy task. Dropping him meant the guy could hit his head on the stone and Archer didn't fancy a murder charge.

Before the others could react, he grabbed his wallet and licence from where Farrell had dropped them on the sidewalk and took off across the street, sprinting hard. There was a saying with any street fight that the loser went to hospital while the winner went to jail, and he didn't fancy being around for when the cops showed up.

As he crossed the street and headed down a side road, he heard a shout from behind him.

'*Hey!*'

He turned, ready to fight, expecting the foursome to have chased him.

40

But they were walking fast up Ditmars, headed the other way and putting distance between themselves and the bar.

None of them were pursuing them.

Although at the end of the street, Farrell had stopped. Archer watched him warily, ready to defend himself.

Then the big man raised a hand in an acknowledgement.

'*Thanks*,' he called.

Archer looked at him for a moment, and nodded back.

Then he turned on his heel and walked off swiftly down the street, disappearing into the night.

THREE

At 10 am the next morning, Archer pulled open the front door to an apartment building across Astoria, having just showered and dressed. He pulled it closed behind him quietly and took in his first breath of fresh morning air.

It was another beautiful day in New York City, the sun warm, the sky blue, not a whisper of wind in the air. He was dressed in a navy blue and white flannel shirt over a white t-shirt and faded jeans, light clothing, not enough to make him sweat but little enough to keep him cool. He slid a pair of sunglasses resting on his towel-dried hair down over his nose and walked forward through a small metal gate. Pulling it open and then sliding it back in place behind him, he stepped out onto the sidewalk and looked each way down 38th Street, left and right.

It was quiet. There were a few people walking down the sidewalk, most of them pulling small metal carriages packed with groceries, but everything was still and calm. He could hear birds chirping and tweeting in the trees that lined the street and the faint shouting and drilling of workmen digging a hole somewhere nearby. Turning right, he started walking down the sidewalk towards the end of 38th Street and the turn to 30th Avenue.

From the apartment he'd just left, he had two choices of subway trains to take. The R service was five minutes away to the left, up on Steinway Street, and the N line ran from the bottom of the hill on 30th Avenue to the right, slightly further away. He wasn't in a hurry, so he opted for the N. It was also over-ground for the first half of the journey and provided a far better view than the dark tunnels and passages of the underground R service. On a morning as beautiful as this it would have to be the N, no question.

He walked to the end of 38th Street and turning left, started to wander down the hill. 30th Avenue was a great stretch of neighbourhood, one of the best in the outer boroughs in Archer's opinion. It had everything. As he walked down, he saw cafes, markets, different kinds of stores. Across the street, he saw people sitting outside a restaurant, enjoying a relaxed morning brunch; it looked like a great place to live. He remembered being told once that Astoria contained the biggest population of Greeks in the world outside of Greece itself. The area certainly had a relaxed European feel to it and definitely had the quality of food.

He made his way down the seven blocks to the subway. It was busier on 30th than it had been on 38th Street and he found himself surrounded by people formally dressed in suits headed towards the station. The rail line itself ran horizontal to the street, looming over 31st Street, and served as direct passage to either the east and Ditmars Boulevard or the west and Manhattan.

As he approached the stairs that led up to the station and platforms up above he heard a Manhattan-bound train arriving, moving into the 30th Avenue station from Astoria Boulevard. He jogged briskly up the steps, pulling a yellow Metrocard from his pocket, and swiped his way through the turnstiles as the train rattled into the station above. He ran up the second flight of steps and arrived on the platform just as the train screeched to a halt.

The doors opened and he stepped past people departing the carriages, moving inside one and joining scores of people already inside. Judging by their clothing, most of them seemed to be headed for work. He took up a position by one of the doors, and turning, watched the carriage next door.

He wanted to get a good look at the guy following him.

He'd picked up the tail the moment he'd turned off 38th. The guy had been waiting for him outside a restaurant across the street, pretending to read a paper. He was sloppy and had picked a bad spot for

43

surveillance. It was also a 50/50 chance that Archer would come this way and not head up Steinway, but then again, there was probably someone else waiting for him up there as well. The guy had been almost directly in Archer's line of sight, an amateur mistake, and behind his sunglasses Archer had seen the man rise from his chair and start to move down the hill the opposite side, watching his mark.

Right on cue, he saw the guy appear, running up the steps, out of breath, and moving forward to just make it inside the carriage next door, jamming his arm in the sliding doors as they closed and then pulling them open and dragging himself inside. Archer examined him quickly before the guy relocated him. He was one of the men from the group at the bar last night.

Not Farrell.

Not the man with longer hair.

The third guy, shaved head and tattoos on his forearms, the one who'd been the first to spot the six guys coming down the street. Archer saw him looking around, trying to relocate his mark, so he turned his back, feeling the man's gaze fall on him. He didn't move. There was no point trying to lose him yet. The trip into the city would take about twenty minutes and he didn't want to alert the guy that he knew he was there.

The train moved off towards the next stop, the streets rolling past down below through the windows. The carriage Archer was standing in was busy, full of people headed to the office, crossing off another day, another step closer to the weekend. People were sitting and standing everywhere, listening to music through headphones, reading newspapers, sipping coffees and tapping away on their cell-phones or just looking out of the window, lost in thought. Archer wasn't impressed to see a number of seats occupied by men as women in heels stood nearby, clutching the rail, some of them fighting to keep their balance. None of the guys on the

44

benches seemed to care though, and he swallowed down his irritation. A small thing, but something that always pissed him off when he saw it. Unlike him, he guessed some guys just didn't give a shit when it came to stuff like that.

The train slowed and came to a halt at the next stop, Broadway. Archer realised the guy next door had no idea where he was getting off. He contemplated deceiving him by stepping outside then back in at the last moment, but decided against it. The guy didn't know he'd been made. It would make it easier to lose him when they got to Manhattan and would avoid a confrontation that Archer could do without. The doors closed and the train pushed on, stopping twice more at 36th and 39th Avenue before swinging a right hook and approaching Queensborough Plaza, the eastern side of Manhattan coming into view up ahead across the East River.

Looking around the carriage to pass the time, he saw a young boy sitting on one of the blue benches, his father standing over him, both in jeans and polo shirts. The kid was no older than five or six but they were already the spitting image of each other; the boy looked excited, as if they had something fun planned for the day, an outing or maybe just a chance to spend time with his father. Archer watched him. His shoelaces were untied, and they swung back and forth in the air as the train moved and slowed, the plastic tips occasionally brushing the ground. His father realised, and knelt down, tying them up, keeping his balance as the train started to slow. Archer smiled, then swallowed and averted his gaze.

There were more people waiting on the platform here, as there always were. Queensborough Plaza was where the N and Q line met the 7 train, the line that ran through all the other neighbourhoods in Queens. The doors opened and everyone on the platform moved inside, the carriage becoming even more crowded, everyone packed in together, the carriage full. Eventually, the doors closed again and the train rolled on. He saw people making last minute texts or ending calls on cell phones. They were about to go into the tunnel, under the river, heading towards 59th Street and Manhattan, and all cellular service would cut out shortly.

The train entered the tunnel and rumbled and rattled on through the darkness. Despite the crowd around him, the sudden change in light made him realise how clean the train was. Archer had seen photos from the 80's and early 90's of the NYC MTA subway system. Graffiti, dirt, scores of homeless people, murders, intimidating gangs waiting for prey and chances to mug passengers. This was a marked change. He'd read in the paper that Mayor Giuliani had cleaned up the streets and the city's transport system during the last decade after 9/11 and he'd done a great job. Archer could think of only one better system that he'd used in his lifetime and that was the subway in Washington D.C. That was about as good as it got. Carpets, no music, no food, everyone sat pretty much in silence, everything clean, no trash. But then again, the New York MTA ran all night, which drew the two just about even.

After another minute or so, the train rolled into 59th Street and Lexington Avenue, the darkness of the tunnels suddenly illuminated by the lights of the station at they flashed past the windows. The train slowed as a female voice announced the station over the train's intercom system, then eventually pulled to a halt, the brakes screeching and stopping the train with an operatic crescendo. The doors opened, and the carriage suddenly started to empty, pretty much everyone inside getting off. Archer saw the boy climb off the bench and grab his father's hand and the two of them joined everyone else exiting the train. The sudden increase in room was pleasant, and Archer saw the few people left inside the carriage visibly relax like himself, enjoying getting their

46

personal space back. After another moment, the doors shut, and the train moved on.

They stopped three more times before the train pulled into Times Square 42nd Street. This station was the central transport hub in Midtown Manhattan, conjoining a series of various subway and transport lines from all sorts of different paths and routes through the city. After the train stopped and the doors opened, Archer stepped out and began walking briskly through the crowd down the platform, headed towards the stairs. He didn't need to look behind him. He knew the guy would be following. He jogged up the steps, quick enough to move up them swiftly but not fast enough to alert the man following him that the game was up.

But the moment he reached the upper tier, he moved fast, gaining some distance. He rushed through a winding turnstile and walked swiftly towards the stairs, taking them two at a time and coming out on the corner of 42nd Street and 7th Avenue.

Up on the busy street, he moved through the crowds of people, ducking into a store to the left of the stairs that led down to the subway. It was some kind of hat-store, all sorts of caps and beanies sitting on racks lining the shelves. He grabbed a navy blue baseball cap from a shelf and moved to the back, pulling it over his head. Taking cover behind a rack, he looked around it and waited.

The guy appeared, rushing up onto the street level from the stairs, looking side-to-side as he searched for any sign of Archer. It was no use. He'd lost him.

After a few more moments, Archer watched the guy curse to himself then visibly give up, disappearing from view as he returned down into the subway, probably headed back to Queens.

Taking no chances, Archer moved to the counter and bought the cap. Ripping off the tag, he pulled it back over his head, took off his flannel shirt and then ducked

47

out of the left side of the store, moving fast down 42nd towards 8th Avenue. As he passed two large cinemas, one either side of the street, he checked behind him to make sure the guy hadn't picked him up again, the peak of the cap low, hiding his face, the sunglasses hiding his eyes. This detour would add to his journey, but he wanted to make sure he'd lost the guy for good.

Once he got to 8th, he crossed the street and ducked into a pizza place on the corner opposite the Port Authority Bus Terminal. There were a few stools near the window, and he sat on one, checking the street, waiting for five minutes. The guy didn't reappear. Still, Archer hung on for a few more minutes, just to make sure he'd ditched the tail, then left the restaurant, crossing the street and walking south. He could see the ugly shape of Madison Square Garden starting to appear up ahead on the corner of 33rd Street. One of the most famous arenas in the world, possibly the most famous, yet it was decidedly unattractive from the outside, looking much like a big, muddy, brown doughnut. If it wasn't for its illustrious history, the place surely would have been demolished and rebuilt a long time ago.

Crossing the streets, he turned to his left, headed back towards 7th.

The walk took him about two minutes and he occasionally checked over his shoulder to make sure that he hadn't been picked up again. As he arrived outside a Starbucks on the corner of 35th and 7th, he took the cap off his head and looked around. He saw a young black kid walking past, his fingers tapping on some buttons as he played some kind of video game.

'Hey, kid.'

The boy stopped and looked at him.

'Want a free hat?' he asked, offering it to him.

The kid looked at him, unsure, then took the cap. He looked at it, checking it out, turning it side-to-side. It was a dark-blue peaked baseball cap, the Yankees team logo on the front, a silver *N* and *Y* on top of each other. He nodded approvingly, then looked up at Archer.

'You for real?'

Archer nodded. The kid pulled it over his head.

'Thanks man,' he said.

'No problem.'

And with that, the kid walked off, returning his attention to the video game in his hands, the cap on his head. Archer watched him go, then turned and pulled open the door to the Starbucks and walked inside.

The coffee shop was moderately full, light jazz music flowing from the speakers, the ambience relaxed and quiet. The early morning mayhem of customers grabbing a drink before work had lessened slightly, and although there was a medium-length queue for the counter, the place was pretty chilled compared to the streets outside. People were sitting around the coffee shop, some working on laptops or reading newspapers, others chatting with friends.

Archer looked across the room and saw a middle-aged man in a smart suit sitting alone near the window. He was wearing sunglasses, but Archer could tell he was looking straight at him. He had two large drinks in front of him on the table, and he picked up the one on the right, taking a sip.

Archer ignored the queue for the counter and moved straight towards the guy. He took a seat across from him, pulling off his sunglasses.

Removing his own sunglasses, Supervisory Special Agent Todd Gerrard of the FBI pushed a cup of tea across the table towards him.

'Good news,' Archer said, checking back over his shoulder.

'What?' Gerrard asked.

'I think I'm in.'

49

FOUR

It had all started four days ago.

Back across the Atlantic in London, Friday morning had begun like any other typical Friday morning for Archer. He'd woken up at 6 am, headed out the door for a 45 minute gym session, returned, showered, then took the Underground to his police station in North London, the Armed Response Unit, for 8:30 am sharp. He'd signed in at the front desk, then headed straight upstairs to their team briefing room to report in with the rest of the team and grab a cup of tea. He saved time every morning by not having to worry about breakfast. He didn't have any semblance of an appetite in the morning and the tea was just about all his stomach could cope with until lunch.

The Armed Response Unit operated in two halves. The first half was an analyst team who gathered intelligence and information from inside these headquarters, and the second was an armed ten-man task force, who used that information out in the field when they were called upon in a crisis. The two teams worked in synergy with each other and during the last eighteen months, despite being a relatively new squad, the ARU had become the premier response and counter-terrorist team in the city. Archer was the youngest man on the task force, still just twenty six, but the events of the past eight months meant his age and relative inexperience was no longer the talking point it had been in the past.

The Unit's headquarters was a two-floored building. The lower level contained locker rooms and interrogation and holding cells for any suspects that were brought in, while the upper level consisted of an operations area to the right, where the intelligence team worked behind high-tech computers and monitors, and a briefing room to the left, which the task force used as their base. That morning, Archer had jogged up the steps and joined the other officers in the Briefing Room, pouring a cup of tea and picking up a newspaper someone had brought in. To an outsider it would have seemed like a pretty good job.

But the work wasn't always this smooth.

Almost nine months ago, a nine-man terrorist cell had waged war on the city on New Year's Eve, with thousands of people gathered all over London for the New Year celebrations. One of the terrorists had managed to get past security at a Premiership football match and had detonated a devastating quantity of home-made explosives hidden under his clothes, killing over a hundred and fifty people and injuring many more.

That had triggered a series of events that unfolded over the next twenty four hours like some kind of nightmare. There had been a number of attempted further bombings, double-crosses, links to a drug cartel in the Middle East and a shooting in Trafalgar Square. The DEA, the American Drugs Enforcement Administration, had also become involved and the ARU team had suddenly found themselves right in the middle of the action, thousands of people's lives depending on them. The Prime Minister had ordered the Unit to be formed after the disastrous riots that had swept across the United Kingdom in the summer of 2011, and that night of chaos on New Year's Eve had been a true baptism of fire for the newly-formed squad.

Prior to those chaotic twenty four hours at the end of last year, 2012 had been pretty quiet. But since then, it was as if the events of that New Year's Eve had opened some kind of floodgates. Every week now something was going down that needed the Unit's attention, things the public mostly never knew about, threats and attempted terrorist acts that would devastate the city if they were successful. The Unit had been set up by the Prime Minister to offer a no-nonsense response to any potential threat, foreign or domestic, to the city and the

51

ten-man task force gathered every morning inside the briefing room at their headquarters with no idea what the day or week ahead held in store.

However, a benefit of all this trouble meant the entire ARU detail had been through some hellacious experiences together which had strengthened their cohesion. When the squad had been formed at the beginning of last year, the PM had demanded that the team be one that would last into the future, long after his tenure at 10 Downing Street had ended. As a consequence, the Unit was a blend of hardened experienced officers and some younger counterparts who would take over once the older officers had moved on. A few of them had been comparatively untested the year before, including Archer, but now they were an experienced outfit that any terrorist would be wise to take very seriously. When people in the city were in trouble, they called the police.

When the police were in trouble, they called the ARU.

Inside the briefing room Archer had just sat down in an empty chair alongside some of the other men when a dark-haired young woman appeared at the door. Her name was Nikki, the only person in the building who was referred to by her first name. She was head of the intelligence team that worked next door. Archer had known her for a long time. They'd started out at the Hammersmith and Fulham Police Station across the city, and were old friends, both the same age. They'd enjoyed a brief romance once, something no one else in the Unit knew about aside from the two of them, but that had fizzled out as so often happened with a relationship in a working environment.

'Arch?' she said.

He looked up.

'Cobb wants to speak to you.'

Archer paused, then nodded and rose, folding the newspaper in half and leaving it on the empty seat. He glanced at his best friend Chalky who was sitting beside him, already eyeing the free newspaper.

'I'm reading that,' Archer told him as he turned away.

Chalky nodded, but the blond man heard a rustle behind him as his friend immediately swiped it up. He shook his head and walked out of the room, heading towards Cobb's office.

Cobb was Director of the Armed Response Unit, the man responsible for taking charge and ownership for the entire detail. He was a good man and an even better leader. The run-in with the terrorist cell during the winter had strengthened the bond between everyone involved in the squad, and especially in their collective gratitude for Cobb's leadership. Everyone who worked here had respected Cobb before, but now they viewed him as a necessity, the perfect man for his role. Cool, collected and dependable, he was one of those people who was born to take charge; it was as if it was in his DNA, a quality you couldn't teach. Archer had never worked with Cobb in the field, but he knew if it ever came to that he'd follow him through fire in a heartbeat if he had to.

Cobb's office was located across the level, overlooking the Operations area and his tech team. The walls to the room were made of transparent glass so Archer saw his boss sitting at his desk, waiting for him, tanned features over a black suit and white shirt with navy-blue tie. Cobb saw the younger man coming, and beckoned him inside. Archer pushed the door open, stepping into the office and letting it close behind him.

'Morning sir.'

'Good morning.'

Archer noticed the expression on Cobb's face.

'Something wrong?' he asked.

Cobb paused, then motioned to a chair the other side of his desk.

'Take a seat.'

Archer sat. He saw Cobb take a deep breath.

'I'm afraid I have some bad news. I just got a call from an FBI detective in New York twenty minutes ago,' he said, slowly. 'He told me the NYPD found a body last night in a parking lot in Queens.'

Pause.

'It was your father.'

Archer looked at him, still, silent. He didn't react, didn't blink, didn't move.

A long silence followed as he absorbed the news.

'I'm sorry Arch,' Cobb added.

Archer swallowed and felt light-headed.

Across the table, Cobb sat still, a compassionate look on his dark-featured face, waiting for the life-altering news to sink in.

'How did he die?' Archer asked, his mouth dry.

Cobb looked across the desk at him. He seemed about to speak, but held back.

'How did he die?' Archer asked again, reading Cobb's hesitance. 'C'mon, sir, I can handle it.'

Cobb nodded. *So be it.*

'He was shot from behind. Point blank. A single shotgun round to the head. Killed him instantly.'

Archer didn't respond. He felt dazed; but against his will, his mind started conjuring up images from what Cobb had just told him. Awful images.

A shotgun round to the head, from behind.

Not an accident.

Not a freak occurrence.

A cold, calculated execution.

Someone murdered him.

Cobb continued, talking quietly.

'I want you to take the week off,' he said. 'Compassionate leave.'

He pushed a printed piece of paper across the table.

'I booked you on a flight to New York from Heathrow. It leaves later on this afternoon. The Bureau have organised the funeral and it's taking place tomorrow so you don't have to worry about setting anything up. But you'll want to be there.'

Archer looked up at him, his mind reeling, a thousand thoughts rushing around his head, all jarring for attention. He didn't respond. Cobb continued.

'I also booked you into a hotel. The Marriott Marquis. Times Square. It's a good spot. I've been there before myself. Stay there until you come back.'

'Sir, I can't accept that.'

'I'm not asking you to. It's an order. Besides, it's on the Unit's funds, marked down as necessary expenses. The Prime Minister told me to handle our budget at my own discretion and that's exactly what I'm doing.'

Archer paused and tracked back mentally in their conversation. He blinked and frowned. He was confused, and about more than just his father's murder.

'You said the Bureau, sir?'

Cobb nodded.

'That doesn't make sense,' Archer continued. 'My father's a- I mean *he was*- a sergeant in the NYPD. The FBI wouldn't organise a funeral for him. Why would they? The cops and the Feds hate each other over there.'

Cobb frowned, then read Archer's face.

'When was the last time you spoke with him?' he asked.

'Not for a long time.'

'So you didn't know?'

'Know what, sir?'

'He was a Federal agent. A Special Agent-in-Charge. Been with them for the last two years. Your father wasn't a cop, Archer. He was working for the FBI.'

Archer and Cobb sat in silence for a few more minutes, Archer absorbing everything he'd just been told. Then he scooped up the flight ticket, thanked Cobb and returned to the briefing room, still stunned. The other officers could immediately see something was wrong and once quiet word spread about what had happened, all nine of them sat there with him in the room. No one left. No one knew what to say. But that didn't matter. Some of them had been in the younger man's situation. They knew that just providing company was enough at that moment. It was all they could do.

Archer had sat in his chair without moving for half an hour, just staring straight ahead. Then his head had started to clear and he'd said his short goodbyes, heading downstairs for his unexpected week off. He made a pit-stop at his apartment in Angel, finding his passport, packing a bag and taking a black suit and shoes from the closet for the funeral. He locked the door to his apartment, stepped out onto the street, hailed a cab and went straight to the airport.

Cobb had booked him on a British Airways flight, which meant he was leaving from Heathrow Terminal Five. As he paid the taxi fare and walked into the huge glass building he realised that the last time he'd been here he'd been face to face with a suicide bomber on New Year's Eve. She'd been a young girl, no older than twenty, but with bricks of C4 plastic explosive packed into her clothes, concealed as a baby bump. Archer had been the first man at the scene to locate and confront her before she was shot and killed just in time by another officer.

He walked across the Departures Hall and checked in at the British Airways desk. His flight was leaving at 2 pm, around three hours from now, direct from Heathrow to JFK. Cobb had booked him a seat in Club Class, which he hadn't needed to do, but Archer appreciated the gesture. He had no luggage to check, just a carry-on and his suit; he moved through the security checkpoints without a problem and headed straight for the Gate as soon as it came up on the screens.

The next three hours felt like the shortest of his life. He'd taken a seat facing the airfield and had been staring out of the window one moment, lost in thought, staring at all the planes on the tarmac. When he finally looked away and checked the time, he realised they'd already opened boarding for the plane.

Three hours, gone in what seemed like a second.

London Heathrow to New York JFK was about a seven hour flight, and all seven seemed to flash past. This was the first time Archer had ever flown Club Class in his life and he could instantly see why people paid the extra money.

The seats had been arranged in pairs, one seat facing the rear of the plane, one facing the front, and they were separated by a screen that you could pull up for some privacy. Archer didn't need to use the screen seeing as there was no-one sitting beside him, but he pulled it up anyway. He had a seat by the window, no one close to him, and the chair was wide and comfortable. It seemed he could press a button to make the seat slide back and turn into a bed if he wanted to.

But during those seven hours he didn't drink a drop of fluid, nor eat a mouthful of food, nor watch a second of any movie. He just sat still, silent, staring at the sky outside the window, watching the wispy white clouds as they drifted past, high above the Atlantic Ocean far below.

This whole thing just felt like some big nightmare. He'd woken up this morning expecting just another day at the Unit and planning what he was going to do over the weekend. Instead, he'd discovered someone had murdered his father and he was now on his way to New York for a week-long compassionate leave. Maybe he was still asleep. Maybe he'd suddenly wake up.

He closed his eyes, then opened them again.

No luck.

He was still on the plane.

This was all real.

He shook his head and glanced away from the window, pulling down the screen next to him and looking at the people occupying the other seats in the cabin. Most of them looked like businessmen and women, probably for whom this trip was a mundane routine or a necessary part of their corporate lifestyle. He saw several tapping into laptops and netbooks, writing and reading documents they'd need for meetings that would take place later or which had already happened. There were also several seats which were empty, but none of the flight attendants had made an effort to upgrade anyone. He figured that only happened very occasionally or in an ideal world in the movies. He pictured everyone farther down the cabin jammed together in Economy, arm-to-arm with strangers, uncomfortable and counting the minutes till the plane landed. One thing was for sure, the extra money for a Club Class ticket was well worth it.

Towards the end of the flight, the blue water of the ocean far below changed into the greenery of the American East Coast and half an hour later they landed smoothly at New York's John F Kennedy International Airport. Once the plane had rolled to a stop and parked and the light for the seatbelt in the cabin dinged off, Archer took his bag and suit from the overhead lockers then disembarked, quickly navigating his way through immigration and through baggage claim to the exit.

His father was an American, so his son had dual citizenship which at that moment meant he could avoid the growing line of people gathering at the non-American immigration line. Walking towards one of the desks for American citizens, he breathed a sigh of relief as he saw the long line of non-Americans increasing by the minute. He'd been in that queue in other countries and they were going to be standing there for a while.

After his passport was checked and stamped, he thanked the woman behind the desk and walked through Customs out into the Arrivals hall. There was the usual crowd gathered behind the cordon, drivers holding name-signs or people eagerly waiting for loved ones or friends to appear, but he made his way past them all and headed to an ATM on the right, pushing his credit card into the slot and withdrawing sixty bucks. That done, he turned and followed the sign for the Airtrain.

The Airtrain was an over-ground service, connecting JFK to the city's MTA subway system and Archer rode it over to Sutphin Boulevard, a hub of a station on the east side of Queens. The time here was five hours behind the U.K, so it was still only early afternoon, and the weather was beautiful, the sun shining over the sea of houses and buildings across Queens, the air warm and summery.

Inside the train Archer stood still, looking out of the window, the sun shining down on him through the glass as he gazed out.

It was a beautiful day.

One that his father would never get to see.

At Sutphin, he bought a Metrocard for the subway and got onto an E train, which would head west through Queens and pass under the East River into Manhattan. It would take him all the way to Times Square, and the Marriott Hotel Cobb had booked him into. Archer sat alone on one of the blue benches, his bag beside him, one of only three people in the carriage, the other two sat down the other end, far away from him. They were underground, but the lights inside the carriage showed Archer's features in the glass window across the carriage and he looked at his reflection. He took most of his looks from his mother, but the one characteristic he'd inherited from his father were piercing blue eyes.

He stared into them in the window across the train, and saw his father staring back.

Someone murdered him echoed in his mind.
And the train rumbled on towards the city.

FIVE

The funeral took place the next day, Saturday, in a picturesque green graveyard across the East River in Queens. Seeing as his father had died in the line of service, the whole thing had already been organised and paid for by the Bureau; there was a good turnout, lots of people he didn't recognise, a couple he did. Archer was standing in his black suit, white shirt and black tie at the front of those gathered, looking over at the polished brown coffin held by levers over the freshly dug grave. He was the only family member present. High above, the sun was shining, not a single cloud in the sky. It was another beautiful day, a strange contrast to his mood. Hollywood often filmed situations like this in the rain to match the mood or the lead character's feelings. Life, however, often wasn't that black and white.

The clergyman conducting the service began a final prayer and those gathered bowed their heads. Archer kept his head up, still staring at the polished wooden coffin, a series of bouquets of white flowers resting on the lacquered wood, small envelopes tucked amongst the flowers with personal notes written to Special-Agent-in-Charge James Archer. Looking at the coffin, his son pictured him inside. He hadn't seen him in over a decade but here they were, ten feet from each other, the last time they would ever be in such close proximity. He swallowed as the clergyman approached the end of the prayer.

He suddenly sensed someone watching him. He looked over and saw a woman with dark-brown hair standing the other side of the freshly-dug grave. She was about his age, attractive and dressed in a dark work suit and was staring at him with a strange look on her face. If anything, she looked tense. Worried. Concerned. Maybe a mix of all three.

61

They held each other's gaze, brown eyes on blue, but that look of concern on her face didn't diminish.

If anything, she looked almost scared.

Maybe she and Dad were friends, he thought. Probably colleagues in the Bureau. She looked the type.

Once the service ended Archer had taken one last look at the coffin, then turned and walked away. He moved slowly over the grass, headed towards the old gates that led out of the graveyard. He'd hailed a taxi to get here and planned to head back into Manhattan. Someone had told him earlier that there was some kind of wake planned but he wasn't going to go. Right now, he just wanted to be alone.

Suddenly a voice called quietly from behind him, cutting into his thoughts and solitude.

'Sam.'

He turned, and saw a man he hadn't seen in over ten years approaching him, dressed in a black suit and tie over a white shirt. His name was Todd Gerrard but all his friends called him Gerry. He and James Archer had been close friends, having come up in the NYPD together in the 80's when the city was nowhere near as safe as it was now. Judging by his suit and demeanour, Gerry had moved on to bigger things. Archer noted streaks of grey in his brown hair but he still looked in good nick, lean-faced and alert.

'Hey Gerry,' Archer said. 'It's been a while.'

Gerrard offered his hand and the younger man shook it, as other mourners passed them.

'Damn it's good to see you kid,' he said. 'I didn't think you'd make it.'

Archer shrugged. 'Here I am.'

Gerrard glanced around. 'Where's your sister?'

'In D.C. She couldn't get time off.'

'Your mother?'

'She's gone. Two years ago. Blood clot in her lung.'

There was a pause. Archer started to walk on towards the gate, his father's old friend keeping pace alongside him. There was a brief silence. Then Gerry broke it.

'You want to get some coffee?' he asked.

Archer looked over at him. He decided he could probably use some company, especially with an old friend of his father.

Gerry read his expression and took it as affirmation.

'C'mon, it's on me,' he said. 'We've got some catching up to do.'

Twenty minutes later they were inside a Starbucks in Manhattan, on the corner of 35th and 7th Avenue. Gerry had driven them here. Inside the Bureau car, Archer had watched the streets flash past through the tinted windows of the black Mercedes as they drove over the Queensborough and then into Manhattan. Traffic was lighter considering it was the weekend and the journey was a relatively quick one, but neither man said a word during the ride. They were saving the conversation for the coffee.

Once Gerrard had parked near Herald Square and put a Bureau marker on the dashboard that would save him from being clamped, they'd walked into the coffee shop. Gerrard headed to the counter while Archer found them a table across the room by the window, asking for tea instead of coffee. He couldn't abide the black stuff. Once Gerrard had placed their order, the barista took a few moments to prepare the drinks then passed them over the counter. Gerrard paid and approached the table, taking a seat across from the younger man and placing the two cups on the table-top. Archer noticed that the older man had brought something with him from the car, an A4 sized yellow folder containing some white documents.

He nodded *thanks* for his drink but more silence followed. Archer looked out of the window, lost in thought, watching people walk past on the sunny street.

Much like yesterday, today just felt surreal, as if it wasn't really happening.

'You're looking well kid. Your dad said you'd ended up a cop in the UK?' Gerrard asked.

'Yeah. That's right.'

'Forget that, you should be a damn model with a face like that,' the older man added, trying to lighten the mood.

Archer forced a smile, but said nothing.

'Where are you staying?'

'Marriott. Times Square.'

Gerrard whistled. 'Who's picking up the bill?'

'My boss.'

Gerrard went to say more but suddenly remembered something, and reached into his pocket, pulling out a pair of keys wrapped in a small piece of paper. He slid them across the table.

'These are for your Dad's place in Astoria,' he said. 'He'd been renting an apartment off 30th Avenue for the past few years. I figured there might be some stuff there you'd want. He was on a lease so there'll be new tenants moving in there soon. I figured you'd be the best person to take what you want and leave the rest to be thrown out. The address is on the paper.'

Archer nodded and took the keys and scrap of paper, tucking them into his pocket, saying nothing. Light guitar music flowed from speakers around the Starbucks, filling the moments of silence between the two men as people chatted around them, all sorts of ethnicities enjoying all sorts of different drinks and specials from the counter. It was busy with weekend activity, but the coffee shop still felt relaxed.

Archer looked down at his tea, at the circular green Starbucks logo printed on the side of the cup. A mermaid wearing a crown, two stars either side of her, with the company's name printed in a semi-circular shape underneath.

'Shit, I'm sorry, Sam,' Gerrard said, sighing. 'Jimmy didn't deserve to go out like that.'

'No. He didn't.'

'When was the last time you saw him?'

Archer glanced out the window. 'About eleven years ago.'

'He always talked about you, you know. That terrorist thing in London at Christmas? He wouldn't stop going on about it. It made the front page of the New York Times. When it was over, he kept saying *that's my son, my son did that.* He was real proud of you, you know.'

'No. I didn't know.'

There was a pause. Archer loosened the long black tie around his neck and unbuttoned his top button, then lifted the white cap off his tea. Steam swirled up from the cup, the water tinted and infused. He lifted the string on the bag and dunked it up and down, watching the water darken as it soaked up the tea leaves inside the bag. He dropped the bag inside and watched it sink to the bottom. His mood felt just as low.

'I know he screwed up,' Gerrard said. 'Made some mistakes. But he turned his life around. He quit the booze. He joined the Bureau. Neither one is easy to do. He hadn't taken a sip in almost two years.'

Archer listened but didn't respond. He looked back out of the window again, at the people walking past on the street, each with their own cares and concerns. There was such a wide variety of people out there. Tourists distracted as they looked at maps and tried to establish their bearings, looking for the way to Macy's or the Empire State Building. Locals accustomed to the sights, impatiently stepping around them. A young street busker on the corner, singing and strumming a guitar, people tossing the odd coin or spare dollar note into the open guitar case beside him. This place really was a melting pot. If he took a photo right now, he could probably point out about fifteen or twenty different nationalities.

65

But despite the wandering meander of his mind, a voice was constantly echoing in there, a voice he couldn't shake, as if someone had shouted into a cave and three words kept reverberating back to him. The echo was saying the same thing over and over again. Three words, five syllables.

Someone murdered him.

'How long are you in town for?' Gerrard asked.

'Until next Sunday,' Archer said. 'A week tomorrow.'

He shifted his gaze from the window to Gerrard, sensing something in his voice.

He looked as if he had more to say.

'Why?'

'Did you speak to anyone about the murder? Or read the coroner's report?'

'No. But I know what happened. Twelve gauge, point blank, back of the skull. Took most of his head off. No suspects, no witnesses. The FBI is handling the investigation and its going absolutely nowhere. Why?'

Gerrard looked across the table at him.

Didn't speak.

'Why, Gerry?' Archer repeated, his face hardening. 'Don't waste my time.'

Gerrard nodded.

'Because I think I know who pulled the trigger,' he said.

SIX

'Do you know when the first documented bank robbery in New York City took place?' Gerrard asked.

Archer shook his head, watching the other man closely. 'No. I don't.'

'1831. City Bank, on Wall Street. Workers turned up on Monday morning and found two hundred and fifty thousand dollars missing. To this day, we've only got back about three quarters of that cash haul. And it's been them versus us ever since. It started with steam trains and Federal reserves, now its armoured trucks and bank vaults. Cops and robbers, Butch and Sundance, Jesse James, Bonnie and Clyde, you know the names. We all do.'

He paused.

'I'm head of a Violent Crimes detail downtown in Federal Plaza. A six man team, including myself, in a squad called the Bank Robbery Task Force. We're in charge of all the major bank robbery investigations in New York City, in each of the five boroughs.'

He cast his arm in the direction of the window.

'This place is a dream target for bank robbers, Sam. There are thousands of banks here, endless escape routes and the wealth of this city means thieves know every bank is guaranteed to be stocked up with cash.'

He paused to drink from his coffee, then continued.

'Most people who try to hold up banks are either incredibly dumb or incredibly desperate. They don't think clearly or rationally. No disguises, no weapons, no real plan. Every witness inside the bank can ID them later, and even if they can't, every security camera in the building documents the whole thing. Some of the more stupid thieves even look up, staring straight into the lens, no mask, no disguise. No common sense. No chance of success.'

Archer drank from his tea and nodded, watching the older man closely.

'The most common M.O is a note-job, where a thief will slide a note to the teller,' Gerrard continued. 'On the paper, they write *Give me all the cash in the register or I'll shoot you*, shit like that. Tellers have a protocol for this. They always hand over the cash, but most of them have panic-buttons by their feet, silent-alarms that go straight to the NYPD. They push that while stalling and complying with the robber's demands, and the thief will walk outside to find an entire police Precinct waiting for him. And if the teller doesn't have a panic button within reach, they'll hand over the cash but include bait money or dye packs deliberately camouflaged and placed within reach. Once the thief tries to leave, a transmitter reacts with a radio by the door and detonates the dye. The money is ruined, and the thief is covered with the red dye which is an absolute bitch to get off. They'll spend the next three days trying to scrub it off their skin, and by the third day pretty much every one of them is doing it in handcuffs.'

He shook his head.

'Most of these people are complete clowns. The NYPD usually rounds them all up the same day as the heists and retrieve the stolen cash. Those security protocols I mentioned have been incredibly effective, especially in this city. At the end of the last decade, things were going real good. Our clearance rate was going up and up and the heists were going down. In 1979, the Bureau logged 319 separate incidents of bank robbery in the five boroughs of New York City. By 2010, there were only 26.'

He paused, sipping his coffee again. Archer listened closely, intrigued.

'Any bank robbery in the Unites States is classed as a Federal crime, which means we automatically get involved and take over jurisdiction,' Gerrard said. 'We normally work together with local law enforcement and put together a team of FBI agents and local P.D in each town and city. We had the same thing going here, but things were going so well that the NYPD decided to pull their guys from the Task Force. We were six-and-six, half cops, half FBI. Well, the cops took back their six guys from the detail, leaving our six FBI agents to handle the caseload themselves. They claimed that the crimes would continue to dwindle and that surely the FBI could handle the reduced number of heists alone.'

'Getting out when the going's good,' Archer said.

Gerrard nodded. 'Exactly. They jumped ship. And since then, pretty much everything that could go wrong has gone wrong. It's just been one thing after another. We're in some seriously deep shit and it's rising every day. The thefts are back on the rise all over the city. And the people pulling the jobs are getting smarter. Even the idiots now know what to look for. Things got so bad last year that the Bureau pulled me from Washington and sent me up here to take over the Task Force and boost the clearance rate. Start catching these guys instead of constantly chasing after them.'

'So have you?' Archer asked.

Gerrard sighed and shook his head.

'We're down to 34 per cent, Sam. Thirty. Four. A third of our case load. It's shameful. That's an all-time low. Every other city across the United States looks to us to set an example. The Bureau has to publish a report to the public every quarter. The reports give exact details on all bank robbery crimes and statistics for each city in the country. Ours are the first people look at. And right now, those numbers are dismal. It's causing a stir within the entire organisation, a black-eye on the face of the FBI. My team and I are catching hell for it. Soon people are going to start getting fired.'

He drained the rest of his coffee, shaking his head.

'And there's one crew that's causing me all this grief.'

'Who?'

Gerrard didn't reply. He just slid the yellow folder across the table instead.

Archer looked down at it.

'Take a look,' Gerrard said, lowering his voice. 'They're killing me, Sam. Every job they pull knocks us down a rung, in the reports and in the public's estimation. They're humiliating me, my team and the entire Bureau. We can't get close to them. They're taking New York City for millions.'

Archer looked at him for a moment, then lifted open the yellow folder. A series of paper-clipped files were inside, five separate documents pulled or photocopied from police and Bureau department files. He thumbed through them and saw each separately-stapled stack had a mug-shot stuck to the top right corner of the page. Five separate profiles and rap-sheets.

Returning to the first page, Archer looked down at the first photo. It was a man. He looked tough and mean, a flattened nose and uncompromising dark eyes over a stubbled jaw-line and a mouth that showed not even a hint of a smile. He had a closely shaved head and a hard face that looked pissed off that he had to stand there and have his mug-shot taken. The black and white height-chart behind him said he was six-two.

Archer shifted his gaze, looking at the name on the file printed in a box on the left.

Sean Farrell.

'You want to talk me through them?' he asked, looking down at the file.

Gerrard nodded. 'That's Sean Farrell, the leader of the bunch. Rough piece of work. He did eight years on Rikers for murder. He was convicted a month before his eighteenth birthday.'

'Who did he kill?'

'Another kid his age. Walked up behind him on a basketball court and blew his head off with a shotgun from behind. Sound familiar?'

Archer looked up at him sharply.

Now Gerry had his attention.

'Motive?'

'The guy slept with his ex-girlfriend. Farrell didn't like it and decided to let the kid know how he felt.'

Archer dropped his gaze back to the sheet, looking at the man's list of convictions. It was long.

'He was an up and coming boxer once, hence the nose that looks like a pancake. He wasn't good enough to turn pro, so he started cornering other fighters. He owns a gym over in Queens.'

Archer scanned the other details on the page as Gerrard continued to talk. His D.O.B, place of residence, family, rap-sheet.

'He did another six months last year for GBH, so he's two strikes down,' Gerrard said. 'And let me tell you, it's just a matter of time before he swings dry for a third. He is walking, talking trouble, that man. Bad shit follows him everywhere he goes. He's got a lot of enemies both Federal and police-wise, not to mention people from his own neighbourhood that he's managed to piss off over the years. He's one of those guys that never backs down to anyone, no matter the situation, no matter the odds. Legacy of being a fighter. A good thing in the boxing ring, but not so good out on the street. That attitude's already landed him almost ten years in prison.'

Archer nodded. He took another look at the guy's photo, repeating his name in his head.

Sean Farrell.

Then he turned his file to one side, examining the next in the pile.

To his surprise, this one was a woman, but in her mug-shot she looked just as tough as Farrell. Maybe even meaner. Her dark hair was tightly drawn back in corn-rows lining her head, and she had a lean, hard face, rock-solid cheekbones and angry brown eyes. She looked Hispanic or Mexican and tough as the nails that had been hammered into his father's coffin.

'That's Farrell's girlfriend. Carmen Ortiz.'

'Latina?'

'Dominican. As you can tell by the photo, she makes her boyfriend look like a damn teddy bear. She cage fights out in New Jersey every few weeks, Farrell as her corner-man. She's got a perfect record as a pro, fifteen wins, no losses. She finished all but one of those fights and handed out a string of concussions and three broken arms on her way. She's a savage, Sam. Difference between her and her boyfriend is that she does it legally inside the cage.'

Archer listened, but continued to examine the woman's photograph.

'In the bank, she works as muscle,' Gerrard said. 'Farrell controls the room while she makes sure everyone inside listens to what he says. Her signature is busting up bank managers and armoured truck drivers. Breaks their nose, puts a shotgun to their balls and tells them to open up. Gets them compliant real fast. She's sent nine of them to the emergency room since we began this case.'

Archer looked at her stats and history on the file.

Father killed in gang-shooting, 2001.

Mother raped and shot dead, 2003.

'Jesus. Rough upbringing.'

Gerrard nodded. 'Product of her environment I guess. Doesn't give her an excuse to start robbing banks or smacking around truck drivers though. But needless to say, that's one bad bitch.'

Archer took one last look at her photo, then turned over the next file. He saw another hard face and closely-shaved head. This man was like a smaller version of

Farrell, the same flattened nose, the same harsh expression but slightly thinner. He glanced at the name.

Billy Regan, the file told him.

'That's Regan. Farrell met him in the joint on Riker's. He was only on a five monther for breaking and entering, but he and Farrell were cell-mates towards the end of Farrell's bid. They got real tight. Farrell treats him like he's his little brother. They're always knocking about together.'

'His role?'

'In the bank, he gets the tapes, takes care of any security guards and helps Ortiz with the cash in the vault.'

Archer took a good look at the guy, then nodded, turning over. The next man was different. He had brown hair, normal length, but the same angry expression. Like the others, he looked to be in his late-twenties, and looked just as pissed off about life in general.

'That's Tate. Muscle. He's a local kid, grew up in the neighbourhood with Farrell before he went to prison. They've used him as a hostage before, seeing as he looks less threatening than the others. He goes inside the bank before the job. The crew run in, Farrell picks him out, puts an empty gun to his head, says *don't move or I pull the trigger*. Gets everyone obedient and means they can take him with them.'

'And make a clean getaway,' Archer finished. 'Smart moves for a group of fighters.'

Gerrard nodded as the younger man turned the page. He found himself looking at the last member of the crew. This guy looked kind of like Tate, but had black hair instead of brown and more stubble.

'That's Brown. The wheelman. Another local kid from the block. He'll lift a getaway car a couple hours before the job, then after they hit the bank or truck, Brown will get them the hell out of there. We've been trying to work out where they're dumping the bent cars, but so far, no luck. It's like the damn things are vanishing into mid-air. Hard to run Forensics over a stolen getaway car when you can't even find it.'

Gerrard shook his head and finished his coffee as Archer scanned each file again, one-by-one.

'They're eight jobs down with a 100 per cent success rate,' Gerrard told him. '*One hundred per cent*. Five trucks, three banks. Totalled up, they've snatched close to three million dollars.'

'Are they working for anyone higher up?' Archer asked. 'Someone who's setting up the jobs, buying off information, providing truck rotas, blueprints of the banks?'

Gerrard shook his head.

'For the most part, they seem to be working alone,' he said. 'They do their research, and I'm sure they're paying people off to give them the info you just mentioned. They're smart and slick as hell. They're always disguised, and they know our response times and security measures. They take Tate as a pretend hostage so no one moves, and are five miles away before anyone face-down inside the bank so much as coughs. They leave the bait money and dye packs and work to the clock.'

Archer looked up at him, confused.

'You said they use Tate as a fake hostage? Witnesses can't ID him later?'

'He's always disguised, shades and baseball cap. Not enough to alert suspicion, but enough to cover his face and head. The crew are never there long enough for the witnesses to get a good look, and that's not including the fact that everyone inside is shit scared and face-down on the floor. We've tried perp walks, but no one we've brought in has ever been able to make an ID.'

He paused.

'But I thought we made a breakthrough ten days ago.'

'How so?'

74

'I got Brown talking.'

'How?'

'He's got a kid. List of charges against him would take his boy away forever if we wanted to contact child services. I dialled the number in front of him and pressed *Call*. It opened him up straight away.'

'What did he tell you?'

Gerrard checked over his shoulder, making sure they weren't being overheard. They were speaking in lowered tones already, but he spoke more quietly. He leaned forward over the table.

'A week today, there's a world title fight at MSG,' he said. 'Welterweight strap. Biggest fight of the year. Brown said Farrell's planning to hit the place during the fight.'

'MSG? As in Madison Square Garden?'

'The very same.'

Archer turned and looked out of the window over his shoulder. The Garden was a two minute walk from here, on the corner of 33rd and 8th. He'd passed it on his way here.

'Hit it how?' he asked.

'Get in the stash room. There's a big rock concert taking place the night before, this coming Friday night. The money rooms will be packed from the concession stands. There will be millions of dollars in there, easy, and it's not scheduled to be transported out of there until Sunday. They'll find a way of getting inside, or will pay someone off at that gate and head straight for those rooms.'

Archer thought about it for a moment, then all of a sudden realised they'd drifted off topic. He'd been too swept up in what Gerry was telling him. He turned back to Farrell's file, and examined the man's harsh photo again, memorising his features, trying to picture him in his head doing the deed, pulling the trigger of the shotgun against his father's head.

He pointed at the file. 'So you think he's the one who murdered my dad?'

Gerrard nodded. 'Yes. Or someone in his crew did. Let's just say they all fit the bill.'

'But that makes no sense. My father was based in D.C. This is your gig. How the hell would he get dragged into this?'

'An Assistant Director sent him up here. I didn't know about it until later, but apparently he was ordered to see what the hell was going on with my team. Observe my five agents and me from a distance and report back what he saw to the offices in Washington. Like I told you, the clearance rates are published in national reports every three months. New York's stats are bringing a shitload of shame and blame on the Bureau. Thirty-four per cent isn't going to cut it.'

'But why would they kill him? They wouldn't have any idea who he was.'

Gerrard shook his head.

'After he died, I learned that he'd been investigating them too, by way of association.' He paused, looking Archer in the eye. 'I think he found something, Sam. Something that could close this case and bring them all down. And I think somebody killed him before he could tell anyone what it was.'

Archer thought for a moment.

'Any proof?' he asked.

'The method of execution. This crew, they only ever use sawn-off shotguns. It's their signature, their calling-card, their bread and butter. Shotguns are a nightmare for ballistics fingerprinting. The buckshot scatters everywhere when you pull the trigger, so it's impossible to get a sample and match it to a particular weapon. Our only hope would be if they racked the pump and left a shell behind, but they haven't had to fire the weapons on a job yet. There's a credo in the Bureau that *every bullet is another piece of evidence to convict you.* But whoever killed Jimmy didn't reload. The empty cartridge stayed in the weapon. And he took it up close, when his back was turned. Farrell did eight years for killing a guy the exact same way. Shotgun, point-blank, back of the head. Tell me there isn't a pattern and a correlation there.'

Archer thought hard, picturing the scenario. He shook his head.

'I know my dad. Or, knew him,' he corrected. 'He wouldn't turn his back on Farrell or anyone on his team. Especially if he had something that could close this case and bring him in. And why would he meet with him if he had the evidence?'

'Maybe he got the drop on him,' Gerrard answered. 'Maybe Jimmy was meeting someone else and Farrell ambushed him.'

'That's a lot of maybes.'

Gerrard pointed at the file. 'That's a lot of motive.'

Archer didn't respond. He glanced down at the guy's photograph again, memorising his features.

The hard, tough jaw-line.

The pudgy, flat nose.

Sean Farrell.

He pictured him with a sawn-off shotgun in his hands. Stalking up behind his father or ambushing him, ordering his hands in the air and for him to turn. The barrel of the shotgun nestling into the back of James Archer's head.

And Farrell pulling the trigger.

He felt his mood darken.

'OK. Suppose it's the way you say it is. I'm out of my jurisdiction Gerry. I'm UK police, not NYPD. I can't go after these people.'

'I'm not asking you to.' Gerrard looked at him for a long moment. 'But I am asking you for something else.'

'What?'

'My team and I have conducted raids,' Gerrard said. 'Made arrests. Brought each one of these assholes in for questioning. They know exactly what each and every agent in my team looks like. They even know our names.'

He paused.

'But they don't know you.'

Archer picked up where this was going straight away. He leaned back in his seat and shook his head.

'No way. Absolutely no way. It won't work,' he said. 'They're planning to pull the Madison Square Garden job a week from today. That's seven days from now. I'm good but I'm not that good, Gerry. I'll never get near them.'

Gerry leaned forward, pressing him.

'I'm not asking you to. But you'll be in Astoria anyway, clearing out your Dad's place. All I'm asking for is another set of eyes on them in their neighbourhood. There's a pub called McCann's on Ditmars Boulevard. They're in there basically every night. Get inside and grab a beer. If you make contact, try to strike up a conversation with Farrell. Get him to trust you. They're getting their money out and cleaning it and we have no idea how they're doing it. It's untraceable and it's been baffling me for months. I need to find out how they manage it, or at least get something that could give me a goddamned break in this case. I'm out of solutions, kid. I need your help.'

He paused.

'We've made armed arrests. Unlike them, we don't wear disguises. They know what every member of my team looks like, and they'll be expecting NYPD attention. They'd sniff out an undercover cop or Fed a mile off. But they'll never guess who you are. Your accent, your cover story. You don't even look like Jimmy, so they won't realise the two of you are related. It all checks out.'

Archer looked back out the window, shaking his head. Gerrard pressed harder.

'I need you, Sam. They're killing me and my team. You're going to be around for the next week or so anyway. Please help me out. That's all I'm asking.' He tapped the folder. 'I swear to you that someone in this group knows who killed your father. One of them probably did it. Surely that's enough?'

Silence followed.

Archer eventually looked across at him, eye-to-eye, his face hard.

'Listen. If I find out one of these people pulled the trigger on my dad, I can't make promises to you that I can't keep,' he said quietly. 'I need you to know that before I get involved.'

Gerrard nodded. 'That's OK. I'll handle the case file if that happens. I'll take responsibility for it. It won't be an issue.'

Archer looked at him across the table, then out of the window. Gerrard stayed quiet, hopeful, waiting to see if his approach had worked. In the silence light jazz music filled the air. Duke Ellington, or Miles Davis, all saxophone and drums and melody.

Looking out into the street, Archer's mind weighed up his options, like a set of scales, Farrell and his team on one side, Gerry and his father on the other. As he mulled over the facts, his gaze suddenly fell on a father and son, hand-in-hand, crossing the street. He watched as they headed across the street and into a café opposite the Starbucks called *Andrew's*. He watched the man open the door and let his son in first, then the two of them disappeared out of sight.

He turned back to Gerrard. 'My dad's apartment. Do you have the phone number?'

'Of course.'

'Call me at 7pm. I'll give you an answer then.'

Before Gerrard could reply, Archer rose, not waiting for a response.

Tossing his empty cup in the trash, he strode out of the coffee shop.

SEVEN

The Marriott Marquis Hotel Cobb had booked Archer into was located on the west side of Times Square on Broadway. It was only ten blocks uptown from the Starbucks, a ten minute walk but Archer walked straight past the doors, moving on through the bright and busy Times Square, threading his way through the sea of people. Everywhere you looked there were tourists, vendors, tour operators or someone trying to sell you something, and Archer made his way through as fast as he could, past all the commotion, past all the noise.

He needed to think.

Eleven years. Eleven years since he and his father had last said a word to each other. Aside from a birthday card in the mail most years, that was it. After one too many arguments with his wife inside their family home, Jim Archer had packed his bags in a fit of fury one night and left when his son was sixteen. Watching him walk out of the front door all those years ago back in London, standing in the hallway as he watched him go, his son figured that he'd see him again in a couple of weeks, or in a month or two. It was one of those spats that would just need a little dose of time to heal. His parents were both strong-minded and strong-willed people. They'd resolve it soon enough once tempers had cooled. He'd never have realised it at the time, but that was the last time he'd ever see him alive. Jim Archer had gone straight to Heathrow that night, booked himself onto the next flight to New York and had never returned.

Archer walked on, past Times Square, past 50th Street, headed up Broadway. It was slightly quieter and less frenzied here, but he moved on, headed for Central Park.

In one way, that whole phase of his life seemed like a different lifetime. So much had happened since then. He'd joined the police two years later, done his training, spent five years at Hammersmith and Fulham before being reassigned to the Armed Response Unit. He had grown into a man, his own person, independent and strong. But then again, in another way, it seemed as if it had all happened yesterday. The wounds remained raw. He still felt betrayed and angry that his father had never even picked up the phone and called once in the eleven years since. His parents had fallen out, but severing speaking terms with each other didn't mean they could do the same to the kids.

In the years since, Archer had often thought about re-establishing contact with his father. But he never had. He'd always waited, promising himself he'd do it soon. And now that he was gone, there were suddenly a million things he wanted to tell him that now he could never say. He shook his head and walked on up the street, his hands in the pockets of his suit, up Broadway towards the Park.

This whole situation was troubling. He'd known Gerry for as long as he could remember. They hadn't seen each other since Archer was a teenager, but time didn't matter with a guy like Gerry. If you were friends with him, you were friends for life. He was as reliable as anyone he'd ever met, and an old acquaintance to boot. If he was convinced that Farrell or someone in his crew had killed his father, then he was probably right. The young cop glanced up at the sky as he walked. He'd lost his mother a couple of years ago, but they'd all known that was coming. She'd passed in her sleep, not in any pain and Archer was at peace with that. Goodbyes had been exchanged. They'd been prepared, and everything that needed to be said had been said.

But this wasn't gentle or peaceful. Someone had got the jump on his father and executed him. Whoever did it didn't even have the courage to look him in the eye as he pulled the trigger. Not the way a person should leave this world. And whoever did it was out there right now, walking around, figuring they'd got away with it, moving on with their lives and forgetting about the one they'd just ended.

He shook his head again, his anger rising.

He arrived on 59th, the entrance to Central Park across the street. Twenty four blocks, just like that. The Park looked stunning in the afternoon light, green, verdant and welcoming.

Looking left and right, he saw there were scores of people up here, tourists and wealthy residents, tour operators and people in athletic gear headed into the Park for a workout. Archer was standing at a crossing beside a group of other pedestrians, waiting for the lights to change. Once the orange hand on the crossing lights flashed to the white man walking, he made his way over the white lines on the tarmac and continued onto a footpath that led into Central Park.

From the exterior, the place had looked special, but it was even more beautiful inside. The grass and trees were a vibrant green, golden sunlight streaming through the branches and leaving dark shadows on the ground. People of all shapes and sizes were wandering along the dusty winding paths, some licking ice-creams, others snapping photographs of family and friends, others like Archer just here for a quiet stroll and a chance to get some private thinking done.

Alongside the bike path, Archer sat on a bench facing the Upper West Side, alone, and loosened his tie further, taking in a deep breath of the clean air.

Gerry was right. He was going to be in town anyway. His return flight wasn't until Sunday, a week tomorrow, and Cobb didn't want him back before then anyway. And he couldn't just pack his bags and leave knowing that he hadn't helped in any way to catch the killer.

Waking up every day in London knowing that the person who did it was still out there.

Knowing that they were still robbing banks, stealing themselves rich and living the lavish life.

His knuckles whitened and his eyes narrowed, and he shook his head slowly, staring straight ahead through the trees to the street.

He couldn't live with himself if he just left and didn't at least try to find the culprit.

But this wasn't going to end well, whatever happened. These were tough, brutal, dangerous people. Gerrard said Farrell had already served time for murder and from what he'd told Archer about Ortiz, it sounded as if she was a homicide charge waiting to happen. They wouldn't go down without a fight or without taking other people with them. They'd duke it out if they got cornered and anyone who got in the way would be necessary collateral damage. He knew the type from back home in London. Criminals like this didn't care who they killed, be it other crooks, Federal agents, city cops or just innocent bystanders.

As he watched the cyclists and joggers move past him, he tried to picture his father in his head, and to hear his voice.

What would he say?

What would he want me to do?

He closed his eyes, listening for anything, something.

But there was nothing.

All he could hear were the birds in the park.

He sat there on the bench for a further thirty minutes, then walked back to where he'd entered the Park at the south entrance and got on an Astoria-bound R train at the 5th Avenue subway stop. The train rumbled and rattled as it moved under Manhattan, the East River and into Queens, and Archer stood inside gripping the rail for support. The carriage was quiet, and there were only a handful of other people sitting inside.

After fifteen minutes or so and several stops, they arrived at Steinway Street in Astoria. Once the doors opened, Archer stepped out and moved along the platform, walking up two flights of stairs and arriving up on the sidewalk.

He paused for a moment and looked at the neighbourhood around him. He hadn't been here in a long time, not since he was twelve or thirteen, but he knew the area well. His father used to own a place in Woodside, Queens, and Archer had stayed there often as a kid on summer visits from the UK. He pulled the piece of paper Gerrard had given him and glanced at the address in his hand. The apartment was just a five minute walk from here, and he headed off down the street towards it.

Seeing as it was a Saturday afternoon, Astoria was busy. He'd loved this neighbourhood as a boy. It was a separate little community, just like Williamsburg in Brooklyn or Flushing further east in Queens, and if someone wanted to avoid Manhattan, they could find everything they'd ever need right here in these streets. As he walked down Steinway, crossing over Broadway and headed towards 30th Avenue, he passed vendors on street corners, one of them an old war vet with a red USMC Korea hat, sitting or standing beside stalls containing electrical goods. He saw kids running in and out of gaming and shoe stores, their parents talking with each other nearby while trying to keep their children out of trouble.

His father had told him a long time ago that the world-famous *Steinway* pianos originated from this street and were still made here to this very day. Archer liked that. Amongst any potential Manhattan snobbery that figured Queens was a neighbourhood not worth coming out to, there was a little piece of the area in every concert hall around the world that used a *Steinway* piano.

Soon he arrived at the corner of 31st Avenue and Steinway. A grill station was parked on the corner, a small line formed in front as people waited to order cooked meats from the counter. Archer walked through the smoke and steam from the grill and walked north a block to arrive on 38th Street, where the address on the piece of paper Gerry had given him was located.

Shortly afterwards he arrived at the building matching the address on the scrap of paper, to his right. He pulled the slip of paper from his pocket and double-checked, looking at the number on the front door.

This was the place.

It was a semi-detached building, three levels inside a small gated yard. Each side of the street was lined with these three-floor places, structures made from wood and brick, put up probably some fifty odd years ago and gradually renovated since then to keep up with the times.

Looking at the building in front of him, he saw that the upper two floors each had a balcony guarded by black railings. On the second floor he saw a guy in a t-shirt and shorts using a grill, the sizzle and smell of cooking meat in the air. The man saw Archer on the street below and they nodded a greeting to each other.

'Can I help?' the man said.

'Yeah. I think my dad was renting a place here. His name's Archer. James, or Jim, or Jimmy.'

The guy nodded. 'Top floor. Want me to buzz you in?'

'I've got a key. Thanks.'

'No problem.'

Archer pushed open the gate as the guy returned his attention to the grill and walked towards the front door. He slid one of the two keys in the lock and twisted, pushing the door open and shutting it behind him.

Inside, it was quiet. The sounds of birdsong from the trees and sizzling meat from the grill were suddenly gone. He moved up the stairs, past the second floor, and continued up to arrive outside the door to the third floor apartment.

He took the second key and slid it into the lock.

It fitted.

This was the place.

86

Archer paused.

Then he took a deep breath, twisting the handle and opening the door, he stepped inside the apartment.

EIGHT

The first thing that struck him about the place was the cleanliness. It was tidy and organised, unusually so considering the traits of the man who had formerly lived here. The air smelt of polished wood and cigars, oaky but fresh. He shut the door gently behind him, and examined the interior around him.

It was a medium sized apartment. Straight ahead of him was a kitchen, a living area to the right with a couch and television, none of it separated by walls or doors. To the right, a screen door led out to the balcony he'd seen from the street and to the left was the main bedroom and bathroom. The floor was wooden and polished, the walls white and equally clean. It was a nice place and it had been immaculately maintained. Archer figured an apartment like this in this neighbourhood would cost around a thousand-five a month in rent, maybe closer to two. In Manhattan, it would be two, three or four times that.

Archer walked into the kitchen. It was also surprisingly tidy, every pot, pan and plate put away, no washing-up left in the sink, the countertops clean. He turned to the fridge and reached for the handle. As he went to pull it open, something caught his eye and made him pause. There was a newspaper clipping from The New York Times stuck to the door by a fridge magnet. He read the headline.

British police foil terrorist attacks in London.

Gerrard's voice echoed in his mind. *He always talked about you, you know. He was proud. He kept saying 'that's my son'.*

Archer looked at the cutting for a moment longer, then pulled the door open. It was sparsely filled, just a carton of eggs, some milk and some preserves on the shelves.

No beer.

Closing the door, he moved out of the kitchen into the living area on the right. A table was pushed against the wall facing the kitchen, knick knacks and odd items placed on the surface. Standing by the table, Archer saw something he recognised resting there and picked it up. It was a wallet. Jim Archer had used the same one for twenty years. He felt the soft leather in his hands. The texture. The smell. Memories flooded back. His dad giving him money to spend at the weekend with his friends. Buying his son a bottle of Coke then sitting outside a pub in the English summer, the leathery wallet resting on the wooden table. Asking his dad for some spare coins for sweets, and seeing him pretend to consider refusing, knowing he'd always end up saying yes and helping him out.

He flipped it open and saw a New York State driver's licence.

James Anthony Archer. D.O.B: 05/10/1957.

He thumbed through the cards. He found a couple of pictures of him when he was a kid and his sister, Sarah, tucked into the back. He stared at them for a moment then returned them, putting the wallet back where he'd found it.

He turned and moved to the main bedroom. This too was surprisingly tidy, the bed made, the sheets white and clean. He pulled open the closet. A series of suits hung there, lined up neatly on the rail alongside some shirts with ties hung over the coat-hangers. Several pairs of shoes had been lined up side-by-side underneath, some of the laces still tied. Clothes and shoes that would never be used again by their owner, Archer thought. Like everything else in this apartment.

He sat back on the bed. It was comfy and springy. He turned his attention to the nightstand by the bed and reached for the top drawer. It was jammed. He grabbed the side of the stand with his free hand and pulled hard and the drawer suddenly opened. There were a couple of books in there with the memory card to a digital camera laid on top. It had a small square of tape on the underside, as if it had been stuck to something. Archer ignored it as something else caught his eye.

There was a steel pistol in there, resting on the small stack of books towards the back of the drawer. Archer reached inside and took it out. It was a Sig Sauer P226, FBI issue, smelling of gun oil. His father's service weapon. It was still here in the drawer which meant he hadn't taken it the night he'd been murdered.

Possibly meaning he hadn't been expecting any trouble.

It was unloaded, no round in the pipe, no magazine in the base. Archer pulled the drawer open all the way and found three mags at the back, each one fully loaded. He took one of them out and thumbed the bullets out of the clip one-by-one, each round landing in a metal huddle on the bed, *dinging* as they dropped onto each other on the pile. Fifteen bullets in total landed on the bed. He pushed them all back into the magazine one-by-one, then slotted it into the base of the weapon and pulled the slide, loading the pistol.

The gun in his hand, Archer lay back on the bed. Everything that had happened in the past two days suddenly caught up with him. He realised he was pretty worn out. Learning of his father's death, the flight, the funeral, the meeting with Gerrard and the collective weight of it all on his mind had left him way more tired than he thought. He stared up at the ceiling, his arms stretched out to the sides, the pistol in his right hand, the soft mattress supporting his back.

And before he knew it, he drifted off to sleep.

A sudden noise brought him back to consciousness and he stirred awake. Opening his eyes he stared at the ceiling, briefly wondering where he was. The phone on the bed-side table was ringing. He blinked, looking at it sleepily, then glanced at a clock on the dresser.

7:00 pm.

It was Gerry.

Archer reached for the receiver and sat up.

'Yeah?'

'It's me,' Gerrard's voice said. *'What's the answer?'*

Archer looked at the gun in his hand. He shifted his gaze through the bedroom door at the empty, silent apartment ahead of him.

'OK. I'm in.'

He didn't wait for Gerry to respond. He just returned the phone to the cradle, and looked down at the steel Sig Sauer pistol in his right hand again.

Someone had murdered James Archer. They thought they'd get away with it.

But his son was going to make sure they didn't.

NINE

'I think I'm in,' Archer told Gerrard, back in that same Starbucks on 35th and 7th, three days later. Across the table, Gerry's eyes widened.

'Already? How?'

'There was a fight. Outside the pub on Ditmars. They pulled me out to the street to find out who I was but then they got jumped. Six guys, out of nowhere. I backed Farrell and his friends up, and flipped it on its head.'

Gerrard nodded. 'Good move. I told you he's trouble.'

'That's for damn sure.'

'Anyone hurt?'

'No one killed. And you were spot on about Ortiz. She took two of them down like they were practice. There'll be some sore heads walking into Accident and Emergency at Mount Sinai this morning. She put both of them away in about twenty seconds.'

Gerrard nodded, sipping his coffee.

'They pulled another job yesterday.'

'Where?'

'Chase bank, Upper East Side. Hit the place when the time-lock on the vault was off. When you saw them, they were probably celebrating.'

'What was the damage?'

'Five hundred thousand. Over half a mil.'

'Wow.'

Gerrard shook his head as Archer reached for his cup of tea. 'Not quite. They screwed up.'

'How so?'

'Two homicides. Or, should I say, two more. Left them both in the getaway car which they then torched. First time they've done both those things. The two bodies were a real mess when we found them. What was left of them, anyway.'

Archer frowned, pulling the cap off his tea and letting the liquid cool. 'That doesn't sound like them. You said they weren't that sloppy. Who were the two victims?'

'Driver of the stolen taxi-cab, the car they used for the job. And Brown.'

'Brown? Their own guy?'

'The very same. Someone blasted him in the back of the head as he pulled up by the switch car.'

'Shotgun?'

Gerrard nodded.

'They unloaded the gear then tossed a match inside the cab,' he said. 'The driver was locked in the trunk and couldn't get out.'

'Wait, hold on. They just killed Brown?' Archer asked, still surprised.

Gerrard nodded. 'Yeah, they did. I guess they found out he was talking to us.'

Archer shook his head in disbelief. From the report in the file he knew that Brown was a childhood friend of Farrell's, a man who'd been part of every job they'd pulled together. But they'd killed him in a heartbeat, shotgun, point blank, back of the head, the same method of execution as his father.

'Jesus,' he said. 'These people are a different breed.'

Gerry nodded in agreement and took a long gulp of coffee.

'OK, so why not move in right now and take them?' Archer asked. 'That's two more corpses to work with. Surely you have enough of a case to make something stick?'

Gerrard shook his head.

'That's the damn problem. I don't,' he said. 'Everything we have is circumstantial. We know they hit the bank. We know they torched the car. We know they blew Brown's head off and killed the cab driver. I know one of them killed your father. But we can't *prove* any of it. Their alibis will have been bought and paid for weeks ago. They never leave any evidence or traces of DNA, and are always fully disguised so nobody can make an ID. And we can't match the two shotgun blasts with ballistics. So until we actually physically catch them in the act or until they screw up and leave something we can pin on them, it's just not happening. They don't make mistakes, Sam. And that's what is pissing me off.'

He shook his head, looking out the window, cursing under his breath. He looked wearier than the last time Archer had seen him, which was only a matter of days. Judging by his complexion and demeanour the investigation seemed to be really taking its toll.

'OK, so let's think,' Archer said, forming a plan, trying to be positive and help his father's old friend out. 'The last thing Brown told you was the job at Madison Square Garden on Saturday, right?'

'That's right.'

'Today's Tuesday. That's four days from now. You said you needed to catch them in the act, so here's your chance. It's right there on a plate, Gerry. It's the perfect opportunity.'

Gerrard shook his head. 'They knew he was talking to us. That's why they killed him. They'll have changed their plans.'

Archer shook his head.

'Not necessarily. They have no idea how much or what he told you. They're nine for nine so far. One hundred per cent. They won't change. They'll figure they can get it done anyway, even if he did tell you something. These people are fighters, not brain surgeons. They'll love the challenge. The juice'll be worth the squeeze. You can set up a team at the stadium, and be ready and waiting for them. Maybe call in back up from D.C. and get some extra cavalry. Have an entire division on call.'

He paused, picturing the heist in his head.

'How do you think they'll try it?'

Gerrard shrugged.

94

'Disguises, of course. Probably dressed as stadium employees, or cops. They may even have bought tickets and will get inside that way. The concessions stands from the concert the previous night will have brought in close to four million. They'll either buy their way in or force it. If they plan smartly, the take could be monumental. And the Garden is on the corner of the big traffic junction on 33rd and 8th. There are going to be a lot of cops down there, so they'll need to get out of the area quickly. They won't walk or use the subway. They'll want to get off the island and get across the water as fast as possible, but Brown was their wheelman.'

'Surely one of them will take over?'

Gerrard shook his head.

'I don't think so. Farrell and Ortiz will definitely want to be inside, pulling the job,' he said. 'Regan too. The only question mark is Tate. They might conceivably put him behind the wheel, but I don't think so. He's a hothead. Brown was a rough piece of work, but he was cool under pressure. Tate's too volatile and erratic to be reliable in the driver's seat.'

'So with Brown dead, they'll be looking for a new driver.'

Gerrard nodded. 'If they go ahead with it, then yeah, I'd say so.'

Archer glanced out of the window, absorbing everything they'd discussed, picturing the job and each member of the crew in his mind.

'I had a tail, by the way. On the way here.'

Gerrard's eyes widened suddenly. 'What? Who?'

'Regan. He followed me after I left Dad's apartment. He was waiting for me on 38th Street. Farrell must have put him there.'

Gerrard looked outside the window, anxious. 'Did you ditch him?'

'Of course. Relax,' Archer said, noting the sudden alarm in the older man's behaviour. 'Take it easy.'

'Jesus, you had me worried there kid,' Gerrard said, exhaling a long breath, glancing out of the window again. 'They see you talking to me, its game over.'

'Well don't worry. I lost him.' He saw the stress and anxiety on his father's old friend's face. He looked like he'd aged a few years in just the past few days. 'Stay cool, Gerry. It's all good. We're already making progress.'

Gerrard nodded and checked his watch as Archer drank his tea.

'By the way, do you have a cell phone?' he asked.

Archer nodded, and gave him the number.

'I need to get back downtown,' Gerrard continued. 'I've got my team working the Chase job and they'll be wondering where I am. But I'll give you a call later.'

'OK. I'll get out of here too,' Archer said.

'Great work so far, kid. You've done me proud. Maybe head back to McCann's tonight. Try to establish contact with Farrell again and gain some trust. But sleep with one eye open, Sam. You'll have got his attention. He and his team will be watching you, I guarantee.'

Archer looked across the table at him and nodded. Then the two men rose and shook hands. Without another word Archer turned and headed to the exit first, tossing his half-filled cup of tea in the trash and pushing open the front door, walked out and headed uptown.

But neither man realised at that moment that the game was up.

Someone was already watching them.

She was standing across the street on 35th outside a *Vitamin Shoppe*, leaning on a pay-phone, the receiver to her ear. But she wasn't making a call. All she heard the other end was the dial tone.

She was in a good spot for surveillance. The box and post of the payphone were covering her body, the phone and her hand and arm covering one half of her head, but her eyes were looking straight over the metal box at the two men inside the Starbucks.

She'd been up early, despite a late night and had followed Gerrard from Federal Plaza, seeing what he was up to. She'd followed him here and she'd been taken aback when the English guy had shown up ten minutes later. But this definitely wasn't a social call. Around them, every other person going in and out of that place looked, for the most part, pretty chilled and relaxed and unsuspecting or preoccupied. But Gerrard and the Brit looked wary, occasionally checking around them, making sure nobody was watching, leaning over the table, talking in low voices.

She'd watched them speak like that for ten minutes or so then she saw the two men suddenly rise, the English guy walking to the door, leaving and heading uptown. Gerrard strode outside soon after, readjusting his tie and sliding sunglasses over his nose, then put his hand in the air and hailed a taxi.

The woman turned, huddling over the receiver as if she was struggling to hear what was being said the other end. He knew who she was and she didn't fancy him seeing her. Her head down, she risked a glance and saw him step into a taxi, pulling the door shut then watched the taxi speed off downtown.

Once he was gone, she placed the receiver back with a *ding*. Amongst everyone on the sidewalks up ahead, she could still see the British guy walking uptown three blocks away. Although she'd only had a brief interaction with him he'd looked and acted solid, but she didn't know if she could trust him. His private meeting with Gerrard was making her uneasy and unsure.

Something was going on here. Something that she didn't know about.

But before the end of the week, she was going to find out what it was.

TEN

After he left the coffee shop Archer turned left and headed uptown, straight towards Times Square seven blocks ahead. He was intending to go to the hotel and relax there for a bit. He figured a few hours resting up would be just what he needed, getting in some down-time and thinking-time before he headed back to McCann's on Ditmars and tried to re-establish contact with Farrell and his crew.

But before he could go to the hotel, he knew he needed to salvage what he could from his father's apartment. There was stuff in there that should be kept, stuff that his sister might want. The clothes and shoes, all that crap could go to the Goodwill store. It wasn't a job that he was looking forward to, throwing out all his father's stuff, cleaning out the place and ditching any non-essentials. But he knew he'd have to do it at some point and now seemed as good a time as any to get it over and done with.

He crossed the street to the right, headed past a large Chase bank on the corner of 40th and 7th, and ducked down the steps leading to the subway, pulling his flannel shirt back on that he'd removed earlier. He could wear it again, seeing as he no longer had anyone tailing him.

He got on a Queens-bound train and headed back to Astoria. It was an R train, so he stepped off on Steinway and walked up to the street level, heading straight to his father's apartment. He would try to get everything done in an hour or so, working fast. It would probably take longer, but the quicker he did it, the quicker he could forget about it and move on. He walked down Steinway, past the food stand on the corner and through the smoke from the grill, then turned left and walked north a block, crossing the street.

He started moving down 38th but as he approached the apartment, he saw someone sitting on the steps outside.

He could see straight away it wasn't the guy from the second floor, the one who'd been using the grill. This man was a hulking figure, dressed in jeans and a white zip-up tracksuit top with red stripes down each arm, a cigarette in his mouth.

Archer saw who it was immediately, no mistake.

Farrell.

The bigger man saw Archer approaching and rose to his feet, flicking the butt of the cigarette onto the ground. Archer stopped on the sidewalk twenty feet away, outside the gate. In daylight and standing across from him, Farrell seemed even bigger than he had the night before. He was an intimidating figure. Archer suddenly wished he hadn't left his dad's 9mm Sig upstairs in the apartment.

'What the hell do you want?' Archer asked.

Farrell raised his hands. 'Relax. I come in peace.'

'Like you did last night? I don't give a shit. How did you know I was staying here?'

'I had Regan follow you home after the fight,' Farrell replied, honestly.

Silence. Both men stood there, either side of the small gate, staring at each other testily. There seemed to be a mutual respect in the air, but no secure trust had yet been earned on either side.

'So what do you want?' Archer asked.

'To go for a drive,' Farrell said.

*

Farrell's car was a silver Ford, a nice model, sleek and fast. Archer didn't know a lot about cars, but it seemed to handle well and his seat was comfortable. They were headed for the Queensborough Bridge, taking the kind of intricate route through Astoria that only a local who'd lived here his whole life would know.

The Ford had been parked on the kerb outside Jim Archer's apartment and the only reason Archer had got in the car with the guy was to further their contact and to

100

try and build some kind of rapport. Archer was under no illusions; much as Gerry wanted his help, he was doing this for himself. The man in the driver's seat could very well have murdered his father or if not knew who had and Archer wanted to find out everything Farrell knew about it.

'You know, I had Regan follow you again today. He said he lost you at Times Square,' Farrell said, turning right and headed towards the Queensborough.

'Really?'

'Where'd you go?'

'Shopping.'

'Where are the bags?'

'Why'd you have him follow me?' Archer asked, deflecting the question.

Pause.

Farrell didn't respond.

'I saw what you did last night,' he said. 'I was impressed. That guy's a real asshole, but he's a big asshole. I'm a boxing trainer; my girl, Carmen, fights out in East Rutherford every few weeks. Mixed martial arts. I corner her. We'd fight in the city, but it's still illegal.'

Like that would stop you, Archer thought.

'You ever fight?' Archer asked him.

'Used to. Boxing though, not MMA. Did some time inside and couldn't do it anymore when I got out the joint. Lost my cardio, my footwork, everything. Started holding the pads instead of hitting them. Couldn't throw a good punch anymore.'

'Looked like you could last night.'

Pause. They started to move over the Queensborough Bridge, Manhattan rolling into view up ahead. Archer looked out of the window at the skyline, trying to stay cool. He was sat next to the man who had quite possibly killed his father. But here they were, having a casual conversation, like two civil strangers. He swallowed, taking a deep breath.

101

Stay cool. Stay in control.
Think of the big picture.
'So England, huh?' Farrell said.
'That's right.'
'I'm Irish, you know. That should make us enemies.'
'You making a point?'
Farrell smiled. 'Just busting your balls. You're tense, man. Relax. I ain't gonna bite.'
Pause.
'So what do you do for a job?' Farrell asked.
'Currently unemployed.'
'You ever serve time?'
'No.'
'Good. Keep it that way, trust me,' Farrell said, as they approached the end of the Bridge. Farrell turned right on 1st and headed uptown, through the Upper East Side and towards Harlem. Archer stayed silent.
'How well do you know the city?' he asked.
'Been here a few times.'
'Can you drive?'
Gerrard's voice flashed into Archer's mind. *They'll be looking for a new driver.*
'Of course.'
They moved on, through the East 60 Streets and the 70's. The Upper East Side.
'Manhattan streets ain't like the U.K, you know,' Farrell said.' It's a chessboard out here. There're no alleyways, no hiding places and you're on an island. It's a grid, and there are cops everywhere. You get jammed up, you'd better make sure you know what the hell you're doing.'
'I came here a lot growing up. I know the streets.'
A couple of minutes later, Farrell turned left on 110th and drove down to Lexington Avenue, then turned left again and pulled the car to a halt on the kerb, right next

to the upper right edge of Central Park, facing south. He applied the handbrake, but kept the engine running.

They sat there in silence, the car facing the long stretch of road heading all the way downtown, the engine humming.

'So what now?' Archer asked.

Farrell didn't reply, and pushed open his door instead.

'I'll show you. Step out.'

Archer opened his door and climbing out, saw Farrell beckon him to his side of the car. He'd left his door open.

'Take a seat. Get a feel for it.'

Archer did so, as Farrell moved to the passenger side. They both took a seat, swapping places and pulled the doors shut as the light behind them turned green and traffic started moving past them on the left. Archer slid his hands over the wheel and got a feel for the car. It was a good size, strong enough to carry its weight yet light enough to knock off some serious mileage.

'What do you think?' Farrell asked.

Archer nodded. He knew nothing about cars, but feigned interest.

'Not bad.'

The next two things Archer did were crucially uncharacteristic. He made two mistakes, mistakes he never normally made.

He dropped his guard for a split-second.

And he looked out the window to his left.

Farrell suddenly reached behind his back. Archer turned in the next instant, but Farrell had a head-start and jammed something into his neck.

It was a 9mm pistol.

Archer froze, looking at it pushed against his neck, then at Farrell.

'What the hell are you doing?'

'We're on 110th and Lex,'' Farrell said. 'I want us in Herald Square in six minutes. If we're a second late, I pull the trigger and you die, pal.'

ELEVEN

Archer didn't move, the gun still to his neck. Farrell stared straight at him, his finger tight on the trigger.

'Are you kidding me?'

Farrell ignored him, lifting his other wrist, the weapon tight in his gun-hand and checked his watch.

'You're wasting time. And I'm not joking. Five minutes and fifty five seconds, I pull this trigger. *Move!*'

Archer paused for one further moment.

Assessed his options.

Then he released the handbrake and pushed his foot down, the tyres squealing as the car lunged forward.

They were on the north east corner of Central Park, on 110th and Lexington Avenue. Herald Square was 76 blocks away. Unless they had an airplane, Archer knew this was going to be close to impossible. But he floored the pedal anyway.

He didn't have a choice.

The quickest way to get there would be Central Park West but that was the other side of the Park. It all depended on luck. He needed to hit a series of green lights. If they were red, he would either have to run them or accept his fate and either scrap with Farrell or take the chance that he wouldn't pull the trigger. But judging from what he'd already learned about the man, the second outcome seemed unlikely.

The car sped forward. Farrell had lowered the gun and jammed it tight in his ribs, a constant reminder of what he was up against. There was no traffic in the road and he did a U turn in the street, swinging a hard left then turning another left to face west down 110th Street. He floored it, the car burning down the road, other cars honking and drivers shouting as Archer cut the car into the lanes. They were moving right to left, across the top of Central Park, and fast. Up here, it would be far easier to get across town. If he tried the same downtown, they'd get clogged up in traffic like a fly in a spider's web and would never make it before his time ran out.

They zoomed along 110th, all the greenery of the Park flashing past Archer's window on the left. Up ahead, he saw a cathedral fast approaching on their right, *The Cathedral of St John the Divine*, a sign told him. Farrell checked the clock on his watch, the pistol still tight in Archer's ribs, uncomfortably so, as the car sped forward.

'Five –thirty to go,' he said.

Archer was in luck with the green light and there was no one on the crossing. He barely slowed as he turned down to face Central Park West, a sliding turn, the wheels skidding on the concrete as the car pulled its way around to face south.

The lights ahead were green and the car scorched forward, knocking off the streets. Alongside them, the sidewalks were dotted with the odd pedestrian or food stall, but Archer kept his eyes peeled for any cops or a squad car lurking in any of the streets they passed. He considered trying to attract their attention, getting them pulled over and the gun out of his ribs but he couldn't risk screwing this up.

Farrell knew who killed his father. And he needed to do this to find out who that person was.

They burnt it down the streets, the sidewalks flashing past. In New York City, the traffic lights system often lit up one after the other sequentially in order to try and alleviate traffic and Archer struck gold, the car torching it down Central Park West, the Park and all its trees flashing past on the left.

106th.
104th.
100th.
95th.
90th.

They flew all the way down to the early 80's. So far, so good, beating the clock.

But then his luck shifted. He hit his first red on 80th and was forced to slow to a halt, just as Farrell called out the time.

'Four-minutes-thirty. Better move.'

Archer swore, willing the light to flick green, sensing each passing second tick away. When it did, the car leapt forward and turned right, speeding over the crossing and moving along 80th, taking another quick turn on the crossing on the next left and headed onto Columbus Avenue, which would turn into 9th Avenue in a few blocks. He hit another series of greens and they roared on downtown.

Past the Dakota, where John Lennon was shot.

Past the Juilliard School.

Past the Lincoln and Time Warner Centres.

'Three-forty-five. Better hurry,' Farrell said.

Archer pushed his foot down and the car sped on faster.

They roared down 9th, boxing Columbus Circle and avoiding the traffic there. But there was a problem, Archer realised, his mind racing as fast as the four wheels on the car. Herald Square was on Sixth, so they needed to be three avenues over. Archer had to keep going down 9th though. If he tried to get across now, he'd hit all the traffic around Times Square and that would be the end of it.

He was forced to slow as a cop car passed the other way, but once it had passed Archer sped on.

50th.

49th.

48th.

Into Hell's Kitchen, the streets suitably sunny and hot.

'Two minutes,' Farrell said, pushing the gun tighter into Archer's ribs.

They hit another red on 47th. Archer swore. Some school-children moved over the crossing slowly, chewing up his time, laughing and playing together, no idea that a man's life was at stake.

The clock ticked on.

'Ninety seconds,' Farrell said.

The light hit green and Archer sped down.

45th.

43rd.

41st.

They zoomed towards the Port Authority Bus Terminal and Archer got lucky. They should have been held up there by the buses moving in and out of the station, but they hit a gap in-between them. Eight blocks later, they hit a red at 34th, Madison Square Garden straight ahead and to the left.

'One minute,' Farrell said.

Archer willed people across the crossings, but there seemed be an endless stream of them.

'Fifty seconds.'

The light turned green, and Archer pulled left.

Pedestrians were starting to cross here, but he roared through a gap, inches from a woman walking over the white-lined tarmac. She started shouting obscenities and flipped them off but Archer ignored her, the car burning down 34th.

They were three Avenues away.

'Thirty seconds!' Farrell said.

Disaster struck.

They hit a red at 7th.

Archer could see Herald Square one avenue away, the giant building of Macy's running the entire block to his left.

He was so close he could see faces of people in the Square ahead.

'Fifteen seconds,' Farrell said, pulling back the hammer on the pistol with a click. 'You're not going to make it.'

Archer couldn't move.

It was a red and people were crossing.

But suddenly, a fire engine appeared from behind them, the lights blaring. It was a gift from heaven. Cars parted, moving out of its way, but Archer waited, ready to pounce.

He took his shot.

As the truck moved forward, he tucked in behind it, crossing over the lights. There was more honking and shouting behind him, but he didn't hear any of it.

He was still a hundred yards from his destination.

'*Seven,*' Farrell said.

Archer floored it.

'*Six!*'

'*Five!*'

'*Four!*'

'*Three!*'

'*Two!*'

'*One!*'

The car skidded to a halt, both men jerked forward in the seat then falling back with the momentum as the car stopped, the pistol still jammed in Archer's side.

They paused and looked around the car.

Macy's was behind them.

Herald Square was in front of them.

They'd made it.

Archer held the wheel tight, panting, then released it slowly. He exhaled, sweat on his brow, taking deep breaths. Farrell looked around them through the windows, then lowered the pistol slowly and tucked it back into his waistband, not saying a word. Outside them on the streets, it was noisy, but the only sound inside the car was Archer catching his breath.

They sat there in silence.
Then Farrell turned to him, and nodded.
'Congratulations,' he said. 'You're our new driver.'

TWELVE

The next morning, Wednesday, Archer stepped out onto Steinway Street from the west entrance to the subway, and started walking north up 34th Avenue. The sun was beating down, with no cloud cover or protective shade from the tall buildings of Manhattan and he felt the intense heat on the back of his neck and arms as he walked up the street.

He wore his sunglasses to protect his eyes from the white glare of the sun off the pavement, but he saw others passing him squinting as it temporarily blinded them. Looking down, he saw that some tarmac filler that had been packed into cracks in the sidewalk had started to melt, black and sticky. That was the way it went in New York City. Freezing cold in the winter, roasting hot in the summer.

He'd come from Times Square, having slept in the hotel, and had spent much of the night letting the break-neck drive through the city fully sink in. Archer and Farrell had sat there in the car at Herald Square for a few further moments, then Farrell had asked him to take them back to Queens.

Archer was pissed. He'd needed to drop his guard in order to let Farrell test him out, but no one put a gun to his head and escaped the consequences. It had taken a hell of a lot of willpower not to retaliate. The journey had taken about twenty minutes and Archer had pulled to a halt on the corner of 30th Avenue, under the subway line. They'd sat there for a moment, Archer trying to stay cool, thinking of the bigger picture, breathing slowly.

'I own a gym,' Farrell said, turning to him. 'It's on 38th Street, just past 34th Avenue. Meet me there tomorrow morning. 11 o'clock.'

Archer looked over at him. Farrell saw his expression.

'Sorry about the gun, man. I needed to see how you were under pressure. You were good.'

111

Archer didn't react. He didn't move.

'Eleven am. Trust me, you'll want to be there. I'll make all this worth your while.'

Archer had held his gaze, then stepped out. Farrell did the same and moved around the car. He climbed into the front seat and shut the door.

'Eleven am,' he'd repeated, through the wound-down window. 'Don't be late.'

And the car had sped off towards Ditmars Boulevard, disappearing out of sight.

The first thing Archer did next was go straight to his father's apartment and get the 9mm Sig Sauer pistol. He couldn't be shooting people seeing as he was an English cop and not an American one, but he needed a security measure, a bargaining tool, something to level the odds. He was angry at himself. Farrell had got the drop on him. He'd had to play along in order to gain their trust and get inside, but he hated being passive and was furious at himself for dropping his guard. But worst of all, he hated someone putting a gun to his head. That sure as hell wasn't going to happen again.

He'd grabbed the Sig from its home in the nightstand and pulled the top-slide back an inch, seeing a bullet there in the chamber, confirming the weapon was loaded. He instantly felt calmer. *Not all men were created equal, but Samuel Colt and his revolvers had made them so.* He'd sat on the bed and breathed a sigh of relief, the gun in his hand.

Everything was OK. He'd passed the test.

He was in.

But it had been close. Razor-close. Way too close. If they'd hit one more red light or a pedestrian had decided to jaywalk, Archer would be with his father right now. The fire engine passing by had been a lucky break. He couldn't count on getting that lucky again.

Regaining his composure, he'd grabbed a bag from the closet and tucked the Sig and two spare mags inside. He

112

whipped around the apartment, grabbing anything that he figured he or his sister would want to keep then walked out, locking the apartment and leaving for the last time. He wouldn't come back here again. Farrell and his team now knew where this place was, and he didn't fancy any more unexpected visits. He'd walked left and fast for the R train on Steinway and headed to the Marriott Hotel in Times Square, staying there for the rest of the day and all night, high up in his hotel room, the 9mm Sig hardly leaving his hand.

But the next day, having cleaned up and calmed down, Archer turned the corner on 34th Avenue and walked left down 38th Street, the same street as his father's apartment but three and a bit Avenues west. He saw the sign to Farrell's gym thirty yards up ahead, white lettering over a blue background. *Astoria Sports Complex*. Simple, and to the point. He approached the entrance and pulling open the door, ducked inside.

As he walked in, the air-conditioning blasted refreshing, frosty air into his face, cooling him and ruffling his hair. It was a couple of seconds of pure bliss, a brief moment's escape from the baking heat outside; he moved through the cold air and walked into the gym. From where he was standing in the reception area, Archer could see that the place was clean and tidy. Straight ahead, he saw a swimming pool behind the windows of the reception desk. To the right of the pool were a series of separate designated lanes where swimmers were doing laps and in the left corner some kids were playing in the water together with their parents. Behind them was another smaller pool, or maybe a Jacuzzi. Several people were in there, arms resting on the tiles, relaxing and chatting, taking a break from the merciless city heat.

To the right were two levels. Downstairs was the weight-room, lots of barbells, dumbbells and mirrors. He could see a load of guys in there working out, lifting weights, dance music pounding from speakers mounted on the walls around them. Upstairs, he could just see the tops of some people's heads as they pedalled away on bikes. The machine room he guessed, the two floors designed to separate the cardio bunnies and the meatheads. The place was clean and industrious, not the glamorous and expensive type of gym one would get in the city, but then again not the gritty and chalky basements you got at the other end of the scale. It was a legit business, a solid cover for Farrell, and Archer guessed it made him look good when he had to fill out his taxes.

The guy on the front desk had been sizing Archer up from the moment he walked in. He was in his mid-twenties with gelled-back hair, a diamond earring in his right earlobe and a tan that looked a little too golden to be real. He was wearing a white vest that was a size too small, making a statement, trying to show off the result of his work in the room next door. He flashed a customary smile as Archer approached the desk, showing polished white teeth.

'Looking to join?' he asked.

Archer shook his head. 'I'm looking for Farrell.'

The guy's eyes narrowed. His courteous manner disappeared.

'Who are you?'

'A friend.'

Before the man could reply, Farrell appeared at the top of the stairs from the cardio room. He whistled down to the guy behind the counter and nodded. The guy with the earring pressed a button, looking back at Archer suspiciously. The turnstile to Archer's right clicked, unlocking, and ignoring the guy behind the desk, Archer turned and passed through the turnstile, walking up the stairs to the second floor.

When he reached the top of the stairs, Farrell didn't bother with a greeting. He just turned and walked off, Archer following him.

'Gimme five more minutes,' Farrell said, turning to him. 'We're just finishing up her workout.'

Looking around the level, Archer had guessed right. Up here there were lines of cycling and elliptical machines and stair-climbers, people in sports-wear on a few of them, working hard as they watched televisions mounted on the wall ahead. The air-conditioning was on full blast up here too, keeping the temperature nice and cool.

Past the lines of exercise equipment, Archer saw a martial arts cage had been set up across the level towards the wall. He saw Ortiz inside, gasping for air, drenched in sweat, her hands on her hips as she prowled around the black-fenced cage like an animal in captivity. She was wearing a black t-shirt, the sleeves jaggedly cut off and white shorts, her feet bare, black four-ounce gloves on her hands.

She paced around in large circles, recovering, but Archer saw her stop and stare at him when she realised he was here. Her face was cold. Another corner-man was standing beside her, an older guy with grey hair, grizzled and sinewy, looking like a former fighter who'd been defeated by Father Time and had stepped outside the ring to corner up-and-comers instead. He was holding a bottle of water and he lifted it, Ortiz tipping her head to take a drink. She swilled and spat the liquid back out to the floor, still glaring at Archer. He got the message.

He may have gained Farrell's trust but she was another matter entirely.

Farrell stepped back inside the cage, scooping up some red striking pads that had been left on the ground and hooking them over his forearms. The older guy with the water stepped outside the cage and moved to a timer, pressing a button. It beeped.

115

'Let's go!' he said.

Farrell had the pads up and Ortiz went to work.

Archer was expecting a spectacle, but she was truly vicious. From where he was standing he was surprised the pads didn't burst considering the force she was hitting them with. She was exhaling sharply with every shot, so each strike was accompanied with a yell that made it more intimidating. *Bambambam.* She was working combos, firing elbows and kicks and fast punch sequences that were crisp, technical and brutally powerful. Farrell was knocked back every now and then by a blow that was really clean, especially her kicks where she torqued her hip and her shin crushed into the pad. Archer watched her work and his memory flashed back to the street-fight on Monday night. He wondered if the guy she'd clinched and kneed in the face had woken up yet. He was probably still unconscious.

The workout upped in intensity as the five minutes went on, Ortiz's stamina not dropping at all. She was in impressive shape. If anything, she actually gained momentum, her yells growing louder as she hammered violent combo after combo, strike after strike, into the pads Farrell had strapped to his arms. On the exercise equipment behind them, Archer noticed a couple of people turning at the noise, then looking away in the next instant, not wanting the woman in the cage to see them staring. After another minute or so, the buzzer sounded and the round ended.

'*Good job!*' the old guy outside called.

Farrell and Ortiz bumped fists and she hunched over, catching her breath, drenched with sweat. Farrell nodded approvingly and stepped outside, pulling off the work-mitts and heading over to Archer.

'She's got a fight coming up?' Archer asked, watching her recover from the workout.

Farrell shook his head. 'No. Just staying sharp.'

Archer nodded, looking over at her inside the cage. She leaned back, hands on her hips, and glared over at him again, her chest heaving as she sucked in oxygen, her body recovering from the exertion. She walked out of the side entrance to the cage which Farrell had opened and the other trainer started pulling her gloves off. Farrell beckoned Archer to follow him and the two men walked over as the grey-haired corner-man pulled off the second glove. Ortiz grabbed the bottle of water resting on a chair with her white-wrapped hands and unscrewed the cap, drinking from it and sucking in gulps of oxygen.

'What's he doing here?' she asked, panting, glaring at Archer, her accent Hispanic.

'Both of you, come with me,' Farrell said, headed for a side door and ignoring her question.

Archer didn't move.

'Ladies first,' he said.

Ortiz stared at him, hostile, sweat dripping down her brow, the odd strand of hair from her corn-rows twisted and frizzed up in the air from the workout. Then she grabbed a white towel from a bench and wrapping it around her glistening shoulders, followed her boyfriend towards the doorway, her t-shirt soaked with sweat.

Archer followed, but made sure to keep his distance.

The door opened onto a flight of stairs that led down through the back of the building. Farrell pushed open another door on the floor below and walked ahead of them into a storage room.

No one was inside. The place was dimly lit, filled with brown boxes, some of them opened, containing white towels and t-shirts with the gym logo on the front. Farrell walked on and pushed a stack of boxes out of the way at the end of the room on the right.

He reached forward and pulled a second panel open on the wall, leading to another level.

117

It was well-camouflaged, painted cream like the rest of the wall. Archer would never have guessed it was there. Farrell led the other two down the steps. Turning, Archer realised the older man, the corner-man, had followed them to the storage room and had shut the secret door behind them. He heard the slide of the boxes being pushed back across the doorway, hiding it once again.

All three of them stood there in the red-brick tunnel, momentarily still, just a solitary light-bulb hanging from the ceiling providing light, the place old and damp and covered with cobwebs. Ahead of them Archer could see a thick metal door with a spin-dial lock, the kind seen on a bank vault. Farrell worked the dial three times.

It clicked, and he reached for the handle, but suddenly turned, looking past his girlfriend at Archer.

'You say a word to anyone about what you see in here, I'll kill you. They'll never find the body. Clear?'

Archer nodded, looking him in the eye.

Farrell looked back at him for a moment, then turned and opened the door.

This room was a basement, but unlike the storage room it wasn't empty. There were a series of tables and chairs in the room, light bulbs hanging from the ceiling, the place gloomy and starkly lit. Across the room Regan and Tate were sitting at two tables in front of sewing machines, each machine purring as the men fed some dark fabric underneath, the needles hammering up and down the lengths of cloth.

The two of them looked up as the trio entered and Archer saw Regan glower under the white light from the bulb above.

'What the hell is he doing here?' he asked Farrell.

'He's joining us,' Farrell said.

'What? Are you crazy? Why?'

'We went for a drive yesterday. He's ten times better than Brown ever was. He's solid.'

'Who's Brown?' Archer asked, interrupting.

'Our old driver,' Farrell explained. 'Unfortunately he had a medical condition.'

'What?'

'He couldn't keep his mouth shut,' Farrell said. 'So Carmen shut it for him.'

Across the room, Regan went to argue but Farrell cut him off.

'Save it, Bill. I don't want to hear about it,' he said.

Archer felt Regan's gaze burning into him as the trio approached him and Tate. Up close, he saw that the cloth under the needle of each sewing machine belonged to two black jackets. Both of them were fully intact, no tears, no rips. It looked as if they were stitching something inside the cloth instead of mending it.

'How's it looking?' Farrell asked Tate.

Tate paused in his work and lifted the black jacket from the machine, raising it upright on the table and grunting from the effort. It seemed heavy. He tapped the front twice with his free hand, and it gave two metallic *thunks*.

'Solid,' Tate said.

Farrell turned to Archer, pointing at the jacket.

'Aramid and steel plates,' he explained. 'Body armour. That thing will stop a twelve gauge round, easy. Put that shit on with a bullet-proof helmet and no cop is ever going to stop you, not with their firepower. You ever see the North Hollywood shootout?'

Archer nodded. 'I remember. 1997, right?'

'That's right. Two guys took on the entire Los Angeles Police Department outside a bank wearing vests like that. The pigs shot over six hundred rounds at them and couldn't put them down.'

'What the hell do you need it for?'

Farrell paused a moment, then beckoned to his right.

'Follow me,' he said.

He moved to a door across the room, Ortiz following, the towel wrapped around her shoulders, taking mouthfuls of water from the plastic bottle as she walked. While Tate got back to work with the sewing machine, Regan was still glaring at Archer, contempt written all over his face.

'Asshole,' he said.

'Go for a nice walk yesterday?' Archer replied, with a grin.

He saw the other man's eyes narrow as he turned to follow Farrell and Ortiz into the side room to the right. There was just a single table and four chairs under a light hanging from the ceiling in here, the walls and ceilings unadorned and unpainted, all dusty red brick and grey cement. There were a series of wide sheets of paper on the desk, harshly illuminated by the naked bulb above.

'Shut the door,' Farrell said.

Archer did so and glanced down at the sheets. He realised what they were.

Blueprints.

He looked closer. They were extensive floor plans, four pages stacked on top of each other which would mean four levels or floors. He examined the uppermost sheet. He saw designated seating areas, the boxes numbered from 1 to 428, around a central rectangular area. He saw four towers, A to D, on each corner.

And he saw the name of the building in the top right corner of the page. Gerry's voice echoed in his head, three words, matching the three on the blueprint.

Madison Square Garden.

'Take a seat,' Farrell said.

THIRTEEN

'It was Carmen's idea,' Farrell said. Archer was sitting across from him, Ortiz leaning against the wall between the two men. 'We were making shit from fighting, and this place isn't gonna make us rich any time soon. So we started casing houses over in Long Island. It was easy. The owners are hardly ever there, always on vacation in the Hamptons or stuck in some office in the city. Bypass the alarms, avoid the places with guard-dogs and it's Christmas. We hit four of them in a row. Take the stolen goods and valuables and trade them for cash. Just like that, we made close to half a mil, easy.'

Archer nodded, glancing up at Ortiz. She sipped her water while watching him closely. The harsh naked light from above was accentuating her rock-hard cheekbones and the muscles on her arms.

Her dark eyes were expressionless as she stared down at him.

'It was so easy that we decided to step it up,' Farrell continued. 'Armoured trucks, on their way to the city, running through Long Island on the I-495. Pay off someone on the inside to give you the rotas and personal info on the guards and hit them out there on the road, in the countryside, all alone. Pull up a road-block, take out the tyres, threaten their families, use their names to show you know who they are. All it takes is a bit of background work, planning and some balls and the stash is yours. Doesn't matter how secure that truck is, you tell the guy inside you'll kill his family if he doesn't open up, you bet your ass he'll open that door.'

Archer nodded.

'So then we stepped it up again. We started hitting banks.'

'In the city?'

He smiled and nodded. 'Not around here. Not our own neighbourhood. But let me tell you, taking a bank, that shit's harder. But it's possible. Managers and tellers are ordered by their bosses to comply with any thieves' demands which gives us an edge. We know they'll co-operate. Make sure we're tooled up, disguised, get the bank when the lock on the vault is off, avoid the dye packs and bait money, take the security tapes and we're home free.'

'What about the getaway car? Surely you have to ditch it? That'll leave tracks?'

'Once we get the money out and into a switch car, Tate takes the bent one over to JFK and parks it in the long-stay parking spots. Right now there are eight of them in there, parked amongst all the other vehicles. No one's gonna find them for months and even when they do, there's no DNA inside that could lead back to us. We make sure of it.'

Archer nodded.

'How do you clean the money? Surely it's still traceable?'

'Once he ditches the car, Tate meets back up with us then does a trip down to Atlantic City with the stash. He stays there for a couple days, trades the money for chips in the different casinos, plays the table for peanuts, then cashes out. Untraceable. The Feds and cops figure the money will reappear somewhere and they can then trace it back to us. But if they try to track any of the bait money, they'll end up tailing some fat housewife from New Jersey or some asshole with a gambling problem living in a motel on the A.C water-front.'

Archer nodded. 'Clever. So how many jobs have you pulled in total?'

'Thirteen. Four houses, five trucks, four banks. We've made almost five million.'

'I'm impressed.'

Farrell nodded.

'But we're running out of time,' he said. 'There's a shitload of heat coming in from the FBI. They've taken us all in, trying to work us over, find a weak link, something they can use. The lead agent is a guy called Gerrard. He's a real asshole. Sooner or later, they'll be waiting for us or he'll find something to pin on me. Our luck won't hold out forever.'

Archer glanced up at Ortiz, who was still staring down at him.

'So why not cut your losses? Get out while you're still ahead,' Archer said.

'That's exactly what we're doing,' Farrell said. 'Come Sunday night, we're leaving this city and never coming back.'

He paused.

'But we've got a big weekend coming up first. This one will go down in the record books. It'll be legendary. Saturday is fight night at the Garden. There's some big concert going on the night before. We're gonna take the joint just before the fight and clean the place out.'

'The Garden? As in Madison Square Garden?'

'The very same.'

Pause.

'And you know what Sunday is?' Farrell added.

Archer shrugged. 'What?'

'End of the first week's play at the U.S Open. The tennis tournament, over in Flushing Meadows. At 7pm, an armoured truck is headed for Long Island with the takings from the first week's play. Millions and millions of dollars. And we're going to be waiting for them.'

Archer looked at him, genuinely surprised.

'Are you serious? Two jobs in two days?'

'Dead serious. The moment after we hit the truck, we're out of here. We'll head down to A.C, clean the cash, then we're going straight to Florida. Get a private jet off-radar to the Dominican, then leapfrog our way all the way to Mexico. Spend the rest of our lives sipping cocktails, living the dream on a beach somewhere, far away from here and the FBI.'

123

He paused, seeing the look on Archer's face.

'You think it can't be done?'

'It sounds like a good plan. I hate to be a downer but these aren't just liquor store hold-ups or house burglaries. You know how many cops are going to be down there at the Garden?'

'Thirty five. But that works in our favour. We'll go in as cops. We'll blend right in.'

'After you hit the tennis truck you can't just drive away. The NYPD and Feds will put up roadblocks. They'll comb the entire State looking for you.'

'We won't drive. We'll fly. We've got a helicopter at Flushing Airport, hidden in one of the old hangars. We bought it with some of our stolen cash and Bill's been taking flying lessons. The place is deserted. No one ever goes in there. We'll fly down to AC over any roadblocks, undetected, right over their heads.'

Archer looked at him, then Ortiz, who sipped her water, still looking into his eyes.

'Check these out,' Farrell said, indicating to the blueprints on the table. Archer pulled his gaze from Ortiz and looked at the sheets on the table-top.

Each page was a layout of the lower levels of Madison Square Garden. The background was blue, everything on top white, and they were extensively detailed showing every room, every area. He saw the two changing rooms, the trophy room, corporate areas, concessions stands.

'Where the hell did you get these?'

'Public Library.'

Archer looked up at him. 'You're kidding?'

Farrell shook his head. 'New York Public Library. Withdrawn under a false name so they won't lead back to us. These are the latest prints too. They were drawn up three months ago.'

Archer looked at the maps. They were Forensically detailed and precise, showing every nook and cranny, every side room, every exit.

124

'The biggest fight of the year,' Farrell continued. 'Not in Vegas. Here. The Mecca of boxing. 20,000 seats and not a single one of them empty. It's going to be so busy down there that it'll work perfectly in our favour. Like I said, we're going in as cops, blending into the crowd. The plan is me, Carmen and Regan go-'

'What about Tate?' Archer interrupted.

'He'll be down in AC cleaning the cash we've got piled up. You saw the boxes upstairs?'

Archer nodded.

'Let's just say not all of them are filled with t-shirts. All that money is backing up and we need to get that shit out of here. Tate'll do it and get back on Sunday for the tennis truck.'

He pointed to the top blueprint on the table.

'Anyway, me, Carmen and Regan will go in. You'll be parked on the kerb on 33rd Street, facing east in a cop car, in uniform,' he continued. 'Carmen and Bill will come out first. They'll load the first batch. They'll come back and help me with the second load. We take the holdings, throw in the bags, then walk straight out. You get us over the water, we switch the car, get away clean and lay low.'

'Alibis?'

'Bought and paid for. We're all going to be at a fight in East Rutherford. At least ten people saw all of us there. Tate'll make himself visible in the casinos in AC that night, so his story will check out.'

'You can't just walk into the place and take the cash. What's your plan when you get inside?'

'Never mind about that. You just worry about getting us out of there.'

Archer thought for a moment.

'And what about the Flushing job?' he asked.

Farrell shook his head.

'Don't worry about that either. We need you for the Garden and that's it.'

125

Pause.

'So are you in?' Farrell said. 'If you do this, you can either disappear or head straight back to the U.K. You can get your money out through an off-shore bank account, or stay in the country and spend it all. I don't care.'

'What's my cut?'

'Fifty thousand.'

Archer looked at him. 'That's it? Two jobs and that's my cut?'

'I need you for one job. Take it or leave it. I recommend you take it.' Archer looked at him, then at Ortiz, whose face hadn't softened an iota as she stared down at him. 'We need you pal.'

Archer paused a suitably long time, seemingly making up his mind.

'OK. I'm in.'

Farrell nodded. 'Good.'

He rose.

'You got a phone?' he asked.

Archer nodded and gave him the number.

'I'll be in touch,' Farrell said. Archer got the message. The meeting was over. Without a word, he rose and moved to the door.

'One more thing. I meant what I said,' Farrell said from behind him. 'You say a word to anyone about this, I'll kill you myself. You'll join that asshole Brown and that Fed from D.C. who got his head blown off.'

Archer kept staring at the door. He didn't turn. It would show the expression on his face.

'You got it.'

Then he twisted the door handle and walked out of the room.

*

'It's a double job,' Archer told Gerrard, as they sat in the back of a white van nine hours later. Each man was munching on a foil-wrapped burrito Gerrard had picked up on the way. They were parked in Union Square; the time was just past 7:30 pm, still Wednesday 31st, the last day of August. The heat was clammy and Mexican food probably wasn't the best choice considering the temperature, but Gerrard had set up a fan in the back of the van and it was keeping them both relatively cool.

'A double job?' Gerrard asked.

He bit down into his food and some guacamole squirted out of the side of the foil and hit him on the shoulder of his black suit jacket.

'Oh shit.'

Archer passed him a napkin and he wiped the green splodge off his shoulder. It had left a stain; Gerrard shook his head and cursed.

'Goddammit, this is my best suit. Anyway, keep going.'

'It's two jobs. The stash-rooms at MSG and the tennis truck in Flushing. The plan is to hit the Garden just before the fight starts. The whole place will be packed and distracted, the takings at the concessions from the night before will be loaded up in the rooms. They're planning to clean the place out, in-and-out in a couple of minutes. I think they've paid someone off to give them access to the lower levels, then they're going to go in armed in the stash-room and tie and gag everyone inside.'

'Jesus Christ, they're getting cocky,' Gerrard said. 'And stupid. There'll be a shitload of cops down there.'

Archer shook his head. 'Cocky maybe, but not stupid. They're going for an all-time record. Three jobs in one week, then they're going to leave the city forever. Farrell knows your team is trying to take them down. He called you a real asshole.'

'Trust me, the feeling's mutual.'

'He said it's just a matter of time before you manage to pin something on him so he's bailing out. After the

127

two jobs they're going straight to Atlantic City on Sunday, then Florida, and then to the Dominican by private jet. They're headed for Mexico eventually. Trying to steal enough money in one week to live on for the rest of their lives.'

Gerrard nodded, taking another bite from his food.

'What about the Flushing job?' he asked.

'I don't know. Farrell wouldn't tell me much about it, save that there's some kind of armoured truck they're going after. They'll try to hit it before it gets to its destination, either on the I-495 or even in Flushing Corona Park itself. Their transport is hidden at Flushing Airport so they won't have to go far.'

'Transport? A car?'

'A helicopter. They're planning to fly over any roadblocks at the city and State borders and ride all the way down to AC.'

Gerrard looked at him for a moment, then shook his head.

'Son of a bitch. A damn fighter shouldn't be that smart.'

Archer nodded, taking a bite from his burrito.

'Farrell and his team have a couple of hidden rooms at the back of his gym, behind a secret doorway,' he said. 'When I was down there, I saw Regan and Tate stitching some fabric on sewing machines. Tate showed us what he was working on. It was a black, long-sleeved vest, reinforced with Aramid and steel-plated body armour.'

'Like the North Hollywood shootout.'

'Exactly. They've done their homework. I think that's got something to do with Sunday. I'm guessing that armoured truck from the tennis is going to have armed guards inside, maybe more than usual. I think they'll try to take them out head on, duke it out with a gunfight. The body-armour is insurance against getting hit. They wouldn't need it for the Garden heist.'

128

Archer bit into his burrito again, tasting the warm meat, rice and cheese. It was good, if a little too spicy. Across the van Gerrard was thinking hard, then seemed to come to some kind of decision.

'OK. Today's Wednesday,' he said. 'That gives us three days to prepare. We can take them at the Garden. Don't worry about the tennis truck; they won't even make it that far. You said they're going through the Penn Station entrance?'

Archer nodded.

'Farrell, Regan and Ortiz will go inside in cop uniforms, headed for the stash room. It sounds like they've paid off the necessary people to let them inside. Not the guys in the coal room, but the guys who are protecting them I guess.'

'What about Tate?'

Archer took a bite of the burrito and nodded.

'That's the part you'd like. They send him down to Atlantic City every fortnight, packed up with the stolen cash from their previous jobs. He drives slow, breaking no laws, drawing no attention. He spends the weekend down there passing the cash through the chips at the casinos, then settles up and comes straight back. He's headed down there the night of the fight. He's coming back for the main event on Sunday.'

Gerrard nodded, taking a last bite and finishing his burrito, scrunching up the foil.

'So they want you in the car?' he asked.

'Yes. I'll be kerb-side in a cop car, on 33rd, facing east. Plan is to move across town as fast as possible and get to the Midtown Tunnel before anyone can close it off.'

'OK.'

And with that, Archer stayed silent. He took another bite of burrito and looked at Gerry. He'd told him everything he knew.

'Wow,' Gerrard said. 'I'm speechless. Great job kid. This is beyond anything I could have hoped for. You sure as hell take after your father.'

Archer ate his food, saying nothing.

'How are you feeling?'

'OK.'

'Has Farrell talked about Jimmy's murder?'

'He knows about it. He threatened me. Said if I told anyone what I saw or what he told me I'd end up with Brown and the *dead Fed*, as he put it.'

'Did you pursue it?'

'No. It would have set off alarm bells instantly.'

Archer paused. He looked at the older man on the other side of the van.

'But I still mean what I said to you. I'll back off, but if he tells me he did it and I've got a chance to take him out, I'm doing it. He put a gun to my head yesterday, Gerry. I'm not going to forget that.'

Gerrard nodded, wiping his hands with a napkin. 'No argument from me. Get rid of Ortiz too while you're at it.'

And just like that, the conversation had ended. Archer finished his burrito then rolled up the foil, wiping his hands on a napkin.

'Thanks for the grub.'

'Least I can do,' Gerrard said. 'You're certainly a cop, kid. It's in your DNA.'

Archer nodded.

'I'll be in touch,' he said. 'Just start getting your team ready,'

Archer reached for the door handle; he pulled it open and stepped outside into the humid evening air of Union Square.

Slamming it shut behind him, he checked to make sure no-one was watching the van. Satisfied, he tossed the rolled up ball of foil into a trash can beside him and headed off into the night.

Across the street, a woman was slumped down behind the wheel of a silver Ford. She watched the English guy climb out of the white van, slamming the door and heading off across the Square. She stayed still, keeping her eyes on the van, waiting to see who would appear and move into the driver's seat.

After a moment, a figure in a suit emerged.

It was Gerrard.

She watched him fire the ignition and move off uptown. As he left, she raised herself upright in her seat. So they were working together. That much was clear.

Her eyes narrowed as she thought of the situation and its ramifications.

Gerrard was clever, using the English guy. Farrell would never have seen this play coming. She watched the Brit walk to the subway entrance, disappearing down the steps and out of sight.

And wondered how she could use him and all this to her advantage.

FOURTEEN

Thursday. September 1st.

10:05 am.

The bank was a Chase on 40th and 7th Avenue. It was a good location, close to Times Square and convenient for all the tourists, yet also readily available for the businesses and workers operating out of the Midtown area. It was accessible from both sides, located on the ground floor of a tall office building on the corner of the street. From the east, one would walk through a set of double doors from Broadway, through a golden lobby and over a marble floor, then turn left and pass through a doorway that led into the bank.

From the west, access to the bank was a simple wide entrance on the corner of 40th and 7th, right on the doorstep of Times Square. This portion of 7th was also known as Fashion Avenue and was right up there with the wealthiest areas in the city. Over three quarters of every piece of clothing in the entire United States were tailored and put together in this district and once the garments were sold, the profits came straight back. Consequently this bank was another perfectly placed branch for Chase, right in the centre of a money-making and industriously corporate area, and when coupled with all the tourists in the neighbourhood, business thrived every single day.

That Thursday morning, the bank was busy. Customers were using ATMs, both outside on the street and inside the bank itself; tellers were lined up on the north wall behind bullet-proof glass, busy handling cheques and deposits and dealing with other customer requests. A queue of twelve people or so formed a line horizontal to the tellers, each waiting for their turn, some more patient than others. Against the south windows a series of desks ran side-by-side all the way down the wall, several of them occupied with bank employees

132

conducting private, one-on-one discussions with customers, handing out financial advice, organising loans or setting up new accounts.

There were two armed guards inside, as there were in every Chase bank in the city; they were standing on either side of the bank, against the walls, blending into the background, yet alert and vigilant, watching everyone who walked into the branch.

All things considered, they both figured they had a pretty cushy deal. Although the double entrances meant there was a constant stream of people flowing through the bank, and any one of them could be a potential thief, the NYPD had a headquarters set up on the southern edge of Times Square just two blocks away. All five tellers were protected behind bullet-proof glass with a silent alarm button by their feet and each guard had a Glock 17 and two spare mags tucked into a holster on his hip as extra insurance. It would be foolhardy to say that a bank was impossible to hold up, but this branch was up there with the most impenetrable. Armed guards, five panic buttons, bulletproof glass, a vault as strong as a nuclear bomb shelter, not to mention long windows on every wall revealing the interior of the bank to everyone walking outside on the sidewalk.

If anyone came in and tried to use weapons, they'd be spotted by about fifty witnesses outside in an instant, not to mention everyone inside the bank. This was the kind of place that made bank robbers wake up in the middle of the night in a cold sweat. In every aspect it was secure and protected. A couple of thieves had been stupid enough to try note-jobs here in the past and had turned to find the entire south-Midtown NYPD division from Times Square rushing through the west doors, thirty seconds after the tellers had pushed the panic buttons with their feet. There were thousands of banks in Manhattan, but this was most definitely a branch that thieves would be best-served to leave well alone.

But at 10:06 am that September Thursday morning, three cops approached the west entrance to the bank.

They were two men and a woman. They were dressed in full navy-blue NYPD clothing and each had large aviator sunglasses over their noses, sitting snugly under the police caps pulled low over their eyes. It was a bright, sunny day outside, so the sunglasses didn't seem unusual or cause suspicion. Even cops needed protection from the sun.

As they approached the entrance and pulled the doors open, no one outside on the street or standing inside the building as they walked in, gave them a second glance. Cops like this were just as much a part of the city as burgers and baseball. If anything, people in their proximity felt just a little bit more secure by knowing they were there.

The three cops moved across the floor into the heart of the bank. One of the men and the woman stopped, examining the interior of the place and the people around them, their faces impassive and expressionless. Meanwhile, the second man, the biggest of the trio, headed straight for the bank manager, who was just finishing up with a female customer.

The manager was a small, family man called Dean Wileman, thirty nine years old, only five-seven and a hundred and fifty pounds; he was an academic, not an athlete. Wileman had a wife and daughter and a large house over in Long Island which was a benefit of his job in the bank. He'd met his wife when they were both students at Harvard, college sweethearts; she now worked five days a week at an accounting firm in Long Island.

Wileman was physically slight and hated confrontation of any kind, but nature had found a balance and given him a head for numbers and a talent for organisation which made him the perfect man for his job. He'd taken over the role eighteen months ago and he was damn good at it. His unintimidating nature and proficiency with spread-sheets and percentages were reassuring to customers as well as his superiors, and business had thrived since he'd taken over the role as manager of the bank.

He'd noticed the three cops enter through the west entrance and wrapped up his conversation with the customer he was currently attending to. He thanked her for doing business with them, giving her his best smile, then once they had shaken hands and she'd departed, he turned to the big policeman approaching him.

The cop was intimidating, a big man, the kind of guy who'd given Wileman such a hard time at high school all those years ago. He looked at the man's face as he approached, but all he saw was his own reflection in the cop's sunglasses.

'I'm looking for Dean Wileman. The bank manager,' the cop asked.

Not a request, but a statement. Wileman nodded, offering his hand. The cop shook it, his hand enveloping Wileman's.

'That's me. Is there a problem, officer?' Wileman asked.

The cop nodded.

'Yes. There is. I need to speak to you alone for a moment, sir.'

'What's the matter?' he asked.

The cop stepped past him.

'Just come this way and I can explain.'

Wileman nodded and followed the cop to one side, towards the east windows and around the corner. Across the bank the other two cops stayed still, side-by-side, both of them silent. Nearby, the two branch security guards were watching them, curious. The two cops just stood there, stern and expressionless. The guard on the east side of the bank moved off the wall and looked closer at the pair.

135

Their heads turned in unison and he saw the two of them staring back, their eyes hidden behind the sunglasses.

Across the bank, the big cop led Wileman around the corner, then pulled something from his pocket and passed it to the smaller man. It was a cell phone. Wileman looked down at it, confused. He had his back against the wall, the cop standing in front of him, shielding him from everyone else inside the branch.

'What's this?'

'Listen,' the cop said.

Confused, Wileman took the phone from the man's hand and put it to his ear.

'Hello?'

'Dean?' a voice replied, shaky, scared.

Wileman froze.

It was his wife.

He heard her crying down the other end of the phone. She sounded terrified.

Before he could react, the cop interjected, his voice low, his eyes hidden behind the sunglasses.

'If you make a sound or react or do anything that pisses me off, she dies. So does your daughter. Understand?'

Wileman stared up at him, horrified. Around him, people in the bank continued with their activities, none of them aware of what was happening. Wileman nodded silently, hearing his wife's terrified sobs through the receiver.

'Dean, please do everything they say,' she said, her voice shaky. *'They have me and Kimberly. There's a man here. He's saying he'll rape and kill us if you don't do what they ask.'*

Wileman tried to respond, but he couldn't speak. He was in shock, feeling as if he was going to throw up or faint. The policeman took back the phone and put it in his pocket.

'Get everyone out of here,' he ordered. 'You trip an alarm, alert someone, do anything stupid, your entire family dies in a heartbeat. My man will go to town on them first. Your daughter first. Then your wife. Then your daughter again before he shoots her in the head. Then your wife again before he shoots her too.'

Wileman swallowed, picturing it in his head. He tried not to hurl.

'What do I do?' he whispered.

'I want this place empty.'

'How?'

'Think of something. Tell them there's a gas leak. You've got sixty seconds or you'll never see your family again.'

Wileman nodded, slowly, willing himself not to collapse. He looked up at the man's face, desperate to find some humanity, some part of the man that he could reason with.

But all he saw was his own terrified reflection in the man's aviators.

He stepped past the cop who turned to watch him. The two security guards had moved forward, seeing the cop take Wileman to one side.

'*Excuse me, everyone,*' Wileman suddenly called, thinking on his feet, desperately trying to hide his terror and keep his voice steady. Everyone in the bank turned. 'I'm very sorry, but this officer has just informed me that there is a gas leak in a pipe running under the bank. I'm afraid that you will all need to step outside for your own safety while we investigate the problem further.'

There was a pause. People stood still for a moment, taking the news in; then they started to file through the exits, most of them irritated by the disruption. Chase employees at the desks finished up conversations and the tellers behind the glass locked up their stations and headed for the exits.

One of the two security guards stepped forward to talk to Wileman.

'Is everything OK, sir?' he asked.

Wileman nodded, and managed to keep his voice even, hiding his terror.

'Everything's fine, Ray. Just get everyone outside,' he said.

The guard called Ray looked at him for a moment, then nodded, turned and moved towards the exit, guiding people out.

After about a minute the whole place had been cleared. Wileman turned back to the cop, who'd stood and watched the whole thing, expressionless.

'Very good,' the cop said. 'Now take me to the vault.'

'The vault?'

'I know it's open. You had a delivery six minutes ago. Don't try to lie to me. You waste another second, my man will start on your daughter. I hear she just turned sixteen, correct?'

Wileman paled. He moved unsteadily around the teller counter and headed into a second portion of the room. The design on the vault here was exactly the same as the other Chase banks in the city. He entered the spin lock combination. They were around the corner, out of sight from the street, so no one out there had any idea what was going on.

After entering the six-digit code, he twisted it, and it opened.

'Now the second one,' the cop ordered.

Wileman looked at him then moved forward, taking a key from a keychain around his neck and sliding it into the lock. He twisted this one and pulled open the second door.

The cop was right, but Wileman had no idea how he'd possessed that information. They'd just had a delivery less than ten minutes ago. Most Chase banks did the drop-offs every fortnight on a Monday, but with a spate of bank robberies in the area recently the company had decided to change the routine. As a consequence, that morning the vault was packed with stacks of bricked and banded hundred-dollar bills, fully stocked.

Close to two million dollars, neatly piled on the shelves.

'Over there,' he ordered Wileman, pointing to the corner. 'Face the wall.'

Wileman complied, trembling. But before he turned, he saw the cop do something bizarre.

He unzipped his trousers.

Wileman sneaked a longer glance as he shuffled to the wall and saw that the man had a second pair of dark trousers under his police-issue pair, compartments stitched into the black fabric running all the way up each leg. He proceeded to pack a stack of bills in each slot, ten on each leg, taking them one at a time from the shelf, moving fast. Each stack contained ten thousand dollars, so that was two hundred thousand. He pulled his trousers back up, then unbuttoned his shirt. Wileman glanced over his shoulder and saw the man was wearing a black vest with similar compartments.

He filled them up. Fifteen more.

Three hundred and fifty thousand dollars in total, strapped to his body.

He zipped his coat back up and smoothed down his trousers, making sure none of the shapes of the bill-stacks were visible. Satisfied, he looked at Wileman.

'Don't move or I'll kill you.'

He moved outside and nodded at one of the other two cops. They swapped places, the female officer moving into the back, the big guy taking her position beside the third man on the bank floor. Outside, he could see people were standing just outside the windows, talking to each other, waiting for the issue to be resolved. He saw one of the guards was staring inside but his partner wasn't paying any attention, his head back, enjoying the sunlight and respite from being indoors as he stood with all the other employees and customers.

After a brief spell, the woman reappeared and the third cop took his cue, moving into the back. He did the same thing. Once he re-appeared, the big guy went back into the vault. Wileman was still stood against the wall, trembling.

'Close it,' he ordered.

Wileman nodded, then shuffled outside, locking the second vault, then doing the same with the first. That done, he stood there, facing the cop, who towered over him, twice his size. The big man checked his watch, then turned to the small manager.

'We're leaving. But this isn't over for you. If I hear or see anything suspect, anyone chasing us, any sirens, your family dies. Clear? Face the wall again.'

Wileman trembled and nodded, turning. He pictured his wife and daughter in his mind, taped and gagged, some anonymous man threatening them, a gun in his hand.

'But how-' he started.

He stopped, and risked a quick scared glance over his shoulder, hoping to plead with the man.

The cop was already gone.

Outside on the street, the guard called Ray was standing there in the sunshine, looking into the bank. He could see two of the cops, but Mr Wileman wasn't anywhere to be seen. Around him, the other employees who were enjoying the unexpected break in the morning's work and the handful of customers who were still hoping to complete their business, had their backs turned to the bank and were chatting with each other.

But Ray wasn't so relaxed. There was something about the three cops who'd just arrived that was beginning to set off alarm bells in his mind.

Something just didn't add up.

Through the glass he saw the third cop reappear then watched as the three of them walked towards the east exit, the opposite side from where they'd entered, but no sign of Mr Wileman. The guard walked around the corner on Broadway and 40th and over to the doors to the building, waiting for them to exit. When they passed through the doors, he noticed none of them were carrying anything. Nothing to make him suspicious. They did however seem to be in a hurry, all three of them moving fast.

'Everything OK, officers?' he asked, as the trio moved out into the street.

The lead cop nodded.

'It's just a maintenance issue,' he said. 'Ruptured pipe. We're going to get back-up and call maintenance to come fix it. Stay here and keep everyone outside, sir. We'll be back soon.'

Ray looked at the three of them, their faces expressionless, their eyes covered by the aviators. He nodded, satisfied, and watched as the three of them walked off swiftly down the street, headed towards Bryant Park and 6th Avenue.

Watching them go, Ray thought for a moment then decided to go check on Mr Wileman and see if he could shed some light on the situation and an estimation of when it was likely be fixed. He wasn't intruding, he was just doing his job.

He pulled open the east entrance, moving through the lobby and then moved left and pulled open the second door, walking back into the Chase bank.

It was quiet, strangely so. He was so used to seeing the place full, but it was empty and silent, all the activity outside on the street.

Mr Wileman wasn't around. No sign of him.

'Sir?' he called. *'Sir?'*

No response.

He walked through to the back, behind the teller desks.

He found him.

It was bizarre. He was standing there, facing the wall, like he was a kid who had been in trouble and put there as a punishment. He looked absurd. To his right, Ray saw the vault door was shut.

'Are you OK, sir?' Ray asked.

Wileman didn't move. Ray moved forward and lightly touched his shoulder.

'Sir?'

Wileman jumped and jerked around, looking at him. Ray was shocked.

The small man was pale, his eyes wide and he seemed almost paralysed with fear.

'Sir? Talk to me. What's going on?' he said.

Wileman went to speak, but no words would come.

The only thing he did was flick his eyes to the left and look at the vault.

And Ray realised what had just happened.

*

The response was as fast as lightning.

Despite Mr Wileman's sudden and unexplained panic and frantic protestations begging him to stop, Ray rushed back into the bank floor and pushed the silent alarm button on the teller station. The NYPD were there in less than a minute from Times Square, six cops in bulletproof vests bursting in through the East entrance, shotguns in their hands. Ray told them three cops had just held up the bank and that they were somewhere in the area, headed towards Bryant Park. He couldn't give any detailed descriptions seeing as each had been disguised, but he confirmed the trio were two men and one woman. One of the cops who'd arrived instantly made a call over the radio instantly; the information was immediately passed on to the FBI Bank Robbery Task Force Office at 26 Federal Plaza.

Gerrard was nearest to the phone and he took the call. The moment he heard what had happened he raced for his car with the rest of his team, ordering all bridges and tunnels off Manhattan to be closed. His orders were carried out within minutes and traffic in and out of the island ground to a halt. The word was put out over every NYPD and Federal frequency in Manhattan that they were searching for three cops, each of whom had approximately three hundred and fifty thousand dollars hidden about their person.

Inside his Mercedes, Gerrard headed straight for the scene of the crime, Katic in the car beside him, Siletti and Parker following close behind while O'Hara and Lock headed for the roadblocks at the Midtown Tunnel. They figured geographically that would be the trio's best bet for an escape.

But twenty minutes after Ray made the call, a NYC MTA M train pulled into the 36th Avenue station in Astoria, across the East River. The doors slid open and passengers stepped out, the doors shutting behind them after a few seconds and the train moving out of the station and on into the tunnel. Everyone who'd disembarked proceeded to walk towards the two exits and the place slowly emptied.

However, three people stayed where they were, leaning against the wall as everyone else passed. They'd been in separate carriages and were standing around thirty feet from each other.

Three cops.

Once the last person had gone, they stood still for a moment longer, then the officer on the far right turned and started walking down the platform. Once he passed the officer in the middle, she started walking beside him and they approached the third man.

They each high-fived as they finally joined up in a three, and together, the trio headed for the stairs that would lead up to the maze of streets in Queens. One of them, the biggest one, looked behind them and smiled.

No one was following them.

No one knew who they were.
They'd done it.

FIFTEEN

Later that day Archer opened his eyes, waking up from a deep sleep. He blinked, yawning, and sat up. He'd been watching the television across the room but had passed out on the hotel bed, fully dressed. He yawned again then rose and wandered to the window, pulling open the curtain and looking out at the view.

The sun was setting in the distance, the buildings ahead black and silhouetted against the orange-tinted sky. He'd been out for a while. Moving back into the room, he checked the clock on the bed-side drawer.

7:04 pm. He'd been asleep all afternoon.

He reached for his cell phone which was resting on a chair to see if Gerry had tried to get in touch. He had no missed calls, but saw he had a text message from Farrell. He clicked it open.

MSG, Friday. 8 o'clock. Meet 33rd and 8th. Don't be late.

Archer read the message again, and nodded. That was twenty four hours before the job. Farrell would probably want to walk through it, get a feel for the place and the atmosphere, making sure that Archer knew every detail of his role and that they were both on the same page. Archer tossed the phone onto the bed and sat down in a chair, thinking. Across the room, the television was still on, sound coming from it quietly, and he grabbed the remote and clicked it off.

Suddenly, there was a knock on the door. Three raps, quick. *Taptaptap.* Every knock conveyed something and this one sounded urgent. He wasn't expecting a guest, so he grabbed the Sig from the bedside table and walked over, the pistol in his right hand.

'Who is it?' he asked.

'It's me,' a familiar voice said.

145

Shielding the pistol down his right leg, Archer pulled it open. Gerrard was standing there, still wearing the suit with the guacamole stain on the shoulder, looking stressed and worn out.

'What's wrong?' Archer asked.

'They did it again,' he said.

'I've been called up to D.C. to explain myself,' Gerrard said, sitting on the edge of the bed inside the room. Archer had let him in, then shut and locked the door behind them. 'I'll be back tomorrow or Sunday.'

Archer moved to the minibar and pulling it open, took out two cans of beer from the shelf, kicking the door shut behind him. He passed one to Gerry, who took it with a nod of thanks. The beer was a Miller, All-American, the can golden, the liquid inside cold.

'You're not going to be here Saturday?' Archer asked. He lifted the ring-pull on his can and the beer gave a *tschick* as it opened.

He beckoned Gerrard to follow him and he opened the sliding door leading out to the balcony, stepping outside with the FBI agent then sliding the door shut behind them.

'They summoned me,' Gerrard said in a low voice, taking a seat in a white plastic chair. He continued to speak in lowered tones, seeing as the balconies of rooms adjacent were in earshot. 'When that happens, you know you're in deep shit. Nothing you can do will get you out of it. I tried to explain what the situation was, but they weren't having it.'

'This is bad, Gerry. I need you here on Saturday.'

'I should be back sometime over the weekend. Don't worry. I'm going to brief my team tomorrow on the intel we've gathered and the all details you've provided. They're a good outfit. They can handle it without me. I'll have them set up at the Garden, ready and waiting.'

He shook his head and looked at the beer can in his hand. The sounds of Times Square down below filled the silence, the constant hum of electric lights under the interjections of car horns and the occasional shout.

'Shit. They're going to have me for lunch. This could be the end of my career.'

'Don't think like that. You'll be fine. Tell them you'll have Farrell and his entire crew in hand-cuffs by Sunday. This will all be over by Monday morning.'

Gerrard didn't reply. He opened his can instead, lifting it and taking a mouthful of cold beer.

'Shit, that's good,' he said, savouring the taste and clearing his throat. 'Anyway, they didn't tell you about the job today?'

Archer shook his head.

'They only need me on Saturday,' he said. 'Farrell won't tell me anything other than the absolute essentials, and it's clear that Ortiz and Regan still don't trust me. Tell me what happened.'

'It was another Chase, on 40th. Two minute walk from here. They went in dressed as cops, probably the same outfits they'll use on Saturday.'

Archer pictured the location.

'Wait, I know that bank,' he said. 'I passed it the other day. It's the one on 7th right?'

Gerrard nodded. Archer frowned. 'In a location like that? How the hell did they pull it off? Did they use guns?'

'No. Farrell went straight to the manager. Handed him a cell phone and told him to listen. On the other end, he heard his wife crying, telling them to do everything they say or a man holding her captive would rape her and his daughter then kill them both. It took my detectives two hours just to pull that information from him. Apparently the thieves told him that if he told anyone what had happened, he'd never see his family again.'

'Have you found them?'

147

'Yeah. They're OK, aside from the trauma. We sent a squad car over to the family home in Long Island and the two cops found them duct taped-up in chairs in the main room. Apparently it was one man, wearing a hockey mask and armed with a sawn-off shotgun. Tied them up and sat there with the Ithaca on them, waiting for the job to be done, the phone in his hand. The guy left straight after apparently.'

'He didn't harm them?'

'No. And neither one could tell the cops anything about the guy later. Both are still in shock, and the guy was masked up anyway.'

Archer drank from his beer, thinking.

'OK, so they passed the manager the phone and laid out the threat. What happened next?'

'He was ordered to clear the place out. He got everyone's attention and said there was a pipe leak and that the area needed to be evacuated immediately. Everyone complied, leaving him and the three cops inside. They took the manager round the corner to the vault, out of sight of anyone on the street. Gave him a listen on the phone and told him to open it or they'd open up his daughter. Funnily enough, he did what they asked.'

'Wasn't there some kind of time lock?'

'They got it when it was still open. Given the unpredictability of traffic in the area, the time-lock on the vault in that bank is different. It's unlocked for twenty minutes at a time. There was a delivery a few minutes earlier so the damn thing was packed full. They had fifteen minutes to work with.'

Archer drank from his beer again and shook his head.

'OK, but they couldn't just walk out of there carrying bags. Everyone outside would know in a second that something was up.'

Gerrard nodded, drinking from his Miller. 'That's the thing. They didn't. They walked out the same they walked in. One of the guards approached them but said they looked perfectly normal.'

'So the cash had to be hidden under their clothing then?'

Gerrard nodded. 'Yes. The guard went into the bank to talk to the manager and saw that he was petrified with fear. He pushed the alarm and ran back out to the street, but by the time he got there the three cops had gone.'

'Did you close off the city exits?'

'Of course. But we screwed up. We figured they'd be in a car. But with Brown gone-'

'They used the subway,' Archer finished.

Gerrard nodded.

'I'm an idiot,' he said. 'I wasn't thinking fast enough, otherwise we could have shut down the subway too and trapped them on the island. There are cameras down in Bryant Park Station and we found them on the tapes heading through the station. Looks like they split up and got on an M train headed to Queens, but after that, we lost them. Passed right under all our road blocks, which held up Midtown traffic on a weekday morning. And they got away with the cash. Needless to say, my bosses and the Mayor are seriously pissed. The other jobs have been humiliating enough, but this happened right under our noses. That bank should have been impossible to rob. But they did it. And now I've got to go and explain how.'

He drank more from his beer, a long mouthful, then shook his head and cursed.

'We sent a squad car over to Farrell's gym, but the three of them were all in there, Ortiz working the pads with Farrell, Regan working the timer. They claimed they'd been there all morning. We asked around, but their alibis checked out. It's useless asking the gym staff. They've all been paid off for sure.'

'What was the take?'

Gerrard shook his head in frustration. 'Over a million.'

149

Archer stared at him. There was silence.

'Jesus.'

Gerrard nodded, draining his beer.

'Exactly,' he said. 'Yet more on the total. And down goes my clearance rate another notch. This is beyond a joke now.'

Archer thought for a moment, opting for a positive approach.

'Look, you'll be OK,' he said. 'Explain the operation to everyone in D.C. If you get down there today, you could be back by Saturday and lead the take-down yourself. We now know Tate is going back and forth to Atlantic City with the stolen cash. Get someone to arrest him at the casino or at the hotel. You know he'll be going down there before Sunday. You're in control of this situation, Gerry. You'll get that money back.'

'When was the last time you spoke to Farrell?' he asked.

'Yesterday. But he dropped me a text earlier. He wants to meet tomorrow night at the Garden. I'm guessing he'll want to walk through the job. I'll get in touch afterwards and pass it all on.'

Gerrard nodded, scrunching up the empty beer can in his hand.

'I'll be in D.C, but like I said, there are five other agents on my team. I'll brief them. They can handle it.' Pause. 'Thanks for the beer. I needed it.'

Archer nodded, finishing his own.

'Hang in there, Gerry. Two more days. Then you'll be the one bringing the beer,' he said.

Gerrard nodded and rose.

'I'll see you soon, kid. Keep your phone switched on.'

Archer rose and the two men shook hands.

Then the FBI Supervisory Special Agent pulled open the sliding door, walked across the room to the hotel room door and left.

Downstairs in the lobby, a woman was sitting in a chair facing the reception desk, a newspaper in front of her. The elevators from the upper levels were lined with glass windows, so she saw Gerrard step into one and make his way down. She couldn't work out which floor it was from here, but she'd find out soon enough.

After a few moments, the elevator arrived on the ground floor and she lifted the paper back in front of her, covering her face and upper body in the chair. She sensed him passing her, and glanced past the broadsheet to the right and saw the FBI agent walk through the doors and head out onto the street. He looked stressed.

Once he was out of sight, she folded the newspaper and rose. She walked over to the reception desk, and asked the woman sat behind the counter a question, showing her the appropriate ID. The receptionist nodded and carried out the request, tapping away on the keyboard in front of her.

'Sam Archer. That's the one you're looking for?'

'Yes. He's a friend.'

'He's booked into Room 38C. Would you like me to call and let him know you're coming up?'

'No thank you, I'll come back later.'

The receptionist nodded as the woman turned and walked away from the counter. She looked up at the giant lobby, all the way up the 38th floor.

Now she knew where he was staying.

And she was going to pay him a visit sometime soon.

SIXTEEN

The following day, Archer headed over to Madison Square Garden forty minutes before he was supposed to meet Farrell. He holed up in a bar across the street from the stadium and watched and waited as the time ticked on towards 8 pm.

He saw Farrell appear, right on cue, at 7:55 pm. Archer watched him through the glass, weighing up the other man's demeanour. He was standing on the corner of 33rd, and streams of people moved past him, completely unaware that they were passing the most wanted bank robber in New York State. He looked calm, and judging from the smoothness of his clothing he wasn't carrying a pistol. Archer gave it a couple more minutes, then trapped a five dollar bill under his empty glass of Coke, stepped outside and walked across 8th Avenue towards Farrell.

Farrell turned and saw him coming. As Archer approached, he didn't bother with greetings. He didn't even react. He just turned and started walking east. Archer moved up onto the sidewalk from the road and followed. The streets around them were busy, people and cars everywhere, and they blended right in, two men in an ocean of activity. They walked side-by-side down 33rd, then Farrell stopped by the kerb, the stadium directly to their right, traffic flowing past them in both directions on the road to the left.

'Check it out,' Farrell said. 'You'll be here in the car. Get a feel for it.'

Archer looked straight ahead at the long stretch of road. He'd ridden this route before and knew the street led all the way across town to 1st Avenue and East River Drive, and from there access over the water to Queens or Brooklyn. He saw the Empire State Building looming ahead on Sixth, proud and iconic. He pictured how the stretch of road would look tomorrow night.

Twenty four hours from now, he would be parked here on the kerb in a stolen cop car as the three thieves moved inside the stadium for the biggest heist of their lives. Little did they know that Gerrard's FBI team would be ready and waiting for them. As the thought of Gerry flashed into his mind, he pictured him entering the FBI D.C. main office, headed straight for a gruelling debriefing and a directorial firing squad. He hoped his father's old friend would be OK.

He deserved better than that.

'Straight and true,' Farrell said, standing beside him as people walked past.

Archer nodded.

Farrell then reached into his pocket and pulled something out, passing it to Archer. He looked down and saw it was a piece of card. A ticket for the rock concert set to take place inside the stadium. Archer took it as Farrell pulled out another ticket and beckoned the other man to follow him. They walked to the right up some steps and moved towards the entrance to the stadium, *Madison Square Garden* printed in white letters above the wide doors to the mezzanine.

Inside, it was even busier than the street, people everywhere, buying t-shirts, mementos and snacks and beverages for the concert that was about to begin. There were all sorts of banners and notices announcing upcoming events, everything from concerts to basketball games to a political debate. Farrell led the way and walked on through the crowds of people, heading for some escalators thirty yards ahead.

The two men stepped on and waited as they moved up a level. Upstairs, it was more of the same, lots of concession stands and fans buying concert programmes. On the walls were photos and black and white snapshots from the greatest events in the stadium's history, and Archer glanced at them as he walked past. The first fight between Joe Frazier and Muhammad Ali, the *Fight of the*

Century, where Frazier shocked the world and beat the future greatest of all time. The New York Rangers ice hockey team winning the Stanley Cup in 1994. John Lennon's historic, and sell-out, concert here on August 30th, 1972. Iconic moments and for those who attended, unforgettable memories.

They walked forward and arrived at a set of turnstiles. An usher checked their tickets and they moved through into the heart of the stadium. With seating on four sides of the Garden, there was a long wide corridor that led all the way around the place in a big oval, providing access to each stand and seating area. Farrell turned and started walking left. From the way he was moving, Archer reckoned he could probably do this blindfolded, having studied the blueprints of this place to the point that they were tattooed on his brain. They passed a number of security officials and stadium employees, none of whom gave them a second glance, and walked on down the white corridor, passing people headed into the seating area to take their spots before the concert began.

After a few moments, the two men walked past an entrance to the seating area near Tower D, just past all the press boxes. There was a blue security door there to the right by the stairs that led into the stadium, almost inconspicuous, a lone guard in front of it looking bored, a thick keypad lock on the front. He flicked his eyes over to Farrell and Archer, but they continued to walk past, neither man prolonging his gaze and attracting the man's attention.

They moved on for a further fifteen yards, people passing them from both sides, then Farrell turned to Archer, leaning close so he could hear.

'That's the door,' Farrell said. 'My guy is going to let us in there tomorrow. The asshole there right now won't be on duty.'

Archer nodded.

'What's on the other side?' he asked.

'Flight of stairs and another security door leading to the cash room on the first sub-level. I paid off another guy down there. He'll let us in.'

They moved on through the crowd, but Farrell turned left, moving through one of the turnstiles the other way, Archer following close behind. They moved down the escalator and eventually came out of the East entrance by 7th Avenue, moving to avoid everyone making their way inside.

Although they'd only been inside for a few minutes, Archer was glad to get back out on the street and get some personal space back, taking a deep breath. It was seriously crowded and congested in there. He'd thought the city subway was bad but this was on another level.

Back out on 33rd Street, both men stood still for a moment. Then Farrell turned to Archer.

'Happy?'

Archer nodded.

'Let's go grab a beer. I'm buying,' Farrell said.

They moved on to a pub called Blaggard's, an Irish joint two blocks away on 35th Street. As they approached the place, Archer realised it was ironically pretty much across the street from the Starbucks which he and Gerrard had used as a meeting ground. It was moderately busy inside, the odd customer at the bar or at a table, but the place had a low-key and dull vibe. Music tried to force its way out of old speakers mounted on the walls and the lights were dim. All in all, it was a pretty dreary place.

Farrell went to the bar while Archer walked to a table away from the bar so they could talk without being overheard. The bartender pulled the cap on two beers; Farrell dropped a ten on the bar and carried them over, taking a seat.

Silence followed. Archer didn't feel compelled to speak. He was waiting for Farrell to start. There was a television mounted on the wall behind the bar, but it was showing some kind of sports show, nothing interesting or eye-catching.

'Feels strange, that I'm leaving this city,' Farrell said eventually, taking a long pull from his beer. 'Lived here my whole life. Born in Queens, been here ever since. Never even left the goddamn state before.'

Archer nodded, drinking from his own bottle. The beer was good, just about the only thing that was in this place.

'You know getting out of here isn't going to be straightforward,' Archer told him. 'You said you're taking all kinds of heat from the cops and feds. The FBI won't just let you go or forget what you guys have done.'

Farrell nodded.

'Yeah, I hear you. But we'll make it. Trust me. We've run circles around these assholes so far. We'll keep doing it, all the way to the cabanas.'

He paused.

'Anyway, I can't stay here, man. I'm two strikes in the hole. If I hang around, they'll find a way to put a third on me. That puts me away for life. And I'm never going back to jail.'

He paused. Archer drank from his beer and said nothing.

'We pulled another job yesterday,' Farrell said, his voice low. 'Took two hostages. First time we've ever done that.'

'Seriously? Did you kill them?'

Farrell shook his head.

'Tate was the one who held them,' he said. 'Once the job was done, he just walked out and left them be.'

'Could they ID him?'

'He was wearing a hockey mask. And he also told them what would happen to them if they tried.'

'You ever kill any cops?' Archer suddenly asked. He couldn't help himself.

156

Farrell looked over at him. There was a pause.

Then he shook his head, taking a long deep pull from his beer.

'No. Not yet. Haven't needed to.'

Archer read his face. He wasn't lying.

'What about Feds? Surely robbing banks puts you in their crosshairs?' he asked.

Farrell nodded. 'Of course. If it came down to it, then yeah, we'd probably have to take some of them out. But I try to make sure it never comes to that. Not because I'm a pussy. Because if you kill a cop, you get the entire damn NYPD on your ass. You better leave town immediately and never come back. And if you kill a Fed? That's even worse. Don't be fooled, guy. We may be fighters, but we ain't dumb. Last thing I need is an army of pigs or feds tearing apart my gym looking for answers.'

Archer drank from his beer, thinking.

'You mentioned a dead Fed the other day? You said if I talked I'd join him and Brown. Who was he?'

'I don't know. None of us put a move on him.'

'Then how'd you hear about it?'

Pause.

Archer's face stayed expressionless, but inside his common sense was screaming at him to shut up.

He had to be careful.

He was getting carried away and asking too many questions.

Farrell turned to him. 'I can trust you, right?'

'Of course.'

'We had some inside help.'

Archer managed to hide his expression behind a pull of beer.

'The cops?' he asked.

'No. Bigger. The Feds.'

This time Archer couldn't hide his shock.

'Who?'

'Someone on the Bank Robbery Task Force. They tipped us off. Telling us what to look for. That's the main reason why we've been so successful. That's why they couldn't get near us and build a case.'

Archer blinked.

'You still working with them?' he asked.

Farrell shook his head. 'No. Not anymore. I cut them out.'

'Why?'

'They got greedy. Wanted a bigger cut. So I told them to go screw themselves and that was the end of it. We always met in secure locations and checked for any wires or recording equipment so they didn't have anything they could put on me. If anything, it was the other way round. I said I'd go to the other feds and tell them there was a rat in the Task Force.'

'When was this?'

'Six weeks ago, give or take.'

'You haven't been in touch since?'

Farrell shook his head. 'No. They've got no idea what we've got planned this weekend. If they did, they'd probably try to screw us for the cash. But they can't arrest me. If I go down, I'll start talking and take them with me.'

'What's his name?'

Farrell grinned, drinking from his beer. 'Now I can't tell you that. And I didn't say *he*.'

He paused.

'Anyway, apparently the Fed who got shot was some asshole sent down here to see what was going on in their team. He found something but the rat took him out before he had a chance to squeal. They called and told me last week. Said they did me a favour and that I owed them to continue our partnership. But I told them where to get off. I don't need them anymore.'

158

Archer kept looking straight ahead, seemingly impassive. Farrell drained his beer, then looked over at the other man.

'Another one?' he asked, nodding at the beer.

Archer shook his head, keeping his eyes on the door ahead.

'No. Think I'll head out. Big day tomorrow, right?'

Farrell nodded.

'OK. I'll be in touch. Stay near your phone.'

Archer nodded, finishing his beer.

Then he rose and walked to the exit and left.

Outside on the street and out of sight of Farrell, Archer walked fast up 7th, headed uptown.

We had some inside help.

Oh shit, shit, shit.

Someone in Gerrard's team had flipped. That's why Farrell and his crew had been so successful. That's why Gerry was bashing his head against a brick wall trying to build a case against them. It all made sense.

And whoever they were, they were the ones who killed his father. Farrell had just confirmed it. A Federal agent murdered by another Federal agent.

That's why he'd left his service weapon at his apartment.

He hadn't been expecting any trouble.

Archer kicked an empty box as he walked up the street, cursing, worried. This whole thing had just been flipped upside down. Gerry had mentioned there were five agents plus himself in his team. Archer didn't know any of their names, or anything about them. He couldn't just walk down to Federal Plaza and claim that one of them was on the take or file a complaint. He needed Gerry's help and he needed it now.

He swore. The only good thing Farrell had said in there was that he had severed communications with the

Federal rat. Otherwise the moment Gerrard finished briefing his squad, whoever was dirty would most likely call Farrell and tell him the game was up. He'd said whoever the rat was needed to protect their own identity, so maybe they'd warn them off, tell them where the feds would be, or just tell them to bail on this job.

And depending on what Gerrard told his team, Farrell would know that Archer was the one who passed on the information.

He suddenly ducked into a Cosi coffee shop and headed straight through the café for the bathroom. He moved into the toilet and locking the door, pulled his phone from his pocket, trying to stay calm. He dialled Gerrard's number and lifted it to his ear.

Waited.

But it rang out.

No one picked up.

He tried twice more.

C'mon Gerry, pick up.

Pick up.

Nothing.

Shit.

Archer looked at his reflection in the mirror, taking a deep breath and trying to think straight.

Maybe it was a bad connection. Maybe Gerry was still in a meeting.

Or maybe it was something else.

He tried Gerrard again.

But no one picked up.

SEVENTEEN

Saturday night on 33rd Street was always busy, but fight night gave those evenings an extra buzz. The Garden wasn't called the Mecca of boxing for nothing. All the greats and world champions had fought there, from Ali to Frazier, Sugar Ray Leonard to Roy Jones Jr, Joe Calzaghe to Sugar Shane Mosley. The list went on and on. Las Vegas was the fight capital of the world, but tonight the sporting eyes of the world would be focused solely on a square 20x20 roped-off ring inside the Garden. As much a social occasion for the rich and famous as it was a sporting event for others, from the moment the opening bell rang till the moment the winner got his hand raised, Madison Square Garden was the place to be in the city tonight.

The streets outside were busy. Spectators and those lucky enough to have tickets made their way inside, excited, looking forward to the evening, while scalpers worked those wandering around on the hunt for last-minute tickets, desperate to get inside and watch the fight. Amongst the fight crowd was the usual mix of people out on a Saturday night, headed both ways down 33rd and 8th Avenue.

Inside a police car parked on 33rd, facing east and dressed in an NYPD officer's uniform, Archer checked the clock on the dashboard and wondered what the hell he was doing here.

9:47 pm.

The fight would start in thirteen minutes.

Which meant that Farrell, Ortiz and Regan had just gone inside.

He scanned the streets, looking for any sign of extra law enforcement. There were cops behind and to his right, near the stadium. Archer counted eight scattered outside, not including the security that would be stationed at the gates and turnstiles inside, which meant

161

twenty five others were somewhere else in the area. Although he was parked on the kerb next to the stadium, none of the cops on the street approached the car, and rightly so. It was giving no cause for suspicion.

He'd pulled up less than a minute ago and had left the engine running, as if he was waiting for his partner or had just stopped momentarily on the kerb. The car had been stolen earlier in the day, the plates changed and Farrell had left it in a parking lot in Queens for Archer to pick up, with a uniform concealed inside.

To his left, traffic moved past, headed down 33rd towards 7th, Broadway, 6th and the Empire State Building. He peered through the front windshield and looked at its tall, unmistakeable outline up ahead on the left. There were some LED lights set up on the upper levels, illuminating them with three different colours, and tonight it was red, white and blue. Patriotic and proud. Speaking of which, he peered through the windshield, looking for any possible FBI agents lurking, tooled up, ready to pounce. People wearing earpieces, or hanging around near the vicinity of the car.

No one he saw gave him suspicion.

Hopefully they were all inside, ready and waiting for the three thieves.

Nevertheless, Archer felt extremely uneasy.

He couldn't back out now.

He'd been trying Gerrard all night on the cell phone but he still wasn't picking up. Archer had spent the last twenty four hours high up in his hotel room deciding whether to go through with this, his phone in one hand, the 9mm Sig in the other. He'd been up most of the night thinking about it. Anyone thinking clearly and sensibly would jump ship in a heartbeat.

But he'd decided yes.

Farrell knew who killed his father.

Archer needed to stay close to him to find out who did it.

162

And he owed it to Gerry to take down the thieves. They'd come too far. He couldn't pull the rug from under him now.

If he's still alive.

Looking down the street ahead, he took a deep breath and reasoned with himself.

It's fine. Gerry's just being debriefed. He can't have his phone on because he's in meetings all day.

He'll be in touch soon.

If Gerry had managed to brief his team, Archer realised that the agent who'd flipped might expose him or herself. He could kill two birds with one stone and take the agent down as well as Farrell and his team. If he hadn't managed to brief them, Archer would get the three thieves and the cash out of here then take matters into his own hands. Somehow get the drop and subdue the three of them, then call the FBI or NYPD straight away, returning every stolen dollar.

So, against all his instincts telling him to bail and against his instincts as a cop, he decided to go through with it.

Stay cool, stay in control.

If he played his hand correctly he could bring down the whole team in one night, and get Farrell to tell him who the rat was.

He checked the clock again.

9:48 pm.

They would be inside the concessions stores now, the door closed, subduing the guys inside and packing up the cash.

Archer hadn't driven here with the other three. They'd all arrived separately to avoid any NYPD suspicion, legitimate officers wondering who the hell these four strangers in uniform were. He glanced either side of the car again, but he still couldn't see any sign of an FBI ambush. When to approach the thieves was possibly a logistical problem. On this job, none of the robbers had shotguns or heavy weaponry on them, but each had a pistol and bad intentions to go with it. He checked the time again and realised the trio might never even make it back from the stash room. An FBI team would be waiting in there with shotguns and assault rifles to make sure they didn't, surprising them and trapping them down there.

But just as the thought came into his mind, the trunk to the car was suddenly pulled open. He turned and saw two cops standing there, each carrying a large black holdall swung over the shoulder.

It was Ortiz and Regan.

They dumped them inside and pushed down the trunk quickly, shutting it, then turned and headed back towards the stadium for the second portion of the haul.

Shit.

So far so good.

No intervention.

He started planning ahead, working out a strategy to take the crew down himself and return the stolen cash. *But now might be when they get snatched*, his mind reasoned. Maybe Gerry's team already had Farrell in handcuffs and were waiting for Bonnie and Clyde to return. They were greedy. He guessed there was close to a million dollars already in the trunk. A fortune for anyone, a career heist for most thieves. Now they were just toying with fate, riding their success, figuring they could cheat the security and the odds again and again.

He checked the clock.

9:49 pm.

Shit.

This was bad.

All of a sudden, the front passenger door opened.

Archer turned, expecting to see Farrell.

But it wasn't him. It wasn't Regan or Ortiz. It wasn't Gerrard.

It was a dark-haired woman.

He instantly recognised her. He'd seen her a week ago at his father's funeral. She had been staring at him the other side of the coffin.

'Who the hell are you?' he asked.

She pulled the door shut and jammed something into his ribs quickly. He looked down and saw a Sig Sauer P226 pistol, FBI issue, same as his father's, fourteen rounds in the magazine, one in the pipe.

'Drive,' she ordered, glancing over her shoulder.

He looked at her.

Didn't move.

'*Drive man!*' she ordered, pulling back the hammer on the weapon with her thumb. One twitch of her trigger finger and Archer would die. 'I don't want to kill you but if I have to, I will.'

He looked over at the kerb and the entrance to the stadium. He couldn't see Regan or Ortiz.

And there was no sign of the FBI.

The woman jammed the gun higher and harder into his ribs.

'*Drive!*' she ordered for a third time.

Shit.

He had no choice.

Cursing, he put his foot down and the police car sped off down the street.

EIGHTEEN

They moved fast down 33rd, headed east, Archer's mind racing as he saw the stadium shrinking in the rear-view mirror. This wasn't part of the plan.

'You're messing with the wrong people, lady,' he told her, feeling the barrel of the gun digging into his side. 'Do yourself a favour and let yourself out. Walk away.'

'Shut up. And drive faster,' she said, checking behind them.

'This isn't what you think it is.'

'*Shut up!*'

Archer sped on. He pulled a left at Greeley Square and burned up Sixth Avenue. He hit a run of green lights and they moved fast, past Bryant Park. There was some kind of movie showing going on in the Park. He saw a large crowd gathered on the grass, the New York Public Library behind them, a large movie screen set up in front of them.

'Who the hell are you?' he asked.

'Just keep driving,' the woman said, turning and looking behind them, checking to see if they were being followed. She seemed edgy, but the pistol was strong and firm, digging into his side. The police car barely slowed as they raced on uptown.

'Where am I going?'

'What?'

'Where am I going?'

She paused.

'Upper East Side.'

Archer obliged and turned a sudden right on 45th, speeding down to 3rd Avenue. After he got there, he turned left and moved on, headed uptown. They drove on in silence, catching another series of green lights. They were moving fast, but being in a cop car no one they passed reacted. The woman kept looking behind them anxiously, the gun jammed into Archer's ribs, her manner tense and edgy. Behind the wheel, Archer was thinking fast.

After five minutes of silence and a journey that took them further and further uptown, they passed 90th Street.

91st.

'Turn here,' the woman said, the gun now held to Archer's neck. 'Here!'

Archer complied and turned right down 92nd. It was a residential street, but there were a series of empty spaces on the kerb. He figured she had some kind of safe house here, or there would be a switch car parked on the street. She'd either pull the trigger and leave him in the car, pieces of his neck and brain all over the interior, or she'd keep him as a hostage and take him with her. He felt the pistol in the woman's grip soften slightly, no longer pressed as hard against his neck.

She thought she was home free.

He made his move.

He suddenly put his foot down all the way, and the car leapt forward. Then he slammed down on the brake pedal as hard as he could. The woman wasn't expecting it and she wasn't wearing a seat-belt. It threw her forward, her pistol momentarily jarred free from his neck. In a flash, he let go of the wheel and grabbed her arm with his left hand, pushing and holding it to one side. With his right, he pulled his father's Sig from the holster on his cop uniform, jamming it into her neck, right under her chin. He gripped her right arm tightly with his left hand, the limb fully extended, her pistol now aimed uselessly at the windshield.

Archer's Sig was now pushed under her neck, his hand and stronger grip clamped on her left arm, holding her in place.

The tables had turned.

With her head tilted to one side from the pistol, she looked over at him, scared.

'My turn,' he said. 'Now let's have a talk.'

'Who are you?' he asked.

'My names Katic. Mina Katic. I'm a Special Agent. I work for the FBI,' she said fast, trying to shift her position. He tightened his grip on her left arm and kept the Sig nestled in her neck.

'Bullshit. You're after the cash. Do FBI agents hold up getaway drivers?'

'You're not a getaway driver. You're an English cop.'

Pause.

'How did you know that?'

'I was at your father's funeral. You saw me, remember? I was standing across from you. I knew who you were before then. I'd checked up on you. Found you on the UK Met system. I've been tailing you ever since.'

'Are you Farrell's inside man?'

Her head tilted away, he saw her frown, then her eyes widen.

'What? No? Did he tell you he had one?'

'I don't believe you.'

'Listen to me. Please. I need your help.'

'With what?'

She tried to shift, but he kept her where she was.

'With what?' he repeated.

'I know there's a leak in our team. You just confirmed it.'

'And it's not you?'

She shook her head slightly, as much as the Sig would allow. 'I swear. I got the jump on you because I had to get you out of there. You're being played.'

'By who?'

Pause.

'By Gerrard, I think.'

Archer looked at her for a moment, incredulous. 'Are you serious?'

'Yes.'

'What complete bullshit. I've known Gerry almost my whole life. He's clean as a choirboy.'

She shook her head.

'He's flipped. He's working with the bank team. He had a deal worked out with Farrell and his crew, but Farrell won't co-operate with him anymore. Gerrard's trying to find out where they're keeping their money and take it for himself. He's using you to get to the cash.'

'Bullshit. He's straight as an arrow.'

Pause. He tightened his grip on her arm.

'Anyway, you're the one holding me up. Maybe you're the leak in the detail,' he said.

'Does anyone know you're working with him?'

Archer went to respond.

But he didn't.

'Has he ever taken you to Federal Plaza?' she asked.

Archer didn't reply.

'Does anyone else in the detail apart from me know who you are?'

Pause.

'Yes. He briefed your team. He told you all what the deal was.'

She shook her head. 'No he didn't. We weren't even on duty tonight.'

Pause.

But despite the heat, Archer's blood started going cold.

'Show me your ID,' he said. 'Now.'

He eased back slightly as she reached down to her hip with her left hand and pulled it slowly, flipping it open for him to see. He glanced at it. It looked legit.

'I'm trying to help you, I promise,' she said, her head pushed back from the Sig in her neck. 'Can you put the gun down? It's hard to talk like this.'

He thought for a moment, weighing her up.

'Drop yours first.'

169

She complied straight away. The other Sig clattered onto the dashboard and slid down, dropping into the front passenger foot-space.

And he let her go.

She panted in the seat, rubbing her neck, leaning back.

'You don't need that,' she said, looking at the gun in his hand, which was still aimed at her stomach. 'Right now I'm one of only two people in the entire United States who know that you're on our side. If you kill me, you really are screwed.'

Suddenly, headlights lit them up from behind. Both of them jerked around but it wasn't a threat, just someone trying to get past. Archer pulled into a parking slot to his left and let the car pass. Katic stayed where she was, making no attempt to reach for her pistol, rubbing her neck and arm instead. On the kerb in an empty slot, Archer switched off the engine and took a deep breath. He glanced over at the woman. She looked far too troubled for this to be a play. She wasn't messing him around.

'Right,' he said, the pistol still in his hand. 'Please tell me what the hell is going on.'

NINETEEN

'We're a six man team. Used to be twelve, but eighteen months ago, finally, our clearance rate improved,' Katie said. 'We were six -and-six, six FBI, six NYPD. The cops pulled their guys from the squad. Claimed the clearance was so high that their work was done, that we could handle it and their resources would be better used elsewhere.'

'Yeah, I know all this. Gerrard explained this to me. You felt like they ditched you.'

'Exactly. Since they left, the number of heists have risen. But that means we're the ones taking all the flak for it. The cops have their own bank robbery detectives, but they handle note-jobs and liquor-store stick-ups, petty stuff like that. The big heists get sent our way, with just six of us asked to handle every single one in the five boroughs.'

They were momentarily lit up as another car passed them down the street, but after a quick glance neither reacted, satisfied it wasn't after them. Archer listened closely as Katic explained.

'I was with the old team. One of the originals. Once we'd got that heist level down to just 26 in a calendar year our old boss figured his work was done too. No better note to retire on. He packed his bags and headed back to Virginia for his retirement. Two of the others were promoted and transferred back to D.C. So there were three of us from the old team. Myself, O'Hara and Lock. And last summer, three new agents were brought in. Siletti, Parker-'

'And Gerry.'

She nodded. 'Yes. And we couldn't have asked for three more different guys.'

'How so?'

'First of all, Gerrard was bitter as hell when he arrived. We all noticed it straight away. There were a lot of

171

rumours circulating, but word on the grapevine was he got demoted from his old position at Quantico.'

'What did he do?

'I don't know for sure. But whatever he did, it pissed off everyone above him something severe. They demoted him, screwed up his pension, his $401k. Everyone Gerrard came up with had climbed the ladder, or stayed where they were, but he got pushed straight back down. Not just down a level, but down several. Almost twenty years of service, gone just like that. They knew the role here was a poisoned chalice. It was a ticking bomb waiting to go off. After Williams retired, no one in D.C. wanted it. So they gave it to Gerrard and sent him up here as punishment.'

Archer didn't respond. But he listened closely.

'Siletti came with him. They transferred him from Finance. He's a moaner, but he's reliable.'

'And Parker?'

'The golden boy, fresh from the farm at Quantico. His family are crazy wealthy, but he decided he wanted to become a Federal agent. He's young, younger than me. Everyone likes Parker. He could have taken the easy route, and lived on a yacht or in the Hamptons off his family's money, but he started from the bottom. Wanted to carve out his own path. He went through the training at Quantico, aced it, and they transferred him here a month later.'

She paused.

'I'll say it again. Before they all joined, our clearance rate had been rising. It was rock solid, you know? Over fifty per cent, the highest it's ever been. We were on a roll. But since Gerrard's been at the helm, it's plummeted. I kept thinking that it had to stop, that the decline would end. We've got some good people on the team. But it just kept dropping and dropping. Farrell and his crew have been running riot. Someone on the inside has to be helping them.'

172

'And you think Gerrard is the rat?' he asked.

'It makes sense, doesn't it?'

Archer shook his head. He wasn't convinced.

'That's one possible, if highly unlikely scenario. You don't understand, Katic. I've known that man for over twenty years. He's been a cop or a Federal agent his entire life. He's a good guy. He wouldn't cheat the game and betray his own people like that.'

Katic nodded. 'You'd put your life on that?'

'Yes, I would.'

Katic took a deep breath. 'Look, don't think that I have a vendetta against him. I don't. I'm not saying that he is the leak for sure. He's just been the one that I've been watching most closely. But someone in the team has dirt on them. Maybe more than one of them.'

Archer thought for a moment.

'What about the three of you that were already here?' he asked 'The originals. Was anyone bent out of shape by Gerrard taking the post?'

'Of course. All three of us were. We all wanted that spot as head of the detail. We'd put all the work in and then they just pass us all over for Gerrard. It was bullshit. We were pissed. For him, it was a demotion. For myself, O'Hara and Lock, it would have been the promotion of a lifetime.'

'Think cold, unemotional. Take out any personal relationships. Could O'Hara or Lock have flipped?'

She nodded. 'Yes. Conceivably so. O'Hara is a father of three. He's got a lot of mouths to feed. And Lock is a single guy with extravagant tastes. He could be after some extracurricular income.'

She shook her head, looking at him.

'Farrell's crew are good. But they're not that good,' she said. 'We should have rung them up and got them courtside by now. But it's been over a year, ten successful jobs in the city and we still haven't got a set

173

of cuffs on any of them. They're taking the city for millions.'

Another car passed, but again, neither reacted. Archer didn't take his eyes off her.

'It's uncanny,' she continued. 'They know exactly what to look out for and where to strike. Farrell and Ortiz, they're fighters, not brain surgeons or college grads. Someone is helping them out. We upped surveillance on certain banks and trucks we thought they'd go after, but they always manage to hit the ones we aren't tailing and box our counter-measures. Someone is telling them our game-plan. And tipping them off. They're always one step ahead of us.'

Pause.

'Maybe Farrell has something on one of you? Maybe he's made some threats?' Archer said.

She nodded. 'That makes sense. We've brought them all in for questioning. They know who we are. They even know our names. It wouldn't be hard for one of them to dig deeper and try to find some leverage.'

Katic looked over at him in the driver seat.

'Look, you probably think I'm full of shit. No one from the Bureau would ever go against their own team, right? How could that ever happen? But I'm not the only one with my suspicions.'

'Who else has them?'

She looked him in the eye.

'*Had* them. Your father. He agreed with everything I just said.'

TWENTY

'I made contact with him ten days ago,' Katic explained, as Archer listened closely. 'He'd been sent from D.C. anonymously. No one in our office knew he was here. His superiors knew that he and Gerrard were old friends. Something wasn't adding up with our numbers, and everyone in the Bureau knows about it. It's an embarrassment. The NYPD Chiefs were aware of it from the reports and were using it as cannon fodder, taking shots at our organisation, like bragging rights. So they sent your father down here to investigate. Stay in the shadows and find out what the hell was going wrong.'

'How did you know he was here?'

She paused.

'Because I followed Gerrard home one night.'

'What? Are you serious?' he asked. 'That could get you fired, Katic. You could get in some serious shit for this.'

'I know. But I picked up something else instead. I saw your father, in a car outside Gerrard's apartment. I recognised him from D.C. Couldn't miss him, face like his. I approached him, tapped on the window, and asked if we could go for a coffee. He said yes. When we got there, we spoke. I outlined my suspicions straight away, put all my cards on the table. And he agreed with everything I just told you and told me why he was here. He agreed that something definitely wasn't right. Bank robbery clearance rates in major cities are usually bad, but never this catastrophic. Something was very wrong.'

She paused.

'And he agreed with you about Gerrard. He was so mad that the Assistant Directors thought that Gerrard could be doing something shady. It made him even more upset that they'd wanted to send him down here to tail him. *It's all bullshit,* he told me. *Gerry would never do a thing like that.* He was adamant. I think he took the post

175

because he wanted to build a case to show that Gerrard *hadn't* flipped. That was his intention.'

She paused.

'Anyway, he called me last Thursday. Late, around 10 pm. Told me he'd found something, solid proof that Gerry wasn't the guy. He wouldn't tell me what it was over the phone. Said I'd find out soon enough, and that he was leaving later on that night. But before morning, his body was found in the parking lot in Queens. He found something on someone. He confirmed it to me, over the phone. And the timing tells me that whatever it was got him killed.'

Archer leaned forward, cursing quietly. Katic looked at him, concerned.

'What do you think?' she asked.

'I think you're telling the truth. Because Farrell told me the same damn thing. He said someone out of your team slotted my father before he left town.'

He paused and looked over at her, the pistol still in his hand.

'But maybe it was you.'

'How so?'

'You were here before the others. Clearly you're tough and career driven. I'm guessing you wanted that promotion as head of the Task Force really badly. But they passed you over, probably not because you're a woman, but you probably thought that was why. I don't see a wedding ring, so you're single. Not much money. So you decided to work with Farrell. You picked up my dad and tailed him, covering your tracks. My father called you and told you he'd found something and you killed him before he could tell anyone what it was. Then you decided to rip Farrell off, and hold me up for the cash in the trunk.'

She didn't answer. Silence filled the car. He looked over at her. She'd been wearing that exact same expression on her face the first time he ever saw her, at the funeral a week ago. He was pretty good at spotting a liar, but this woman wasn't lying. She looked too worried to be faking. She wasn't a professional actress.

She looked just like an FBI agent who was in some extremely deep shit.

'It's not me,' she said. 'All I can do is promise you that. But someone in the team is for sure.'

'Not Gerry.'

She shrugged. 'I'm just looking at every scenario. But this thing could go up way above me, Archer. I was doing this with your father before he got killed. Now I'm doing it alone.'

Silence. Both of them sat there, a thousand thoughts racing through each of their minds.

Archer went to speak, but a phone suddenly rang, breaking the silence in the car.

It was Katic's.

She pulled it from her pocket. He saw her glance at the display.

'It's Siletti,' she said. 'He's off duty. Maybe he can help?'

The phone continued to ring. She looked at Archer, her face asking permission because of the gun in his hand.

'OK. Answer it,' he said.

She pressed the button and lifted it to her ear.

'Hey.'

Archer heard murmuring the other end.

After a moment, Katic frowned. 'What?'

'What is it?' Archer asked quietly.

She listened further, then covered the lower half of the phone, turning to him.

'He's saying the NYPD have been informed that you're a suspect in the heist. Every cop in the city is searching for you.'

She lifted her hand and turned back to the call.

'No, I'm with him,' she told Siletti. 'He's innocent. He was working with Gerrard.'

Archer didn't move. From his seat, he heard a quiet murmuring over the receiver as Siletti continued to talk down the line.

'Where is he?' Archer asked.

Katic heard this, then asked Siletti. There was a pause.

'Columbus Circle.'

'There's a cinema by 67th and Broadway. Loews. Tell him to meet us there in fifteen minutes.'

Katic looked at him, covering the receiver. 'That's the other side of the Park? Why not around here?'

'Just tell him.'

She thought about it, then nodded and told Siletti the plan. Beside her, Archer pulled his own phone from his pocket and tried Gerrard again, lifting it to his ear, silently willing him to pick up.

But there was no response.

67th and Broadway was a logistical problem for Katic and Archer to get to being the other side of Central Park. Katic wanted to drive there in the cop car, but Archer refused. He knew the plates would be going out over every NYPD radio in the city. They wouldn't even get halfway there before someone made the stolen vehicle and pulled them over. Katic argued, saying that all she had to do was show her badge, but Archer demanded they left the vehicle parked where it was.

Archer didn't tell her, but he was more worried than he was showing. Not only was every cop in the city looking for him, but the FBI were all-powerful here. If any of them were on the wrong side or had their own agenda, it would only be a matter of time before they tracked them down. And considering everything they now both knew, it was a certainty that someone out there would be desperate to silence them for good.

So the three options for transport were either walking, subway or taxi. The subway was out, as was walking. Both would take too long and Archer didn't fancy getting cornered underground on a platform as they waited for a train. So they opted for a taxi.

Before they left, Archer quickly changed out of the cop uniform, pulling on a grey t-shirt, blue jeans and a pair of black Converse sneakers he had stashed under the front seat of the car. He grabbed a thin navy blue raincoat from the back-seat to go over it all, a cheap one he'd picked up at JC Penney's the other day. It was a warm night, but he needed it to help conceal his pistol. He pulled it over his shoulders and stepped outside onto the sidewalk and shut and locked the car.

Katic had also wanted to take the money with them, but Archer had refused that too. Strange as it felt, the money would be safer here. They couldn't walk around the city carrying duffel bags containing almost a million dollars. No one would ever guess what was in the trunk, and car-jackings were close to non-existent up here, especially on an NYPD squad car. So, much to Katic's displeasure and against her sense of duty, the money stayed where it was. It felt unnatural to leave it, but she quickly realised it was the right thing to do in the circumstances.

There was another reason why Archer demanded they leave it behind. It had been a chaotic night so far and from now on, he didn't trust anybody but himself. Archer wanted to find someone they knew they could trust before handing over a single dollar. From what Katic had told him, everyone could be a suspect.

And that included this guy Siletti.

As he locked the car, she walked to the sidewalk and stood beside him.

'Ready?' he asked, tucking the keys into his pocket.

'Wait,' she said. 'Your pistol.'

'What about it?'

'I need it.'

He looked at her, ready to refuse.

'You can't be running round town with a gun, Archer,' she said. 'You're in deep shit already. You shoot someone, nothing I can do or say will help you.'

He looked at her for a long moment, weighing her up.

'Can I trust you?' he asked.

'With your life.'

He believed her. So he pulled the Sig from his belt and passed it over.

If she was the rat, he was a dead man. She'd kill him right there and then and make off with the cash.

But she nodded a small nod of gratitude and tucked it into the back of her waistband.

Archer hid a small smile.

Their level of trust had just gone up a notch.

TWENTY ONE

Once they headed up the hill, it took a couple of minutes walking downtown before a taxi approached. Archer was on his guard, looking for any cops on patrol or any squad cars speeding down the road but they didn't encounter any law enforcement. Katic hailed the cab, which slowed and pulled to a halt on the kerb beside them. They both climbed inside, Archer pulling the door shut behind them. Katic told the driver their destination and the vehicle moved off downtown, headed south towards 59th where they could pass under the Park and move up the other side in a big U.

As they moved down the Upper East Side, the occasional police car flashed past the window but Archer kept his face looking inside the cab. They sat in silence. Neither wanted to talk within earshot of the cabbie, so Archer took the chance to get a closer look and sense of the woman beside him.

She was a great combination, tough and feminine, long dark brown hair tied back in a ponytail and rich brown eyes. Her name was Eastern European, Croatian maybe, but her accent told him she was the product of an upbringing in the States. Not New York or New Jersey. She didn't have the twang. He guessed somewhere else, like Chicago or Philly. She had the street-smarts of a city girl and the strength and resolve of her predecessors, folks who had most likely packed their meagre belongings and headed to the United States for a new life sometime in the last century after World War II. He imagined she'd broken a few hearts in her time but figured she also took precisely zero shit from other guys at the Bureau who wanted to test her out. He could smell her perfume and could see her tanned legs protruding from the black skirt of her work-suit. She was a scorcher, that was for sure.

As they moved through the mid-60 streets towards 59th, Archer's thoughts turned from Katic to Gerrard. He pulled his phone from the pocket of his coat and tried calling him again, but it rang straight through and went to voicemail.

This wasn't good.

Everything Katic had told him could conceivably make sense, but it was so unlikely Gerry was the fall guy that Archer just couldn't believe it. Gerry was a good man. He'd been caring and thoughtful to Archer the boy and had extended the same courtesy to him as a man, and had always been a good friend to James Archer.

There were a number of reasons why he could not be picking up his phone and not all of them were bad. If he was in D.C, stuck in meetings and debriefings, he wouldn't have a chance to answer any calls. He'd be back tomorrow and Archer figured he'd just have to make it through the night until he returned. Gerry would have an explanation and a solution for all this. It wasn't his fault his bosses pulled him from the city tonight.

But he wasn't picking up his phone.

And that didn't sit right.

This past week, Gerry had always answered his phone, usually by the third ring. Archer's father had been duped by someone and shot in the back of the head. Archer sent up a silent prayer that Gerry hadn't suffered the same fate and that someone wouldn't suddenly find his body in a parking lot missing a head. Good men didn't deserve to die like that. Especially not men like James Archer and Todd Gerrard.

They turned right and started heading along 59th towards Columbus Circle, the Park sliding past Katic's window on the right. To the left were a series of absurdly expensive-looking buildings and hotels that ran all the way along the street. 59th was where the thoroughfare of Midtown offices ended and the wealth of Uptown Manhattan started. Archer didn't want to think how much dinner and a night in a hotel in one of the places up here would cost. Probably more than a month's salary for him.

To the right, the Park looked surprisingly foreboding. During the day, nothing was more pleasant than a stroll inside, but at night it looked like a place that no one would want to enter. He'd heard stories from the past when armed gangs would wait in the shadows to mug pedestrians, and there'd been a fair amount of murders back when the city was a far rougher place to live. Archer looked at the Park move past the window, all shadows and darkness. He was going to be on the run all night, and if it came down to it, he figured he could always hide out in there. But he'd make sure to get his Sig back from Katic first.

The car arrived at Columbus Circle and held at the red light. After a few moments, it flicked green and they moved around the circular roundabout from the left. Archer watched the water splash in the fountain below the marble statue of Christopher Columbus as they slid around him and headed up Broadway.

'Drop us off on 70th,' Archer told the driver. Katic turned to him as Archer saw the driver's head nod.

'Why?' she asked. 'The cinema is on 67th.'

'We'll come in from the top. I want to see what we're walking into.'

'You don't trust Siletti?'

He shook his head.

'Tonight, I don't trust anyone.'

They stopped on the corner of 70th and Broadway as requested and Katic paid the fare. The two of them stepped out, shutting the doors and the taxi sped off uptown, leaving them there alone.

The streets were relatively busy, not heaving, but there were quite a few pedestrians headed to bars and the cinema or just outside enjoying the warm night air.

Archer stepped up onto the sidewalk beside Katic and didn't move.

He stared down the street ahead, looking for anything unusual. It didn't matter if Siletti was clean or dirty, he could still have called for back-up.

Up ahead, he saw a big digital clock in red letters mounted on a CNN building on the south side of Columbus Circle.

10:15 pm.

'What do you think?' he asked Katic.

She nodded. 'Let's go.'

They walked down slowly, side-by-side, checking for anything unusual. Any vans or people sitting in cars. Anyone nearby wearing an earpiece.

Any sign of a trap.

'Recognise any vehicles?' Archer asked her.

She shook her head and turned to him.

'Relax, Archer. We can trust Siletti. He's one of the good guys.'

'Even if he is, he might have called for back-up.'

'That's OK. We'll go downtown and I can explain what the hell is going on.'

They crossed the street, thirty feet from the Loews cinema ahead to their left. Archer looked up and saw the names and show-times of different movies scrolling across a digital black background in red lettering. All the summer blockbusters still on show, the studios eager to squeeze every cent they could from the paying public before they pulled the movie reels from the cinemas and started packaging them into DVDs.

The first door to the large dark foyer of the cinema appeared on their left. Archer quickly checked both ways up and down the street, then opened the door and letting Katic precede him, followed her inside.

Inside, it was dark and busy. There were people all over the place. A long queue had formed in front of the ticket desks, people waiting in line to purchase stubs for

184

whatever movie they were seeing, while others were walking to the escalators near the two newcomers and stepping onto the metal steps, making their way upstairs and towards the concession stands and screens.

The place felt like a disco or one of those laser tag places Archer had gone to as a kid, dark with occasional glowing lights piercing the gloom. Katic stepped into the north-west corner, Archer beside her. They were in a good spot, an exit either side of them, inconspicuous, not attracting any attention but with a good view of the place. Nevertheless Archer still felt uneasy and on edge. All of a sudden he was starting to regret handing his pistol to Katic.

He guessed who Siletti was the moment he saw him. He was a slim, wiry guy, tall, six two or three maybe. He was dressed in a suit that was a bit too big for him, a shirt and tie, and had a thin moustache and freshly slicked-back dark hair. Katic mentioned her team had been given the night off so his attire seemed unusual, but maybe he'd just dressed up before he left his place, anticipating a long night at Federal Plaza.

Archer's suspicions that he was looking at an FBI agent were confirmed when he saw the man clock Katic across the room. He stepped through the line of people queuing for tickets and made his way swiftly towards them. Concern was written all over his face. He glanced over at Archer in the darkness; Archer saw his right hand was by his hip, close to a pistol that would be surely tucked under the suit jacket.

Archer eased himself back a hair. If Siletti pulled it, Archer could probably grab the Sig from the back of Katic's waistband before she reacted.

'There you are,' he said to Katic.

He glanced at Archer, hostile.

'He's on our side,' Katic said, reading the look in his eyes. 'Like I told you, he's been working with Gerrard.'

'No way,' Siletti said, his hand still by his hip.

185

'Yes way. Take your hand away from there. You pull your gun, I'll pull mine and we'll be stuck here wondering what to do next.'

Siletti stared at Archer for a long moment.

Archer stared straight back.

Eventually, Siletti turned his attention to Katic.

'You're in deep shit, Mina. Why the hell did you hitch a ride and not just take him in? And where the hell is the money?'

'In a safe place. Look, I had to intervene. I think someone on our team has flipped.'

'What?'

'Someone's flipped.'

He stepped closer to the corner, lowering his voice. Archer looked past him, seeing if anyone was watching, making doubly sure the guy had come alone.

'Who?' Siletti asked.

'I don't know. But think about it. Surely you've got your suspicions. Farrell and his crew have been one step ahead of us every time.'

'Yeah, I know,' Siletti said. 'But to say one of us is working with them? That's pretty extreme.'

'Just hear me out. Look, I promise you I'm legit. And I can trust you, right?'

'Of course.'

'So it's either O'Hara, Lock, Parker. Or Gerrard.'

'Gerrard. Are you nuts?' Siletti said, still not convinced. 'He's head of the Task Force. He's an SSA. Guys like that don't turn on their own. It's unheard of.'

'When was the last time you spoke to him?'

'Thursday. Why?'

'We've been trying to call him for over a day now but we can't get through. Whoever the leak is might have got to him first.'

Siletti shook his head. 'You're serious about all this?'

'As a heart attack.'

186

He cursed and ran his hand back over his slick hair. Then he looked over at Archer.

'Speaking of deep shit, I should take you in right now. You're on the casebook of every cop and Federal agent in the city. I could land a promotion by bringing in your ass.'

'Go ahead and try.'

'He's good,' said Katic, interjecting as the two men stared at each other again. 'I can vouch for him.'

Siletti kept looking at Archer, then turned back to Katic.

'OK. So how much was in the car?' he asked.

'Close to a mil,' Archer said.

In the darkness, Archer saw Siletti's eyes widen.

'Jesus Christ. So where is it? That's stolen money. It needs to be returned straight away,' he said. 'Right now, you two count as thieves. Badge or not, Mina, you've still got almost a million stolen dollars in your possession. That's as illegal as you can get.'

She nodded and looked at his suit.

'Were you at the Plaza?'

He nodded.

'So do you know what happened with Farrell and his crew?'

He nodded again. 'The cops took them at the Garden. The operation's over.'

'Really?'

'Yeah. Let's go get the money, head downtown and sort this all out.'

Katic looked at Archer for approval, encouraged.

'C'mon, my car's a couple blocks away,' Siletti said.

They headed outside, pushing open the doors. Katic looked to Archer, reassured, but noticed he didn't seem as upbeat. The trio headed up the street. Siletti drove a small Mercedes and it was parked on the kerb, an FBI badge on the dashboard. He pulled a set of keys and the lights flashed as it clicked open.

'Let's go get the cash first,' he said. 'We need to get it in safe hands as soon as possible. Where did you stash it?'

Archer went to reply, but his phone suddenly rang in his pocket. He pulled it out and looked at the display. *Private Number.*

Oh shit. This could be Gerry.

He clicked *Answer* quickly, hopeful.

'Hello?'

'I'm going to kill you, you piece of shit,' a voice said.

It wasn't Gerry.

It was Farrell.

TWENTY TWO

Katic and Siletti had opened their doors, but turned, watching Archer take the call. He hid his shock at hearing Farrell's voice and smiled.

'Oh hey, how are you?' Archer said, warmly, his mind racing.

'You're a dead man.'

'Why's that?'

'You ditched us.'

'Really?' he said, still cordial, thinking hard.

'Where are you?' Farrell asked.

'Around.'

'Bring us the money and I'll let you live.'

Archer smiled, as he looked at Katic. His mind was racing as fast as he'd driven from the Garden, Katic's gun in his ribs.

'OK. I'll be in touch,' he said. He ended the call.

'Who was that?' Katic asked.

'Just a friend. Let's go.'

Siletti looked at him for a moment, his face unreadable. Archer didn't make eye contact.

He took another look at the man's suit instead.

They all climbed into the car, shutting the doors.

What happened next was fast and violent. In the front passenger seat, Archer smashed his left forearm into Siletti's face, then slammed his head forward against the steering wheel as hard as he could. He wasn't ready for it and his head smashed into the wheel like they'd been in an accident; he pulled back, gasping from the pain.

Archer grabbed Siletti's pistol from the holster on his hip, jamming it into the man's ribs just like Katic had done to him. It was a Heckler and Koch USP, not FBI issue, not his service weapon. He flicked off the safety catch and pushed it into the man's side hard, grabbing him by the slick hair.

189

'*What the hell are you doing?*' Katic yelled. She pulled her own pistol and put it on Archer. 'Drop the gun!'

'That was Farrell. They're not locked up. He called me from the street.'

'What?'

Archer looked at Siletti, who was covering his nose, blood leaking through his fingers and soaking his thin moustache.

'He's lying, Katic. They didn't take down the thieves. They're still out there. He's the rat. Did you murder my father?' Archer asked, jamming the gun into his ribs harder, causing him to gasp. Siletti's nose was bleeding profusely, staining his shirt. 'Was it you?'

'You're a dead man,' he said. 'We're going to kill you.'

Archer punched him with his left fist, hard, spraying blood from Siletti's nose onto the dashboard. Then Archer hesitated for a split-second.

He'd said *we*.

'Who are you working with? Who else is in on it?' he demanded.

'What are you going to do, kill a Federal agent? You just assaulted me, asshole. You're screwed.'

Archer paused, thinking, as Katic watched from the back, her Sig still aimed at Archer. He then jerked forward and grabbed Siletti's tie, pulling it off roughly.

'Keep a gun on him,' he told Katic. She looked at him, confused. 'Do it.'

She complied, and nestled her pistol against Siletti's neck.

'Hands at 10 and 2,' Archer said. Siletti swore at him and spat blood. Archer hit him again, hard, and reeling from the blow, Siletti complied, blood spilling from his nose. He grabbed the tie and wrapped Siletti's hands up, tying them to the steering wheel and pulling the knots tight.

190

Next, he grabbed the keys and turned to Katic, who looked scared and confused.

'We're out of here.'

'You can't hide. We'll find you,' Siletti snarled at him.

Both of them looked at him; Archer hit him again, then he and Katic stepped out, slamming the doors. But before she did so, Katic holstered her pistol and Archer pushed the magazine release catch on Siletti's weapon and caught the mag. He pushed the top-slide, catching the bullet that popped out, and then tossed the unloaded pistol on the backseat, tucking the mag and spare round in his pocket.

Stepping outside, Archer slammed the door and moved to the trunk of the car and slid the keys into the lock, Katic beside him, confused. He twisted and pulled it open and they both looked inside.

There were a number of items in the trunk. Items that alone wouldn't have cause for concern, but at that moment painted a terrible picture.

A roll of duct tape.

Ten or so red bricks.

A load of plastic bags.

And a power saw. The sharp serrated blade of the saw was red with wet blood.

It had been used recently.

Beside him, Katic gasped. A taxi passed them on the right and Archer hailed it. The driver stopped, and looked through the open window.

'Where to?' he asked.

'Anywhere,' Archer said. The guy looked at him, then shrugged and nodded.

Archer and Katic climbed in quickly, and the vehicle sped off down the street and into the night.

TWENTY THREE

'What the hell is going on?' Katic asked, as the taxi sped downtown. 'Siletti's the rat?'

'He lied. About Farrell. Why would he do that? And you saw all the shit in the trunk. He was waiting for us to show him where the money was. Then he was going to kill us both, chop us up with the saw and probably dump the pieces in the sea, weighed down with the bricks. And my guess is Gerrard is already down there.'

'What? Why?'

'He was wearing Gerry's suit.'

Katic looked at him, her eyes wide in disbelief, trying to process the situation.

'Are you sure? How could you know that?'

'Positive. Had the same stain on the right collar. I saw him get that stain on Wednesday. He killed Gerrard tonight, probably within the hour. He got some of the mess on him. He didn't have time to get home and change, so he swapped clothes with Gerrard instead. That's why his hair was wet. He had to clean himself off.'

Katic thought for a moment. Realised she'd been played.

'That son of a bitch. I trusted him.'

'And it almost got you killed. I didn't like that guy the moment I saw him. And he said *we*. He's not the only one involved'

Katic didn't respond. She shook her head slowly, her eyes unfocused, still trying to wrap her mind around it all. Archer pulled his phone and tried Gerrard again, more out of vain hope than anything else.

No one picked up.

Oh shit, Gerry, Archer thought, the image of Siletti executing him flashing into his mind.

'Wait,' Katic suddenly told the driver, regaining her clarity. 'Stop here, please.'

The driver complied. They were just before Columbus Circle, on 60th and Broadway. Archer and Katic got out on the Park side, both shuffling out through Archer's door. She paid the fare and the taxi departed, and she rushed across the street, Archer following. As they stepped onto the sidewalk on the other side of the street, Archer took Siletti's car keys, the magazine to the USP and the spare bullet, wiped them off with the lapel of his coat and dropped them all in a trash can as they passed.

'Where are we going?' he asked her.

'Siletti's going to be looking for us,' she said. 'Especially you. He was right. You just assaulted a Federal agent, unprovoked. If we don't find justifiable cause for that, you are going to be in a whole new world of problems.'

'So where are we going?' he asked again.

They had stopped outside a huge building on the west side of Columbus Circle. He glanced to his left and saw a silver-coloured giant globe mounted on a marble block, then looked back up at the structure in front of them. He knew what it was. His father had taken him here for a slice of cake one Saturday afternoon almost twenty years ago. He looked straight ahead and saw the name of the place printed on the awning above the wide entrance.

Trump International Hotel and Tower.

'Parker lives here,' Katic said.

'Parker? As in the guy from your team.'

'The very same.'

Archer looked up at the building.

'He lives here?'

Katic nodded. 'He's Siletti's partner on the team. Let's go up there and talk to him. Tell him what just happened. Perhaps Parker can tell us more and we can get some back-up. Three's better than two, right?'

'He might be in on it.'

193

She pointed up at the expensive hotel. 'Do you really think he needs the money?'

The building was impressive from the street, but Archer was stunned as he walked into the lobby of the Trump hotel. It looked like a movie set or something out of a dream.

Inside the lobby and reception area, the polished walls and decorations were lined with golden metal, the floor and reception desk fashioned from immaculately cut marble, not a single speck of dirt in sight. Crystal chandeliers hung from the ceiling, opulent and beautiful, extravagantly luxurious. To the left was a seating area, couches and armchairs with embroidered cushions that all together would probably cost him a year's salary. Neat bouquets of white flowers had been placed on the tables in front of the seating area and also on the marble desktop of the reception counter, their fresh smell scenting the air.

As he saw guests moving past him through to the exit or headed to the bar and restaurant up ahead, he suddenly became aware of how scruffy he looked in his overcoat, t-shirt and sneakers. He figured there could be cops or security lurking who might have access to the NYPD scanner, or maybe a report had gone out over the television networks breaking the news on the Garden heist, so he kept back and let Katic take the lead. His feelings of sartorial inadequacy were confirmed when he saw the expression on the face of the woman behind the reception desk. From her seat he saw her look him up and down; she seemed distinctly unimpressed.

Katic approached the woman, flipping her badge and spoke in lowered tones with her, asking what floor and room Parker occupied. After a brief conversation, Katic thanked the woman and led Archer forward through the lobby to the elevators, walking over the polished marble floor.

Katic pushed the button for the elevators and they waited, Archer looking around the place in awe.

'I need to join the FBI,' he said.

'That's highly unlikely, given our current predicament,' she replied.

He smiled as the elevator arrived. She was right. She turned and winked at him as the doors opened.

They let an elderly couple out of the cart then stepped inside, and Katic pushed the button for the 41st floor.

After the elevator moved up the building and arrived on 41, they got off and Katic led them down the corridor. Up here it was equally impressive, lots of cream-coloured carpets and golden lighting lining the white walls.

'41F,' she told Archer quietly, as they moved over the smooth carpet, headed right from the elevator.

Soon enough, they arrived outside the polished wooden door, *41F* printed on a gold oval-shaped tag on the door.

Katic went to knock, but stopped.

At the same time, she and Archer both looked down.

The door was already open.

It was standing slightly ajar, the lock resting against the metal frame. One simple push from the inside would lock it, but no one seemed to have done so.

Without a word, Katic stepped back and pulled her pistol. She thought for a moment, then reached behind her back into her waistband and passed Archer back his Sig. He nodded appreciation and took it, both of them holding the weapons double-handed. She looked at him, raising a finger to her lips. He nodded.

Then she pushed the door back gently and they moved into the apartment.

It was astonishingly opulent inside, beautifully furnished with a deep-pile cream carpet. Through the windows the view of the Park was spectacular, a sea of

195

greenery alongside the looming building work structures of 59th Street to the right. The room seemed to have a golden glow, like everything else in the hotel and it was silent.

The two newcomers walked in quietly, their pistols moving everywhere their eyes went, avoiding touching anything and not making a sound. Katic didn't call out Parker's name.

They didn't know who else could be in here.

Archer turned left. The door to the main bedroom was open. He moved inside, smooth and quiet, the 9mm Sig up, his finger tight on the trigger, his footfalls soft on the thick carpet. He saw the bed was made, undisturbed, pristine white sheets, duvet and pillows tucked and folded by house-keeping. Like the main room, the bedroom was empty. He glanced over his shoulder and saw Katic reappear. She shook her head, her pistol down by her side.

No one was here.

Inside the main bedroom, to the left of the bed was a door to a bathroom. It was closed. Archer crept forward and listened closely. He couldn't hear anything the other side. No sound of running water. No activity.

He pulled up the corner of his coat to protect against fingerprints and taking hold of the handle, gently twisted it and pushed the door open.

And he found Parker.

Archer could see he was around his own age, mid-twenties, blond hair and tanned. He was slumped over the side of the bathtub, his arms and legs outside. Blood and brains were spattered all over the white walls, shower rail and on one side of the shower curtain.

He could see what had happened. Someone had pushed him headfirst into the bathtub and shielding themselves with the curtain, shot him once in the back of the head. He could see the entry wound, a small maroon hole in the young man's blond hair. It had to be a

196

silenced pistol otherwise the other guests would surely have heard something. He had been executed, his hands and feet duct-taped behind his back, another strip pulled over his mouth. The duct tape was grey. The same colour as the roll in the back of Siletti's car.

The murder had happened recently too. Blood was still sliding down the white tiles.

Archer heard a sharp intake of breath behind him and turned. Katic was standing there, her hand over her mouth, tears welling in her eyes as she stared at the lifeless body of her colleague. Archer pulled the door back and shut it gently, then turned to Katic. Tears were streaming down her cheeks but she didn't make a sound, her brown eyes wide in disbelief.

'We need to go,' Archer said.

'We can't just leave him here,' Katic said, turning on him, anger in her voice and eyes. She was full of shock and grief. Archer was a stranger with no history with the guy, so he was thinking with more clarity. He didn't blame her for what she felt. If it was the other way round and one of his friends, like Chalky, had been murdered he'd have reacted the exact same way.

'We'll call the cops from the street and tip them off. C'mon. Let's get out of here and find somewhere to hole up and think.'

'I can't,' she said, pulling a tissue from her pocket and wiping her eyes. 'Not yet.'

'We can't stay here.'

'No, I mean I can't hole up anywhere yet.'

'Why?'

'My daughter.'

'You have a daughter?'

She nodded.

'Where is she?'

'One of the other mom's from school was looking after her.'

She checked her watch, sniffing, wiping tears from her eyes.

'Shit, I'm meant to be at home. She was due to get dropped off half an hour ago. I can't leave her there by herself Archer. She's only nine.'

'Does anyone in the Bureau know where you live?' Archer asked, his eyes wide.

Katic thought about the question, starting to re-gather her composure.

'Of course. It's on the records.'

Suddenly, she turned to Archer. She realised what he was thinking.

'You think—'

But she didn't even finish the sentence.

The two of them rose and ran for the door instead.

'What the hell happened?' the voice on the phone asked.

Siletti swore as he stuffed gauze up his nose. He'd managed to get help from the street, telling a concerned passer-by he'd just been mugged. The guy saw his nose and realising this wasn't a bluff loosened the tie from the steering wheel, releasing the other man's hands. Siletti had then gone to the trunk and grabbed a first aid kit, slamming the rear shut and walking back to the front seat in a rage.

'Katic is with him. He realised something was up and he got the drop on me. Asshole broke my nose.'

He swore in pain as he pushed the gauze up his nostril.

'Farrell called him too. His crew made it out of the Garden and they're gonna be searching for him. We could give them a call.'

'Forget him. He'll never co-operate with us again.'

A silence followed.

'You're an idiot,' the other man said, struggling to control his temper. *'Eight million people in this city and you had the two of them actually in your car. Why the*

hell didn't you waste them? They could be anywhere by now.'

'I don't need a reminder. I thought I had them.'

There was a pause.

'Where are you?'

'67th. Just north of Columbus.'

'Did you take care of Lock and Parker?'

'Yeah, they're gone. They won't be talking to anyone in D.C. Gave them both one to the back of the head. Used the HK, so it won't land back on us. I chopped Lock up and dumped the bags in the sea, but I got Parker's brains all over me when I shot him. Damn shower curtain didn't work. I had to go and change my clothes with the ones Gerrard was wearing before I met with Katic. I didn't have time to get home.'

'Not like he's going to need them anymore,' the other guy said.

Siletti nodded. There was a pause.

'Wait where you are,' the other man said. *'I'm headed your way. I think I know where the bitch and the English guy are headed. We'll do it properly this time. We'll get them to tell us where the money is, then shoot them and dump them both in the bay.'*

Siletti nodded, wincing as he finished splinting his nose.

'Bring the shotguns,' he said. 'I'm gonna take my time with the British asshole. By the time I'm done, there'll be nothing left of him to throw away.'

'See you in five,' the other man said.

TWENTY FOUR

Katic lived in a small place in the East Village, just off 1st Avenue on 13th Street. The journey from Columbus Circle took about fifteen minutes, the driver weaving his way skilfully across town, avoiding the traffic in and around Times Square. They'd asked the guy to get them there as soon as possible and so far he was definitely earning his tip.

On the back seat, Katic pulled her phone and called her home number.

'Won't the other mum be waiting with her?' Archer asked.

Katic shook her head, holding the phone to her ear. 'The woman has a key. She lets Jessie back in and locks the door and leaves. I work unpredictable hours and I'm not paying her to babysit.'

Thankfully, someone answered the call. But Archer was surprised. Katic didn't start talking to her, or warn her, or tell her to hide. She just said one word.

'Turtle.'

That was it; one word, loudly and clearly.

And with that, she hung up, sliding her phone back into the pocket of her suit.

'Turtle? What was that?' Archer asked.

Katic ignored the question. 'Can you drive faster, please?' she asked the driver, as they moved fast down 2nd Avenue and past 20th Street.

'We're almost there, Miss,' the guy said politely. He didn't need anyone to tell him how to do his job but he also didn't want to sabotage his tip. Katic nodded, her leg jiggling as she released nervous energy. The streets flashed past outside the windows as they moved on downtown.

18th.

16th.

'What the hell is going on, Archer?' she asked him, anxious. The cab driver could hear what they were talking about, but she didn't seem to care.

'Siletti. Had to be.'

'But why?'

'He's tying up loose ends. Parker was his partner. Siletti's covering his tracks. Maybe even the idea that Parker knew something was enough for what happened in the bathroom to happen.'

She looked at him, her face pale. Archer chose to save the rest of the conversation for when they were out of earshot of the driver.

Soon enough, they arrived on East 13th. The driver turned left, and headed across towards 1st Avenue. They hit a red at the end of the road, but it didn't matter. Katic told him to pull up where they were and paid the fare. She and Archer stepped out, shutting the doors, and the taxi sped off, the driver happy with the tip they gave him.

Katic went to walk forward, but Archer grabbed her arm and held her back. He stepped to the left, into the shadows, with her beside him.

'Wait,' he said.

Her maternal instincts were screaming at her to just cross the street and get to her daughter as quickly as possible, but she held back. Just ahead of them, 1st Avenue was busy, people out enjoying the Saturday night. Across the street though, 13th looked quiet. Archer had his Sig back in his hand in the pocket of his coat, and Katic had her own pistol in the holster on her hip. The game had just changed. Any rules that were in place had just gone out the window. If they kept trying to play them, Katic knew it could be the two of them next who would be pushed face-down into the bathtub.

Satisfied that no one was about, the pair of them crossed the street quickly and headed down 13th. Katic said she lived at Number 20 which was within a stone's

throw from the cross street and on the left side. The
street looked pretty empty. Archer scanned the interior of
any cars parked in the area, looking for anyone sitting
inside, or anything that seemed unusual. But it looked
clear. Besides, they'd be in and out in a couple of
minutes. The sooner they got on with it, the sooner
they'd be safe and could hole up somewhere.

Katic walked quickly up the steps to the door as
Archer double-checked the street, watching a man
walking his dog pass them by. She'd already pulled a
key from her jacket and she slotted it into the lock,
pushing the door open. Archer turned and ran up the
steps, moving inside and closing the door behind them.

Inside, out of sight of the street, Katic pulled her pistol
from her holster. Archer lifted his Sig from his pocket.

They both stood there in silence, waiting, listening,
looking at each other.

The building was old, lots of old wooden floorboards
and the two of them were standing next to the lines of
letterboxes.

Archer closed his eyes and listened.

Nothing.

'Which floor?' Archer whispered.

'Third.'

They approached the stairwell and moved up the
flights swiftly. Archer let Katic take the lead. Behind
her, he was impressed. He'd already seen that she was
tough, but the idea of anyone doing harm to her child
seemed to have given her an added layer of resolve that
made a protective mother the toughest fighter in the
world. Her dynamic with Archer had subtly shifted too.
She had gone from ordering and commanding him to
engaging with him and they were now working as a pair.
For the time being, they were partners. She needed his
help as much as he needed hers.

He needed to clear his name.

And she needed to make it through the night alive with her girl.

The stairwell was empty and they moved up the old set of stairs swiftly and silently, arriving on the third floor. Katic still had the wad of keys in her hand and she grabbed one of the keys, letting the others fall away, holding them so they wouldn't make any noise.

She came to a stop outside Apartment 3D and slid the key silently into the lock, the floorboard under her foot creaking as she stepped on it.

In the same instant, Archer pulled her to one side and against the wall in a flash, thinking instinctively.

If anyone was inside, they would have heard the noise.

The way he'd moved her meant they were close, face-to-face, her back against the wall. He looked at her, putting his finger to his lips and they both listened, tense. The two of them stared at each other up close for a moment that felt like a minute.

Moving aside, Archer nodded and she twisted the key, opening the door. The two of them moved inside quickly, weapons up.

The hallway was clear. Archer waited for a little girl to appear, rushing over to her mother.

But she didn't.

Archer shut the door behind them quietly.

They both stood there in silence, listening, pistols up, in the aim.

Katic moved forward and swept the place quickly, Archer staying where he was by the door. She reappeared soon after, looking relieved. There was no one here. They were clear. Katic holstered her sidearm, nodding to Archer, who lowered his and tucked it into his belt hidden under the coat.

'*Turtle*,' Katic suddenly called.

Archer looked at her, then heard a rustling and scuffle from the room next door. The next moment, the door was pulled back and a girl in pink pyjamas appeared, running over to her mother. Katic swept her daughter up into her arms, giving her a tight hug and kiss and exhaling a long sigh of relief.

'Turtle?' Archer asked, watching the mother and child with a smile.

'That's our code word,' Katic said, looking at her daughter proudly. 'What do we do when I say *turtle*?'

'We find a hiding place and curl up in a ball. Like a turtle,' the girl said, beaming, hugging her mother and giving her a kiss.

Archer smiled. It was a good plan. Katic was well-prepared and he liked her even more for it. The two of them turned and headed off to the bedroom, Katic telling her daughter they needed to pack up for a trip. Archer took the opportunity to walk into the living area and examine the apartment around him.

It was cosy, new enough to still be in good condition but old enough to have some atmosphere. Given the East Village's history, he figured this single apartment was probably once home to maybe ten or twenty immigrants fresh from Poland or the Ukraine, long before the hipsters and artists arrived later in the 20th century. Maybe it had been an art studio once. It had that feeling of quiet focus. It was a nice place, just about as good an apartment a mother raising a child in New York City with a monthly Bureau pay-check could afford.

Aside from the living area, there seemed to be two bedrooms and a bathroom. As Katic rustled away in the girl's room, packing some clothes, Archer walked forward and looked closer at the decorations and ornaments in the living room. Plenty of books, which showed Katic was a reader. All kinds too. He saw Shakespeare, Faust, Virgil. The classics. Then some fiction to balance it out. Clancy, Connelly, Child. No chick-lit. Education and thrillers, knowledge and adrenaline.

Below the books, he saw a picture frame holding a photograph of Katic with a man and the child. The father. He had to be. His daughter had his smile. He was young, mid-twenties, around Archer's age and looked like a nice guy. The three of them were together on a playground, smiling at the camera, the brown and golden leaves on the trees and on the ground around them showing it was autumn, or fall as the Americans called it. Archer glanced around, but there were no traces in the apartment of the man in the photo.

He didn't know what had happened, but he guessed that smile on his face had faded at some point since.

He turned to find the girl standing there, staring at him. She was out of her pyjamas, and dressed in a white t-shirt and blue dungarees, white sneakers on her feet.

'Who are you?' she asked.

'My name's Archer.'

He offered his hand. She thought about it, then stepped forward and shook it.

'I'm Jessie.'

'Pleasure to meet you. Do you have all your things?'

'Archer,' she said, ignoring his question. 'Like a bow and arrow.'

'That's right. Where's your Mum?'

'She's finishing packing up. Apparently we're going on a trip tonight.'

'We are.'

'Are you coming?'

'I think I am.'

'I want to stay here, but Mom said I couldn't.'

'Where's your dad?'

'He's not here. He's in Heaven.'

Archer paused.

'I'm sorry.'

She nodded. 'Do you have a dad?'

'I did. He's in Heaven too.'

205

At that moment, Katic reappeared. She had a holdall swung over her shoulder, lightly packed, enough for one night. She was still dressed in her dark work-suit, but her hair was now loose and over her shoulders. She looked great.

'Ready to go?' she asked, with a smile.

Archer went to reply, but something suddenly made him stop.

He paused.

He heard something, a soft noise outside the front door.

A creak.

In the same instant, he ran forward, scooping up the girl, and pushed Katic into her bedroom, slamming the door.

And behind them the lock on the front door exploded.

Houses in the old neighbourhoods like the East Village were often as dry as tinder and fire escapes had been installed to provide safe passage if someone inside the building was trapped. The architects probably hadn't envisaged escaping gunfire when they installed the metal steps, but danger was danger, whatever its form.

Katic ran to the window, pulling it open, while Archer locked the door and grabbed a chair, jamming it under the handle. Katic had swept the girl up in her arms and she was already outside, making her way rapidly down the metal steps.

Archer backed up fast to the window, and heard running footsteps and the reloading of a shotgun, a double-crunch as another shell was racked into the barrel. He grabbed the Sig from his pocket and fired five shots through the wooden door, splinters bursting from the door into the air, the empty shells flying out the ejection port of the weapon, the air stinking of gun-oil and cordite, the gunshots echoing in the air. It would buy them time. Whoever was on the other side of the door didn't know what to expect from inside the bedroom.

Archer ducked outside and hurtled down the metal stairs, hearing another boom as the shotgun blew the lock off the bedroom door.

In the courtyard below, Katic had fired the engine in her car already and Archer jumped off the rail, skipping the last flight and dropping to the ground. He raced over, pulling open the passenger door and jumped inside.

'*Go!*' he said.

She was already flooring it. There was another *boom*, and Archer heard a smash as one of the brake-lights was hit. Jessie screamed, covering her ears, as her mother screeched the car forward. They were facing 1st Avenue on 14th Street, the opposite side they had arrived and the car sped down the street. Archer looked over his shoulder, past the girl on the back seat and looked up at the top of the fire-escape as it came into view.

There were two men standing there. One had white tape and a splint over his nose and a pump-action Ithaca in his hands. Another man was with him. He was older, with red hair and was also brandishing a shotgun.

They stood there, side-by-side, watching them go.

They got lucky with the traffic lights, and hit a green straight away, and Katic sped on over 1st Avenue, speeding down 14th Street towards 2nd, headed towards Union Square. She turned a hard right when they got to 3rd, and they moved off uptown, gaining more and more distance from the apartment. Archer breathed a sigh of relief and checked Katic and the girl in the car beside him. Jessie was in tears, upset and scared, but both of them were unharmed.

'It's OK, baby, it's OK. I'm here,' Katic said, reaching behind and rubbing her daughter's leg as the girl sobbed, terrified. As the girl grabbed her mother's hand, Katic turned to Archer.

'Who the hell was that?'

TWENTY FIVE

As they headed uptown and Jessie began to calm down, Archer and Katic discussed where they could hole up as the car sped on through the streets, putting more and more distance between them and the apartment. Katic had plenty of friends and colleagues in the area but right now neither of them knew who they could trust. They also didn't want to draw anyone else into the danger unnecessarily.

As they talked, the streets flashing past, she realised she'd left her purse and cash at the apartment so Archer would have to cover them financially. He didn't have much on him but he had a room booked in his name at the Marriott in Times Square. They decided to head straight there and then figure out what to do next.

But whatever they did, they had to get off the streets immediately. They had a busted tail-light courtesy of the shotgun blast. If an NYPD cop pulled them over he would be very interested to say the least when he discovered who was inside the car.

To avoid the cops swarming in and around Times Square, Katic drove up 8th Avenue and approached the hotel from the west. They arrived in the parking lot under the Marriott building on 45th and reversed into an empty slot on the first lower level, Katic applying the handbrake and killing the engine.

Before they got out the two of them sat there and figured out a plan, Katic reaching around her seat and holding Jessie's hand to comfort her. They couldn't stay in the room booked under his name. Gerrard had known where he was staying and Siletti would probably have got the information out of him before he killed him; they quickly worked out their options, Jessie climbing over to sit in her mother's arms.

Katic came up with an idea. They examined it from every angle and decided it was the best they could come

208

up with. Satisfied, they stepped out of the car, the rear of the vehicle parked against the wall to conceal the busted tail-light. Katic quickly helped her daughter out and shut the door, smoothing her hair down and wiping away her tears, reassuring and hugging her.

Then taking her daughter's hand, Katic locked the car and the three of them headed up to the lobby.

Upstairs, Archer stayed with the little girl while Katic approached the reception desk. Together, they watched her speak to the receptionist then take her to one side, showing her badge and feeding her a story of how she was in witness protection and was in charge of the man and child with her.

As agreed, she said that they needed to use the reservation under Archer's name, but switch rooms and change his name on the record. Archer saw the receptionist was eager to assist, excited to be involved and with a child present she couldn't be more happy to help. He didn't mind about the room switch; he'd travelled light and apart from a suit, he hadn't left anything in the old room that couldn't be easily replaced.

During the brief conversation between Katic and the receptionist, Archer felt Jessie's hand slide into his. He looked down at her and squeezed it gently, smiling at her reassuringly.

After the receptionist passed them a fresh key-card, the trio walked through the lobby into the heart of the building, Jessie releasing Archer's hand and taking her mother's again. Katic had done a great job calming the girl and Archer saw Jessie's attention was now taken by the giant interior of the building, looking at it in awe, her fear momentarily forgotten. He didn't blame her. It was an incredible sight.

The lobby was spectacular. As you looked up, you could see the floors one-by-one, white and illuminated by lights lining each floor. In the middle of the lobby a square column served as the pillar for the elevators to slide up and down, ferrying guests back and forth in small capsules, like something out of a space-station you'd see in the movies.

Jessie's eyes were as wide as saucers, her mouth open as she stared up. Archer had done something similar when he'd first walked in himself and given their current predicament, staying here was perfect. It was like a giant hive, endless floors with endless rooms, and in a city this big they could tuck themselves away and hide out for the evening, hidden from sight high above the streets.

The three of them moved to the elevators just as one arrived at the ground floor. The doors opened and a group of people stepped out mid-conversation. Archer and Katic let them pass then stepped inside the empty capsule, looking just like a young family arriving back from an evening out. Katic hit the button for 21 and the doors shut. Jessie watched out of the windows, excited, as they moved rapidly up and up into the hotel, her face an inch from the glass pane.

Soon enough they arrived on 21 with a *ding*, and the doors opened to reveal the floor. They walked down the corridor, headed for 21G and arriving outside the door. Katic inserted the card in the lock; it clicked and a small light on the panel turned from red to green and they moved inside,

Archer pushed the door shut behind them and pulled over the latch. If someone the other side really wanted to get in the locks wouldn't hold, but it would buy them an extra few seconds.

The room was freshly cleaned, the bed sheets white and smooth, and the bathroom was spotless. Katic led her daughter to the bed and dumped their bags there. She gave the girl a hug and kiss then moved to the bathroom, switching on the taps and starting to run Jessie a bath.

As water splashed into the bathtub, she came back out and joined Archer who was looking out of the window, checking the view. She walked past him and slid open the door to the balcony, beckoning him to join her. He did so and she drew it shut, out of earshot from the child who was watching the television, the remote in her hand.

Up here they could hear honks from horns far below and the light whisper of the wind.

'Jesus Christ Archer. What the hell is going on?' she said quietly.

'As we drove away, I saw who was on the fire escape. It was Siletti and another guy. Red hair, looked older, in his forties.'

She looked at him.

'You're sure?'

'Positive.'

'Oh shit. That's O'Hara.' She sat down in a white chair behind the table on the balcony and ran her fingers through her hair. 'Jesus Christ, him too?'

'Where does Lock live?' Archer asked her. 'The sixth guy on the team.'

'He's in Brooklyn. I tried him earlier, when you and Jessie were talking in my apartment. He wasn't picking up.'

Archer didn't speak. He watched Katic start piecing things together.

'This is all starting to make sense,' she said. 'It was around November last year when we started bringing Farrell and his team in for questioning. We worked them one-by-one, trying to sweat them. We were a new team so everyone was keen to prove themselves and be the one to make a breakthrough. But they got to know our faces, our names, our personalities. We weren't working as a cohesive unit being a new team and given the competitiveness between us, so there were cracks there.'

She paused.

'Suppose Siletti and O'Hara meet with Farrell one-on-one, well away from our offices at the Plaza. Remind him about all the heat that's coming his way. Suggest

they strike up a deal. He agrees. The two Feds talk
Farrell through what to look for and where the Task
Force is focusing their attention and promise to stall the
investigation as much as they can. In return, Farrell gives
them a slice of the profits so they all get something from
the deal.'

She shook her head and looked up at him.

'What do you think?' she asked.

Archer looked down at her.

'I think they both know that Farrell and his team are
planning to skip town tomorrow. I think they're planning
to leave too. And now they're tying up all the loose ends.
Parker might have known something, or Siletti thought
he might, so that was enough for them to kill him.
Gerrard too. And Lock. Not taking a single chance.'

Katic looked up at him.

'You think?'

'He's not answering his cell phone. How does it look?'

'So they're the ones who killed your father. Jesus,
Archer, it was them. It had to be.'

He took a seat and thought for a moment.

'Yeah. I guess it was,' he said. 'I'm an idiot. All this
time, I was looking at Farrell and his team, but they had
nothing to do with it.'

'You said that Siletti and O'Hara will know Farrell is
leaving tomorrow?'

'I'm sure. They would have sweated Gerry for
everything he knew before they greased him. They'll
know that Farrell and his crew are going after the truck
tomorrow and their plan of escape.'

'After tonight, you think Farrell will still try?'

Archer nodded.

'Tonight was their first ever failure. This time
tomorrow they'll be gone from this city forever. They'll
never come back here. They're definitely going to try.
They're too greedy. The risk will be worth the reward.'

'What about the bodies? Parker? And Gerrard? And Lock? There'll be a big investigation. Huge. That's three Feds waxed in one night.'

'That won't matter. They'll disappear. They'll either take out Farrell and his crew and steal their money and their transport or hitch a ride with them. They wouldn't start killing everyone on the team unless they knew for sure they were never coming back here. They have it all worked out.'

He paused.

'But there are two problems. Three, actually.'

'What are they?'

'You, me and Jessie. They can't leave with us still alive. At any moment you or I could go to the cops or contact people in Washington. They'll be tearing the city apart right now looking for us.'

There was a pause as they both absorbed everything that had just been said. Down below, the sounds of the city provided a familiar background noise, a total contrast to the random and unexpected events of the evening.

And somewhere down there two killers were prowling the streets, searching for them.

'So what now? What do we do?' Katic asked. 'We need to go higher up the chain. We need help from D.C. We have to talk to someone before they track us down.'

'We need to stay here for the night,' Archer replied, looking over the balcony down at Times Square. 'We go back out there, we might not come back. And I'm a fugitive remember? The entire NYPD is after me too, not just those two. I'm staying put, with a gun pointed at that door until morning.'

'We can't just sit here, Archer. They'll find us sooner or later. We need to tell someone about this.'

Archer thought for a moment.

He'd trusted Gerrard, and he was gone.

213

Katic had trusted Siletti and it had almost got them killed.

Their next move had to be perfectly played. Because sooner or later, they were going to run out of luck.

And if they trusted the wrong person, all three of them would die.

'OK.'

She looked up at him. 'OK what?'

'I know who we can call.'

'Who?'

'He's on our side, I guarantee. I'll be right back,' he said.

He slid open the door, moving past the girl who was engrossed in a T.V show on the screen and over to the door. He realised the taps on the bath were still running, so he stepped inside the bathroom first and twisted them off.

Walking to the main door he pulled back the latched lock and stepping outside, shut the door behind him.

Outside in the corridor, he checked both ways. It was quiet.

He pulled his phone from his pocket and dialled a number, walking towards the end of the corridor, checking to make sure no one else was around.

It rang four times.

On the fifth, someone answered.

'Hello?'

'It's Archer,' he said. Pause. 'I'm in deep shit. I need your help.'

There was a pause.

Archer checked left and right, his fingers curled around the grip of the 9mm Sig in his right pocket. He heard a rustling down the phone as the man on the other end moved out of his bedroom.

He heard a door open, then close, and a click as a light was switched on.

And the voice spoke again from the other end.

'OK, Archer. Tell me what's going on,' Director Cobb said.

TWENTY SIX

It took Archer about fifteen minutes to explain his predicament. The United Kingdom was five hours ahead so he'd woken Cobb at just past 5 am London time. But in about ten seconds, from the moment he picked up the phone to walking into the next room and speaking again, the Director of the ARU had all his faculties and was awake and alert. Like most powerful people in senior government and security positions, the time of day was just a series of numbers. It didn't matter. If there was a problem, they were awake and ready to deal with it in seconds.

Cobb listened closely as Archer explained the situation. He told him everything, leaving nothing out. The first meeting with Gerrard. His subsequent involvement with Farrell. Their successful series of bank robberies and armoured truck heists and their planned final getaway. The Garden heist. And everything that had happened since. Siletti double-crossing them, the damning evidence in his trunk. Parker's dead body and Gerrard's disappearance. O'Hara joining Siletti and coming after the three of them at Katic's apartment.

Archer finished and took a breath, continuing to check the corridor around him for any activity. He was standing by the stairwell, but no one else was around. He'd been speaking quietly, so there was no risk of anyone in rooms nearby catching what he was saying.

'I didn't know who else to call, sir,' he added, aware that he had interrupted his sleep. 'We didn't know who to contact higher up. We have no idea who's involved. And right now, I'm a damn fugitive anyway.'

'OK. Stay calm,' Cobb said, thinking coolly and logically, not questioning a single word of what Archer just told him. *'I have a friend in the FBI. He's a solid guy. I worked with him on a joint operation a while ago when I was still at MI5. He's in a senior position now,*

an Assistant Director. His name's Sanderson. I'll call him, and tell him everything you just told me. You said you stored the money in the trunk of the car?'

'Yes, sir.'

'Good. If anyone finds it and reports it, it'll pass through the NYPD and they'll return it straight away.'

He paused.

'Jesus Christ Archer, you're supposed to be on holiday.'

'I know, sir. I'm sorry. Someone involved in this killed my father. I had to try to find out who it was.'

There was a pause.

'This Siletti guy could be a problem. He sounds like a smart man. If his story checks out and he's covered any traces of his involvement, you could be in some deep shit. You beat him up. The FBI won't like that, not on their turf. If he has half a brain he'll have killed Parker, Lock and Gerrard with a stolen weapon so any ballistics fingerprinting will draw a blank. You need solid proof against this guy. He'll have made a mistake somewhere. You just need to find out where.'

The line went quiet as he thought for a moment.

'Could you get a signed testimony from Farrell?' Cobb asked.

'He's planning to leave the city forever tomorrow. If we could get something, we'd need to bring him in in the next twenty four hours or he's gone. And he isn't the type to go down quietly. He told me he's never going back to jail. He'd most likely get shot and killed if he got cornered.'

There was a pause. Archer checked up and down the corridor again, the phone in his left hand, the Sig still in his right in the pocket of the coat.

'OK. Stay near the phone,' Cobb said. *'I'll get in touch with Sanderson and call you back. Where are you?'*

'Marriott. Times Square. Same joint you put me up in, sir.'

217

'Did you switch rooms?'

'Yes, sir. False name, claiming wit sec. No one knows we're here.'

'Good. Lay low, Arch. Don't move. Stay where you are. I'll call you back soon.'

'Yes, sir. Thank you.'

And the call ended.

Archer pushed the phone back into his pocket, then walked back down the corridor towards their room. He checked either side, then pulled the key-card from his pocket and eased it into the slot, letting himself back into the room.

At the moment Cobb ended the call, two men in suits were on their way up in one of the elevators in the hotel. They'd left their shotguns in the back of the car they'd arrived in, but both had pistols in shoulder holsters hidden under their jackets. The weapons were stolen HK USP 9mm's, tape over the trigger and grip and each had a black suppressor screwed onto the barrel to lower the sound and report of the weapon firing.

They arrived on one of the floors. The doors slid open and they walked out. One of the men had a makeshift splint and gauze holding a broken nose in place and as they moved down the corridor, he winced from the pain it was causing him. They saw the hotel room door ahead, and the two men slowed, moving forward quietly and slowly.

Fifteen feet.

Ten.

Five.

They arrived outside the door.

They checked either side, making sure no one was around then both pulled out their pistols, pulling the top-slides back halfway to make sure a round was in the chamber of each weapon.

218

One of them, a man with red hair, had a key-card in his right hand.

He eased it into the slot and the door clicked, a light on the panel flicking green. In the next moment, he pushed down the handle and the two of them burst into the room, pistols up and ready to fire.

But no one was inside.

It was empty.

The man with the splint ran forward and checked the balcony while the man with red hair looked in the bathroom.

'Shit,' he said, as the man with the broken nose re-entered the room from the sliding doors. 'They aren't here.'

'I can see that, dumbass,' the other man said.

He looked around and saw that there was an overnight bag here, a solitary black suit hanging on a hanger in the closet. One man had been staying here, travelling light.

'Shit. Gerrard told me this was his room.'

'Maybe they're somewhere else in the hotel,' the other man suggested. 'Or Katic found somewhere for them to stay, with a friend or something.'

Siletti swore.

'We need to find them. They start talking to people in D.C , we're screwed.'

'You think I don't know that?' O'Hara said.

Siletti pulled a phone from his pocket and pushed *Redial*, lifting it to his ear. The call connected.

'Did you find them?' a voice said.

'No. They weren't here.'

Pause.

'This isn't good. If you two go down, that might implicate me. That would make me very unhappy. You'd better pray you find them before the cops do.'

'Understood.'

The call ended. Siletti looked over at his partner.

'He's pissed.'

'No shit.'

There was a pause. The two men looked at the empty room for a moment longer, then Siletti cursed, blood staining the gauze in his nostrils, caking his moustache.

'Screw this. Let's get the hell out of here,' he said.

The two men slotted their pistols back in their holsters and strode out of the hotel room.

Seventeen floors below the two men, Archer closed the door to 21G quietly behind him and secured the latch. The door to the bathroom was open, the mirror steamed up, the bathtub empty; he saw that Jessie was curled up in bed, fast asleep, exhausted but freshly bathed, the scary events of the evening temporarily forgotten. The shootout at the apartment had terrified her but nothing that some velvet lies couldn't fix. In the car on the way here, Katic had played down the attack, saying it was a training exercise from work and although sceptical at first, the girl had believed it with the conviction that her mother was all-powerful, indestructible, the greatest person in the world.

Archer moved back into the room quietly so as not to wake up Jessie and stretched, taking off his coat and laying it over a chair. He pulled the pistol from the pocket and held it in his hand, cold, hard metallic reassurance. Everywhere he went tonight, the Sig was coming too. Jessie was asleep so he didn't need to hide it.

He saw that Katic was outside on the balcony, sitting in one of the white chairs facing Times Square. He moved out to join her.

She started as he opened the screen door and instinctively reached for the pistol on her hip, but relaxed and smiled when she saw it was him. He stepped out, shutting the door quietly behind him.

'Hey.'

'Hey.'

'Mind if I join you?'

She shook her head and he took a seat beside her.

There was a pause. Down below they could hear the constant hum and activity of Times Square. They were facing the east side and if he sat up straight, Archer could see the tops of some of the billboards, illuminated in the night.

'I spoke to my boss, back in the UK. He's going to call me back.'

She nodded. 'Good.'

Together, the two of them looked out over the city. The bright lights. The dark shapes of the buildings.

'I'm sorry about your husband,' Archer said.

'Yeah. Me too.'

'How did he die?'

'Cancer.'

She paused.

'He was only twenty six. We met the week after I left high school back in Chicago.' Pause. 'You'd have liked him. He was calm. Mature. Kind. Jessie was unexpected to say the least, but he never complained about it once. Didn't desert me, like a lot of other guys his age would have done. After she was born, when other guys his age were out partying, he stayed with me to help look after her.'

'Is Katic his name?'

She shook her head. 'Mine. We got married a couple of years ago, but I couldn't keep his name after he died. It was too hard. A constant reminder.'

'Katic. Is that Croatian?'

She shook her head. 'Serbian. Third generation. Family moved here after the war.'

Archer nodded and leaned back. Both of them looked out over the city in silence.

221

'They're out there right now looking for us,' Katic
said. 'The cops want you for the Garden heist. Farrell
wants you because you abandoned him and his team and
took their money. Siletti and O'Hara want us because we
know about everything they'd done.'

She shook her head.

'I thought there were rules, you know? Two separate
sides. Cops and robbers. We're the good guys, they're
the bad guys. They do bad things, we chase them and try
to stop them. But that's not the case, is it?'

Archer shook his head.

'No, it's not.'

'Suddenly it makes sense. Siletti and O'Hara were
always reluctant. Complaining. Bitching about the pay.
Siletti pissed about getting sent up here, O'Hara for not
getting Gerrard's role in the squad. I got so caught up in
tailing Gerrard that I never stopped to look at those two.
Now he, Parker and Lock are all dead.'

'It's not your fault. You never could have known any
of this was going to happen.'

Silence. Katic shook her head, leaning back, looking
up at the sky.

'Parker had been Siletti's partner for over a year. The
kid never hurt a fly. Yet he shoots him in the back of the
head. Executed. The same probably happened to Lock
and Gerrard. They interacted with these men. Spent time
together. Ate food. Rode in the same cars. How the hell
could they just murder them like that?'

Archer stayed silent as Katic sighed.

The noise of Times Square below filled the silence that
followed

'You're a cop in the UK, right?' she asked, turning to
him.

'That's right.'

'Have you ever been double-crossed?'

He nodded. 'Once.'

She saw the look on his face and decided not to pursue it.

There was a pause.

'It's a horrible feeling,' she said. 'I still don't get why they would do it. I can't get my head around it.'

'One reason. Money. I guess being in Bank Robbery, the two of them had been around a lot of cash. You said Siletti came from the Finance office too, back in D.C. Around all that money, every day, yet being unable to ever get your hands on any of it. Having to nod and smile as you get a monthly cheque that's a fraction of the amount of cash you deal with on a daily basis.'

Silence.

'Your father talked about you, you know.'

Archer looked over at her.

'When?'

'We had a coffee two weeks ago, three or four days before he died. He'd been tailing Parker to make sure he was on our side, and had pulled his files from the database in D.C. Parker was a big high-school football player. Played quarterback. Your dad read it in the file and said he reminded him of you. Apparently you used to play soccer.'

Archer smiled, and nodded. 'Yeah, that's right.'

She turned to him. 'He had a lot of regrets, you know. I could see that in his body language when he spoke about you. I don't know what happened between you, but his eyes lit up when he mentioned you that one time. Then his expression changed. He seemed sad. He tried to hide it, but I could see it.'

She paused.

'I'm guessing he did something to screw up. Maybe a lot of things. I don't know what he did, but I could tell that he regretted it and losing touch with you.'

Archer stayed silent, looking at her.

Suddenly, the cell phone rang in his pocket. Pulling his attention from Katic, he lifted it out of his pocket and pushed *Answer*.

'Hello?'

'It's me,' Cobb said. *'Good news. I spoke to Sanderson. He's on his way to you already from D.C. He'll be there before morning.'*

'Great. How did he take the news?'

'He was shocked, but he wasn't surprised. Seems the FBI team in New York has been under review for quite some time. Their closure numbers are so bad, everyone in the entire organisation had noticed. Sanderson is an Assistant Director. All he needs to do is make one phone call and an entire division from D.C. will be on their way up to help you all out. You can trust him, Arch. He's an old friend.'

'Great. Thank you, sir.'

'How are you holding up?'

'Yeah, I'm OK.'

'The woman and the child?'

Archer looked at Katic. 'They're OK too.'

'Just hang on until morning, Arch. Sanderson will take it from there. He believed everything I told him, everything that you told me. When he realised who your father was, that was enough to convince him. Seems he had a very good reputation over there.'

There was a pause.

'I need to go. But call me if the shit hits the fan again. Do you have a gun?'

'Yes, sir.'

'Sleep with it in your hand. Clear?'

'Yes, sir.'

The call ended. He turned to Katic who was looking at him, her brown eyes hopeful.

'We're in business,' he said. 'A guy called Sanderson is on his way from the capital. He's an Assistant

Director. He wants to talk to me first hand, then it looks like he's going to get us some back up.'

'Great,' she said. 'That's good news.'

There was a pause. Then she rose and stretched.

'I'm spent. I'm going to hit the hay,' she said.

Archer nodded. She walked past him, brushing his shoulder as she passed. He smelt her perfume.

He didn't move as she re-entered the hotel room, sliding the door shut quietly behind her and leaving him out there alone.

Archer sat out on the balcony for another thirty minutes, thinking things through. Then he quietly entered the room. Katic and the girl were asleep in the bed. There was a couch straight ahead of him that looked inviting. He stacked up two cushions on the end closest to the window and sat on the middle.

Suddenly, he realised that he'd left his cell phone on. Siletti and O'Hara would be prowling the streets down below, but he knew the kind of equipment they would have access to back in their offices at Federal Plaza. He didn't fancy getting triangulated by the cell phone's signal. Back in London, he'd seen Nikki do the exact same thing and she could find someone in less than a minute using the technology. He unclipped the back panel of the phone quietly so as not to wake Katic and the girl, then pulled out the battery. He thought for a moment, then rose and tiptoed across the room and did the same with Katic's phone, laying it back gently on the table.

Satisfied, he returned to the couch and lay back, closing his eyes, the pistol in his hand. He heard the deep breathing of the mother and daughter from the bed. He glanced over and saw Katic fast asleep, her dark brown hair behind her head, her jaw-line and neck sleek and feminine.

He watched her for a few moments longer, then closed his own eyes.

And within a minute he was asleep.

TWENTY SEVEN

The next morning, Archer was the first to wake. He opened his eyes and found himself staring at the ceiling, his back flat on the couch, still in his t-shirt, jeans and shoes. In his right hand, the Sig was resting on the couch on its side, but it was aimed straight at the door.

He rose, stretching, and checked the bed. He saw Katic and Jessie still snuggled together, fast asleep amongst the folds of the clean white sheets. He smiled. He figured Katic was the type like himself who would be up at sunrise, getting in a run or a gym session before she started her day, but the events of last night had clearly knocked her body for six. He watched them both for a moment, then glanced at the clock on the bed-side table. The sunlight pouring in through the gap in the curtains already told him it was morning, another beautiful day in the city; the red digits on the clock told him it was *9:29 am*. He realised it was Sunday. He was supposed to be heading back to the UK today. His flight took off in eleven hours.

But there was a hell of lot they'd have to face before he could even think about getting on that plane.

Yawning, he moved to the bathroom as quietly as he could and used the facilities, flushing the toilet and brushing his teeth with the complimentary white hotel brush and paste. He laid the pistol on the marble counter as he brushed and rinsed out his mouth. He examined his reflection in the mirror. He looked tired, but he'd seen himself look a lot worse. He smoothed down his hair, then remembered his phone and took the pieces out of his pocket, sliding the battery back into the slot on the back and reattaching the rear cover. He turned it on. After a few moments, a small phone came up in the left corner of the display. He had a voice message. Archer pushed the button and listened.

It was from Sanderson, the FBI Assistant Director. Cobb must have given him the number. He had a deep voice, a neutral American accent, non-regional. He said he'd just arrived in town and it was around 5 am; he was going to get his head down for a few hours then would meet at 10 am wherever Archer wanted. The message ended. Archer appreciated the gesture. Sanderson and Cobb must have been good friends, or he must have really owed Cobb to drive up here so late at night. Right now, he and Katic needed all the help they could get and Sanderson was the perfect man to help them. Archer tried to call him back, but there was no answer. He let it ring through to the answering machine and left a message, telling the man to meet him on the 8th Floor Marriott Hotel bar at 10. He hung up and took out the battery again, then moved back into the room.

Katic and Jessie were still asleep. Archer grabbed a pen and paper from the desk by the television and scribbled *Gone to meet FBI A.D. Back soon x* on the pad, just under the red hotel logo, address and contact details. He laid it on the couch where he'd been sleeping and grabbed his navy-blue over-coat.

Swinging it over his shoulders, he checked the chamber on the Sig by pulling back the top-slide gently. He saw the copper-coloured gleam of a bullet in the pipe, confirming it was loaded, and then tucked the gun into the pocket of his coat. He grabbed the key-card and taking the latch off the door, quietly slipped out of the room, pulling the door shut behind him as softly as he could.

He stood in the corridor, still for a moment, checking each side. The place was pretty quiet. Down the far end, he saw a family of five troop out of a room and make their way towards the elevators. He waited where he was, watching them. The father of the group pushed the button and they stepped into one of the capsules and the doors shut, probably headed upstairs for the restaurant on the 48th Floor and a view of the Manhattan morning as they enjoyed a Sunday morning breakfast.

Archer walked down the corridor. The coat's deep pockets meant he could look like he had his hands stuffed in there, but actually was holding a pistol in his right hand. It meant he could be armed and ready to fire, and if Siletti and O'Hara got the drop on him he would have something of his own to answer with. The odds were already stacked against him but the Sig would even the playing field if he got cornered.

Arriving by the elevators, he pushed the button and a set of doors opened instantly. He walked over and stepping inside, jabbed the button for 8. After a brief pause, the doors slid shut and the capsule moved down.

He looked out of the glass and saw the lobby far below, gradually increasing in size as the elevator took him down thirteen levels. Looking down, he realised any guests who were afraid of heights would probably leave this hotel more stressed than when they arrived. It certainly was an overwhelming view, a clever and artistic design, but not for sufferers of vertigo that was for sure.

A few seconds later the elevator arrived on 8 and once the doors opened, Archer stepped out. Suddenly, it was far busier around him. He saw the giant bar was straight ahead of him, the rest of the 8th floor a concourse with shops and conference rooms. There were people passing him from each direction and he joined the flow, moving up a couple of steps and entering the large bar area.

The bar was big. Very big. It occupied about a third of the entire 8th floor. It was split into two halves. The floor on this side was all polished marble, dark green with white swirls and whorls. To his immediate left was the main bar itself. It was circular, surrounded by a series of white chairs, televisions mounted above the rows and rows of different liquor bottles, showing the news headlines and weather reports for the day. He was glad to see that neither his face nor any mention of the Garden heist was on the screen. But some footage and a headline suddenly flicked onto the television that made him stop in his tracks.

It was a breaking news report. The screen was showing images from outside the Trump Hotel, sometime last night, lots of lights from both an ambulance and cameras flashing in the dark as a black body-bag was wheeled out of the front entrance on a gurney, down the steps and into a waiting ambulance.

He glanced at the headline under the footage.

FBI Special Agent found murdered in Trump Hotel.

He swallowed. He realised the report only made reference to Parker's body, not Lock's or Gerrard's, which meant either no one had found the other two yet or Siletti and O'Hara had disposed of the bodies. He remembered what he'd seen in the trunk of Siletti's car, the power saw, plastic bags and bricks.

He thought of Gerry, his father's old friend, and swallowed down his anger. He pictured the two men in his head and made a silent promise.

For them, he'd make sure Siletti and O'Hara would pay for everything they'd done.

Averting his gaze from the television, Archer saw that there were stools placed all the way around the circular bar with no one sitting on them yet. 9.30 am was a bit too early to start drinking. He walked on over the marble floor, past tables and chairs with people drinking coffee, reading papers, or chatting with partners or colleagues.

As he moved forward, Archer saw the marble suddenly change into a carpeted area, the second portion of the bar. This place was busier. He saw a lot of businessmen and women in suits, engaged in meetings, drinking cups of coffee and discussing documents or proposals placed on the tables in front of them. Up ahead were long glass windows that ran all the way across the walls revealing the heart of Times Square. From where he was standing, Archer could see the tops of the billboards and advertisements below. McDonalds, Mamma Mia, Chicago and M+M's.

The place was a good spot for meeting someone, especially in Archer's case. It had a number of escape routes and he'd see trouble coming from a mile away. Anyhow, he wasn't concerned about Sanderson. He had Cobb's seal of approval and that was enough. He just didn't want to turn and find Siletti and O'Hara standing there, trying to corner him off. There were a lot of people around and he didn't want to have to pull the Sig and start firing.

He walked through the seating area and took up an empty chair to the left and near the window, side-on so he could see the room but couldn't be approached from behind. A waitress walked over from the bar and he asked her for a cup of tea. She nodded and moved away, stifling a smile at the combination of his request and English accent. Watching her go, he glanced over his left shoulder into Times Square and looked at a clock on one of the screens. It told him the time was 9:45 am.

He looked back into the bar and the direction from which he'd just come, but couldn't see anyone who looked as if they could be an FBI Assistant Director. With the Sig held in his hand, hidden in his pocket, he leant back in the chair and waited.

He'd be here soon enough.

Ten minutes later, he clocked Sanderson from about twenty yards away.

He was in his fifties, probably once fit but moving from the field to behind a desk had added some extra pounds to his waistline. He looked surprisingly fresh for a guy who'd been driving all night, but that was the way it was with people as high up as he was in the food chain. For men like him and Cobb, sleep was a luxury in the way that coffee and caffeine were a necessity. He

231

was dressed in a black suit, white shirt and blue tie, recently cut hair that had once been brown but was now turning grey.

He made Archer immediately too and headed over. Archer rose to greet him, but looked behind the man at the same time. No one had followed him.

Sanderson offered his hand. Archer let the Sig drop in his pocket and pulled his own hand, shaking it.

'Bobby Sanderson.'

'Sam Archer.'

'Yeah, I knew your father. I'm sorry about what happened to him.'

Archer nodded.

'Anyway, Let's take a seat,' Sanderson said.

The waitress from the bar approached again having seen Sanderson arrive and he ordered coffee, black, no sugar, no milk. Once she was gone, he turned back to Archer.

'Right. From the start, tell me everything. I already heard it from Timmy, but I want to hear it first hand from you.'

TWENTY EIGHT

It took Archer ten minutes or so. He gave Sanderson every detail, as he had with Cobb earlier. He paused towards the beginning as the waitress returned with Sanderson's coffee, but then he told him everything that had happened from the moment he got the call in London to them sitting right here.

Once he'd finished, he looked at Sanderson, gauging his response. The FBI Assistant Director didn't move, looking straight back at him. Then he spoke.

'Two words,' he said. 'Holy. Shit.'

'Exactly.'

'First of all, do not say a word to another person about anything you just told me. Understand?'

'Yes.'

'I mean it kid. I'm saying that for your own good. I'm an old friend of Timmy's, but there are a lot of people out there who wouldn't care if you end up locked in a jail cell for the rest of your life. Or worse. The FBI has to maintain its image. I don't need to tell you how damaging this could be if word got out to the public.'

Archer nodded. 'It stays with me. You have my word.'

'I'll need more than that,' he said. 'But we'll deal with that later.'

He drank from his coffee.

'After Timmy called me last night, I pulled the files on the team up here. Their individual folders, the case files, the reports, the whole lot. I saw your father was sent up here to investigate.'

'Yeah. It got him killed. That's why I got involved. And they whacked Parker for sure. Most likely Lock and Gerry too.'

Sanderson thought for a moment, then swore. 'This doesn't shock me as it should. People in Washington have been keeping a close eye on this team for a while.

Let's just say they haven't been conducting themselves in a low-key manner. Before you lost contact with Agent Gerrard, did he tell you what he did to get sent here?'

Archer frowned, then shook his head.

'He mentioned he'd had some kind of demotion. That's all.'

Sanderson snorted.

'That's one way of putting it. He struck an EAD.'

'EAD?'

'Executive Assistant Director.'

'He punched him?'

Sanderson nodded.

'Luckily for him, the guy was an old acquaintance. It wasn't a play fight either. He sucker-punched him. Knocked him out cold.'

'Why?'

'The guy was having an affair with Gerrard's wife.'

Archer paused. 'Wow.'

'Exactly. The guy he struck, Jankowski, admitted that he deserved it which saved Gerrard's career. But you don't hit a senior agent ever, no matter what the provocation. They didn't fire Gerrard but they threw the book at him. He was demoted and sent here to take over the Bank Robbery team. Doesn't seem like a demotion, but trust me, this was a job no one wanted to take. A poisoned chalice, if you will.'

Sanderson sipped his coffee. There was a pause.

'So what's the plan?' Archer asked. 'Can we close this thing out?'

'Before that, there's something else I haven't mentioned,' Sanderson said. 'I read the case-file. The latest report from your father was crucial. He had good news.'

'What?'

'He said he had proof that someone in the Bank Robbery Task Force team was on the other side. Someone who wasn't Agent Gerrard.'

'Great. What kind of proof?'

'Photographic.'

Archer sat forward, interested.

'Shit, that's perfect.'

'He didn't want to reveal over the phone what exactly was in the shots. He wanted to deliver it in person back in D.C, face-to-face. He was due to return the night he was killed.'

Archer thought for a moment.

'Siletti and O'Hara must have found out somehow,' he said.

'Or Sean Farrell. I listened to the recording of the phone-call your father made to his superiors. He said this was enough proof to take them all down for good, everyone involved.'

Archer shook his head. 'It wasn't Farrell.'

'Why do you say that?'

'Because my father left his service weapon at his apartment the night he was murdered. If he was meeting with Farrell, he never would have gone unarmed. And Farrell told me himself he'd never killed anyone from the FBI. He said it would be crazy to. He's not stupid. He knew that if he did, the entire damn Bureau would jump on him.'

Sanderson thought for a moment.

'OK, so we have to assume Siletti and O'Hara are in those photographs. But there are problems. You try and pin anything on the two of them from Katic's apartment, they'll just claim they were trying to detain two fugitives from the Garden heist. You put hands on Siletti prior to that, so he'll also claim he was trying to arrest you for assaulting a Federal agent. Lock, Parker and Gerrard will have been killed with stolen weapons so the ballistics

235

will draw a blank. We need hard, substantial proof. We need the camera your father used.'

'The investigating team couldn't find it?'

'No. Not according to the report. Or if not the camera, then the memory card instead. Unless the bad guys stole it after they killed him.'

Archer thought, then his eyes widened.

'Oh shit.'

Sanderson looked at him. 'What? What is it?'

'I know where the memory card is.'

Across the city inside Jim Archer's third floor apartment in Astoria, Billy Regan leaned back in a chair, a sawn-off shotgun resting on another chair in front of him, his fingers curled around the grip. He'd placed another chair just ahead so the barrel of the weapon was resting on the back, aiming straight at the door.

He was positioned just to the right. Whenever the door opened, whoever was the other side would push it forward and step straight into Regan's firing line. They wouldn't have time to react. They'd be mincemeat in a second.

He took a draw on a cigarette in his mouth and exhaled.

He was looking forward to this.

He'd known something was up with that English prick ever since Farrell had brought him on board. And it was a miracle that he was still sitting here and wasn't in jail. After they'd loaded the first half of the money from the stash room into the cop car, he'd been headed back inside the stadium with Ortiz when they'd turned and seen the car suddenly speed off from the kerb, moving off down 33rd Street and into the night, almost a million of their dollars in the trunk.

He'd ditched them. The son of a bitch ditched them.

After a brief second of hesitation and disbelief, watching the car disappearing into the distance, Regan had grabbed a radio from his pocket and pushed the button.

'Abort,' he said into the receiver, once, clearly. 'Walk away.'

Down below, Farrell was still inside the money room, clearing out the last two lockers of dollar bills, but had heard this over his radio. After pausing and gritting his teeth, fighting the urge to keep going, he dropped the stack of cash in his hand, stepped over the two tied-up and gagged guards and walked straight out of the room, closing it behind him with his gloved hand and locking it. He'd been back up on the street in less than forty seconds, swearing under his breath, as angry as he'd ever been in his life. He moved out of the 33rd Street exit, but Regan and Ortiz weren't there. They'd already split. They'd agreed before the job that if they got jammed up they'd separate and meet back at the gym in Queens, whenever they could get there later in the night.

Farrell had walked east, moving fast, putting distance between himself and the scene of the botched heist. He was absolutely livid. He'd walked down into Penn Station and got on the next train out of the area. Half an hour later, the three of them were inside the concealed brick room through the hidden door in the gym.

The English guy had screwed them, played Farrell like a fool and walked off with almost a million dollars in the back of the car.

Carmen had lost the plot, smashing two chairs to pieces and shouting long streams of expletives in Spanish as Farrell tried to breathe and think clearly across the room. A career heist, the finish line in sight, ended because the English guy screwed them.

Farrell had pulled his phone from his pocket and called him, threatening him, in the vain hope he'd give something away and they could find out where he was with the cash. Farrell's premature departure meant they'd had to abandon a huge chunk of their money, a large portion of their pot of gold. When Regan had made the call over the radio, Farrell was loading up a sixth bag. Each one was holding about four hundred thousand. They just left behind 2.4 million, dollars that had been packed and waiting in his hands.

Now it would be safely locked up again. They'd blown it.

Inside the apartment, Regan leaned back in his chair and shook his head, drawing on the cigarette in the corner of his lips. Once they'd all calmed down, they realised that they'd been able to walk out clean and that they hadn't been sprung on by the NYPD or the FBI. They'd also each made it off Manhattan and to the gym, so at least they hadn't been duped by an undercover cop or a fed. At least the English asshole wasn't working for the cops. Once they'd cooled and started to think rationally again, Farrell had outlined each of their next moves.

First of all, they figured the Brit would cut and run. It would be suicidal of him to hang around the city, so Farrell reckoned he'd try to get the money out, split it up, maybe through a Cayman Islands bank account, then get out of the country as fast as he could or jump in a car and get out of the city. One small blessing was that Farrell had kept the details of the Flushing job confidential, not telling the asshole a word of their plan. He didn't know anything important about their plan of attack on the truck, where it would take place and how. The journey from the Tennis Center up into Long Island to the Chase financial headquarters would take around eighty minutes and that was one long stretch of road. He had no idea where or when they would try, or even if they still would.

However, they'd still put it to a vote. They were three of them there, with Tate out of town, so they knew they'd have a 2:1 majority vote whatever the outcome. Farrell outlined the complications, still pissed off but thinking

238

more clearly. There was the distant chance that the English guy would tip off the cops or feds, either because he was one of them or to give himself breathing space and hopefully get the three of them in handcuffs as he left town with the money. And by now, stadium security would have found the tied up guards, the money loaded in the bags and almost a million of it missing. The whole city would be talking about it. They knew security on the truck was going to be tight, but now it was going to be tighter.

He'd asked for an opinion and decision, one-by-one.

And all three of them agreed that the job should go ahead.

Taking a seat on the last remaining chair in the room, Farrell had called Tate, who was down in the hotel in Atlantic City. At least all his plans were going accordingly. He said that he'd passed most of the cash from the two Chase jobs through the tables, just over a million, separated into wads of a hundred thousand and traded for chips. Tate said he'd even won large at one of the tables, and had earned them an extra forty grand. He'd said he was going to clean the remaining five hundred grand, get his head down then drive up tomorrow with the untraceable cash ready for the final job, the Flushing heist.

So it was agreed.

The job would go ahead.

But the one thing they all wanted a shot at before they left was revenge.

Regan knew where the guy was staying. He'd followed him home on Monday after the street-fight. Judging from all the shit inside it didn't look like it was his place, but nevertheless the guy had definitely been bunking down here. Regan himself had been waiting on 30th Avenue on Tuesday, and had seen the guy walk out the door to this building.

Carmen was up on Steinway, watching the subway and any approach from the west. Farrell was at the gym, finishing up arranging their gear and cleaning up anything they'd need to take with them. They would all leave the city as millionaires tonight, each with enough money to buy whatever they wanted. The shotgun in his hands, aimed at where the door would open, Regan smiled. His bags were all packed. He was good to go, to leave this dump and never return.

But all he wanted was the English asshole before he left.

He'd thought about what he would do if the guy showed up or if Carmen found him down on the street on Steinway and brought him here. He wouldn't fire straight away. That would alert the neighbours and people on the street. He'd put the gun on him and make him wait. Then he'd pull his phone and call Farrell. After he arrived, they'd tie up and gag the pretty-boy then take him somewhere isolated, somewhere with soundproof walls. Probably the lower, thick brick rooms at the back of the gym, behind the steel door. Then they would go to work on him. Leave a nice, nightmare-inducing crime scene for the FBI and NYPD.

He smiled and leaned back in his chair, the barrel of the shotgun aimed flush at the door. He checked the time.

10:31 am.

He was going to come back here one last time.

Regan could sense it.

TWENTY NINE

Back across the city inside the Marriott Marquis Hotel, Archer stepped off the elevator for the 21st floor and stood still for a moment, letting the doors close behind him. Once he'd explained where the memory card was, he and Sanderson had discussed what to do next. Sanderson said he was going to head to Federal Plaza immediately and get back-up, both to find Siletti and O'Hara and to set up an ambush for the Flushing truck heist Farrell and his team were planning for tonight. Archer said he'd handle getting the memory card from the camera. They'd risen, shaking hands and parting ways, Sanderson headed downstairs to the taxi rank, Archer back to the hotel room.

Walking down the corridor to the room, he slid the key-card into the slot and pushing down the handle, walked in. Shutting the door behind him, he saw that Katic and the girl were awake, both enjoying a room-service breakfast. They were perched side by side on the edge of the bed, a table pulled up in front of them with some toast, spreads and cereals on the counter. They looked up and smiled as he entered; he also saw Katic withdraw her left hand from her handbag sitting beside her on the bed, no doubt her 9mm Sig inside. He smiled.

'Morning, ladies,' he said.

'Morning,' Jessie said, through a mouthful of toast.

Archer looked at Katic who got the message that he wanted to talk. She rose and moved outside past the screen door to the balcony, Archer joining her and pulling it shut. The sun was shining across the city and there was the usual chorus of car horns and shouts from the streets twenty one floors below.

'What did he say?' Katic asked, biting off a chunk of toast.

'He's gone to call for back up. An entire Division from D.C. will be here before sundown.'

241

'That's perfect.'

'Also, the proof my father said he had. Apparently it's photographic.'

'Really? That's great. Who were the shots of?'

'He didn't want to reveal any names over the phone. He was getting ready to drive down straight away and deliver it all himself. Then he got killed.'

'Siletti and O'Hara.'

Archer nodded and pictured the pair. Siletti, lanky, that pencil-thin moustache, his slicked back hair. His narrow face, Gerrard's stolen suit too big for him. His broken nose. O'Hara, all red hair and Irish fury, standing on Katic's fire escape, shotgun in hand.

'Sanderson said my father was using a digital camera according to the details of his assignment on the report,' he said. 'The team investigating his death haven't been able to recover it.'

'So we need to find the camera. Or just the memory card.'

'I know where it is.'

Her eyes widened. 'What? Where?'

'Inside the drawer of the nightstand at his apartment. I saw it in there the day I arrived.'

She cursed.

'Shit. You can't just walk over there and retrieve it, Archer. Farrell and Siletti will both have that place staked out, guaranteed. The NYPD will probably be around too. You won't get within thirty yards of the place.'

'I know. But I need that card. We get that, we have actual physical proof. They won't be able to twist themselves out.'

'Why didn't you ask Sanderson for help?'

'I can't hang around and wait on this one. And I don't want to draw him into the danger. This is my mess, not his. He doesn't deserve to be shot at.'

242

'OK. Then I'll come with you,' she said, finishing her toast.

He shook his head. 'You need to stay here with Jessie.'

She went to argue, but the words didn't come. He was right.

'There are people out there looking for both of us, right now,' he added. 'One of us needs to stay with her at all times.'

'But how are you going to get the card?' she asked.

He shrugged.

'I'll figure something out.'

He rose and opened the sliding doors, heading for the door.

'Are you leaving?' Jessie asked, jam and toast crumbs around her mouth, cartoons blaring out of the T.V in front of her.

'Afraid so,' he said. 'But I'll be back soon.'

He took a last look at Katic, who was standing just inside the sliding doors, looking worried. The morning sunlight was beaming down from the sky behind her and it lit up her hair, a deep almond and crimson brown.

She looked breathtaking.

He nodded to her. 'I'll be back soon.'

And he left.

*

The taxi rank for the hotel ran undercover from the street, so Archer joined the line and climbed into one when he hit the front of the queue. There was no sign of Sanderson so he must have already left, on his way downtown to Federal Plaza. There were a couple of hotel security guards standing nearby, but no cops, and he hadn't seen his face on the news report in the bar so he figured he'd be OK for now.

After pulling open the door to the taxi, he took a seat inside and shut the door. The driver turned.

'Where to?'

'Astoria. 30th Avenue,' Archer said.

The man nodded, and the car pulled round the corner and out into the daylight and Times Square. As they started down the street, and Archer saw the NYPD Times Square base of operations approaching on their left, a group of officers standing there on the kerb. He looked the other way as they passed and once the taxi had moved on, he forgot about them and started wondering how the hell he could get into his father's apartment without anyone knowing about it.

There were three possible entrance points. From the right on 38th, from the left on 38th or through the back window, accessible by walking through a shop on Steinway Street. None of the options were appealing. There would be eyes on the front door, guaranteed, and he would make too much noise trying to get through the back window which they were probably covering anyway.

And he was pretty sure that someone would be inside. Probably Regan. Maybe even Farrell, if he was still as angry as the night before, demanding retribution for ditching them on the kerb. And not only would he have to get inside, but he'd also have to get out of the area before they got to him. Ideally, he needed to get in and out without them ever knowing he was there.

But how?

He thought for a moment, the car moving across the city, closer and closer to the apartment.

Suddenly, he had an idea.

'Change of plan,' he told the driver. 'Take me up to the Upper East Side. 92nd and 1st.'

'You got it,' the driver said. He turned left on 3rd Avenue and the car sped uptown through the Sunday morning sunlight towards the Upper East Side.

*

Regan had just sparked his fifth cigarette when he heard the front door downstairs open. His eyes widened.

Stubbing out the cig in a mug beside him he sat up in his chair and took the Ithaca in his hands, aiming right for the door-space.

He heard the door shut and feet coming up the stairs and his pulse quickened.

He tightened his finger on the trigger, taking out most of the slack weight, preparing himself.

He'd changed his mind about taking his time with the guy.

The moment he opened the door and stepped inside, he would fire, aiming for the legs.

But suddenly, someone knocked on the door with the bottom of their fist, hard.

BamBamBam.

A shout followed.

'Police! Open up!'

Oh shit.

Regan froze for a split-second then jumped up, rushing to the fridge. He pulled open the door and pushed the sawn-off shotgun inside, resting it on the door shelf carefully. He pushed the door shut quietly, checking the rest of the room for anything else that could give him away. He suddenly realised he had a small bag of coke in his pocket. He pulled it out and tucked it into his sock, smoothing down his jeans over the top.

'Police! Open up!' the voice called again.

'OK, hang on,' he said, double-checking everything. Then he moved to the door and twisting the lock, opened it.

Outside, two cops were standing there, a man and a woman, both late twenties, both stern-faced. He gave them his best smile, but they didn't smile back.

'Are you the homeowner, sir?' the man asked.

Regan shook his head. 'No, officer. I'm house-sitting for a friend.'

'We just got a call of a domestic disturbance at this location.'

Regan frowned, genuinely surprised.

'That's impossible. I'm the only one here.'

'Mind if we take a look around?' the female cop said. He saw the expression on her face and noted the sharpness in her voice. He guessed any domestic disturbance call rubbed her the wrong way, like it would for any bitch cop.

'Sure,' Regan said, letting them inside. He moved back, watching as they started examining the apartment. The two of them walked in slowly, looking around the place.

'Who's your friend?' the cop asked.

'A guy from high school.'

'Where is he?'

'Baltimore. Wedding.'

At the door, Regan saw two other officers had arrived. The pair already inside the apartment turned and nodded to their colleagues, who themselves separated and started examining the other rooms in the apartment. One of them walked across the floor and into the kitchen. Regan licked his lips as he watched the guy examining the outside of the fridge and silently prayed he wouldn't reach for the handle.

'When's he going to be back?' the female cop asked, across the room. 'Your friend.'

'This afternoon I think.'

They continued to look around, walking slowly, with the complete confidence and authority that their badge bestowed.

Eventually, the female cop turned to her partner. 'There's no one here,' she said and he nodded in agreement. She turned to Regan. 'OK. It was probably a fake call. Happens time to time. Probably some kids or neighbours wanting to stir up trouble.'

The other two cops had heard this and were already moving to the door. The female cop walked up to Regan, looking him in eye.

'Sorry to have bothered you, sir,' she said.

He nodded. 'Not at all. Have a good day, officers.'

The last two cops moved to the door and left, all of them headed down the stairs and out of the building. Regan pushed the door shut, waited for a moment, then breathed a sigh of relief and moved back to the fridge.

He pulled open the top compartment and slid out the shotgun quietly. The metal barrel was already cold.

He moved quietly back to his seat by the door and returned, resting the shotgun on the second chair, and grinned.

The English asshole had probably made the call, figuring the cops would find whoever was inside and clear them out. It hadn't worked. Putting the shotgun to the ground, he grabbed a CD case from the table to his right and walked over to the kitchen, grabbing a thin knife from the drawer. He walked back to the chair, sat back down and pulled the bag of coke from his sock. He'd hit a couple lines to freshen him up. As he poured some of the white powder out of the bag onto the CD case, he glanced back at the door, the shotgun resting on the chair.

Sooner or later, he was going to be here.

And he would be right here waiting for him.

Downstairs on the street, the male and female officers moved to their car, nodding to their two colleagues who'd heard the call over the radio and had arrived on foot. One of them headed right, back to his beat on 30th Avenue while the other officer headed to the left towards 31st Avenue.

The male cop inside the squad car fired the engine and pulled off the kerb, moving away from the apartment and headed left down the street. He tapped the horn as they passed the officer, who raised a hand in acknowledgment as they headed off down the street and turned right, moving out of sight.

The officer arrived at the corner of 38th Street, and crossed over to the other side. He moved through the smoke of the food truck and headed down Steinway, walking fast. He checked behind him to make sure he hadn't been followed, then lifted and opened his hand.

A memory card was sitting there.

Under the police hat of the cop uniform he'd worn at the Garden heist, Archer looked at it and smiled.

It had worked.

THIRTY

The next step was finding a drug-store and that wasn't too hard. There was a big Duane Reade alongside the entrance to the subway on Steinway Street, just a minute's walk away.

Taking another look behind him, Archer headed fast down the street. It was a Sunday and Steinway was relatively quiet, but he realised that many of those he passed were nodding or giving him a wide berth due to his uniform. It made him smile, considering he was probably the most wanted man in the city right now. He walked swiftly down the street and saw the Duane Reade up ahead, the other side of the street.

Minding the traffic he crossed over, approaching the wide doorway and heading inside.

The air-conditioning system inside the store was blistering cold, hitting him as if he'd opened a freezer as the sliding doors parted. Clearly the manager preferred to stay cool over keeping his electricity bill down. Inside, he saw the place was quiet, much like the street outside with just the occasional person wandering the aisles.

The only employee he could see was a bored teenage girl behind the counter, reading a magazine and mechanically chewing on gum. She saw him enter but her eyes moved straight back to whatever article she was engrossed in.

'Photography?' he asked her.

She pointed a manicured nail straight ahead, not bothering to look up from the magazine.

'Far side. By the wall.'

Archer nodded and moved down the aisle. He found the electronic machine he was after mounted on the wall. Checking he hadn't been followed, he took off the policeman's hat and tucked it under his arm and slid the memory stick into the slot. It loaded, and he had to press a few buttons, but suddenly the first shot appeared on the screen, asking him if he wanted to edit it before printing.

He pressed *ignore* and studied the photograph closely instead.

It was a surveillance shot, taken late at night. Three men and a woman, in a parking lot. One of the men was Farrell. That much was immediately clear. He was standing face-on to the camera. Ortiz was standing beside him, dressed in a white vest and black sweatpants, her arms crossed, the light from the lamp-post showing the pronounced curves of the muscles in her arms and the sharp edge of her jaw-line.

They were facing two men in what looked like a meeting. The other two had their backs turned. It was dark, so making out exact distinguishing characteristics was a challenge, but he saw a tall, gangly shape on one of them and fiery red hair in the other.

Siletti and O'Hara. Unmistakeable.

He clicked on. Siletti and O'Hara still had their backs turned. It was evidence, but Archer wanted more. A good lawyer could probably defend this in court, finding a way to get them out of it, but then again any half-decent professional in the D.C. office who was familiar with photography could enhance these in seconds.

Archer clicked on. The shots continued, and he tried to decipher what had happened. Farrell didn't look happy, the street-light above showing him frowning, his mouth open, his face angry. Farrell had mentioned that he'd severed ties with his rat in the Task Force a few weeks ago. These photos were taken in the last two weeks when relations had soured, hence the anger on Farrell's face. Siletti and O'Hara were probably meeting to try and re-establish their working relationship. He clicked on.

Soon enough, the meeting seemed to end and Siletti and O'Hara started to turn in the photographs. He watched in staccato as Farrell and Ortiz turned and walked away, disappearing into the night. Jim Archer hadn't bothered to follow them with the camera. He already had them on the memory card.

Instead, the photographs showed the other two men climb into a dark Mercedes. As they moved off, James Archer had caught the perfect shot. The interior light inside the car hadn't quite gone off yet and it lit up their faces like a beacon.

Siletti and O'Hara.

Three cherries.

The lights flashing, quarters pouring out of the bottom of the machine.

Jackpot.

He reached in his pocket, grabbing his cell phone, and pushed Katic's number. It connected and he lifted it to his ear, looking at the damning shot.

'Katic, it's Archer. I've got great news.'

But he suddenly paused.

Something didn't feel right.

Something was wrong.

'Katic?'

'Katic isn't here right now,' a man's voice said, the voice nasal and creepy.

Archer's blood turned as cold as the air blasted from the air-conditioning system above.

He recognised the voice.

'Listen up,' Siletti said, his voice distorted from his broken nose. *'Or the bitch, kid and Sanderson die.'*

THIRTY ONE

Archer stayed very still, the phone to his ear. The air-conditioning system above blew chilly air over him, but he stood there frozen, the police hat in one hand, the cell phone in the other, the photographic evidence still up on the screen before him.

'You're an idiot,' Siletti told him. *'A real dumb shit.'*

'Why's that?'

'I knew you'd end up back at the hotel. We raided your old room last night, but you weren't there. But we saw Katic's car in the parking lot and knew you were somewhere inside. So we waited. We stayed all night in the lobby. Then Sanderson appeared this morning, headed for the taxi ranks. We couldn't believe it. Bobby Sanderson, an Assistant Director, at the same hotel at the same time as you and Katic. Once we put a gun on him and got him in the trunk of our car, I took the receptionist to one side and asked what room you'd been moved to. I told her what I would do to her if she didn't tell me. Before long she was begging to give me the key.'

Pause.

'So what do you want?' Archer asked.

'What do you think I want? The money. And you. I want you, you piece of shit.'

'You can't have both. Make a choice.'

'You broke my nose, you son of a bitch.' Pause. *'Or maybe I should hang up right now. Maybe I should just kill the bitch and the kid. I'll keep the call connected. You can listen.'*

Archer stayed silent.

'The Garden cash. Where is it?'

'No way. We meet. We exchange. You and I can settle it afterwards.'

A pause.

'Flushing Airport,' Siletti said. *'7:30 pm. A minute late, Katic, the kid and Sanderson die, one after the other. If you go to the cops or the FBI, they die, one after the other. 7:30 pm. If you're a second late, they die.'*

And the call went dead.

Archer stood in that same position, staring straight ahead for the next couple of minutes. Someone came up behind him to use the machine themselves, but realised something was up with the cop and moved away.

They had Sanderson. They had Katic.

And they had Jessie.

He couldn't go to the cops. They'd arrest him in a heartbeat over the Garden job.

He couldn't go to the feds. That was Siletti and O'Hara's world. They'd know in a second and the three hostages would die.

Pulling the memory card from the slot and pushing it into his pocket, Archer wandered to the exit, desperately trying to think of a plan. Suddenly he bumped into someone, not paying attention to where he was going. He looked up from under the hat to apologise.

But he stopped dead.

He was looking into the eyes of a woman.

He saw her eyes widen, the same time as his.

It was Carmen Ortiz.

They stood there for a split-second, just staring at each other, both of them in stunned disbelief. Archer's hand was by his right hip, next to the Sig tucked in the holster there. He didn't reach for it though. There were people all around them on the sidewalk and entering the store.

But Ortiz didn't move.

They stood there in total silence, eye-to-eye, not saying a word.

The uniform was saving him.

She couldn't attack a cop or pull a weapon on him. Everyone on the street would see and the last thing she wanted to do right now was draw attention to herself.

'Walk away,' he told her, staring into her hostile eyes as he'd done that night in the bar when she passed him. 'Pretend you never saw me.'

'Where's the cash?' she asked.

'I can't tell you that,' he said.

'If you don't, you'll die, *pendejo*. I won't let you go.'

Neither moved, both staring at each other. A standoff. If she came at him, Archer would pull his gun. If he came at her, she would use her fists, which were almost as effective.

'You left us.'

'That wasn't my fault. I got held up.'

'By who?'

'A woman.'

'Where is she?'

'She's dead. I killed her.'

'So give us the money. If you run, we'll find you.'

'What if I tell the cops about Flushing? I take it you'll all still be there, right?'

She didn't respond.

'Pretend you never saw me. Or I'll talk to the feds. There'll be an entire division waiting for you when you get there.'

He stepped forward and to the side. She didn't respond or move. He moved around her slowly, keeping eye contact the whole time, moving onto the sidewalk. He was close to her radius where she could hit him, but deliberately kept just out of it.

He saw her arms and fists tense, desperate to strike him.

He kept eye contact on her, his hand close to the Sig.

Suddenly a police car passed on the street alongside, then slowed.

'Hey,' a voice called.

Archer flicked his eyes, risking a quick glance.

There was one cop inside the squad car, a man. He was one of the cops that had just checked out his father's apartment, the first guy inside, the one with the female partner.

'Hey man, I'm headed for a house call in Long Island City,' he told Archer from behind the wheel. 'My partner just had to bounce. Can you give me a hand?'

Archer stared straight at Ortiz.

'Sure,' he called.

He walked across the sidewalk, around the side of the car, and climbed into the front seat, beside the cop. He closed the door and the car moved off, Ortiz still staring at him. He looked through the open window at her as she stood there, her eyes following him as the car moved off down the street. The guy behind the wheel saw her too.

'Damn,' he said. 'That's one chick I wouldn't want to mess with.'

'Haven't seen you before,' the cop behind the wheel said, as he drove through the streets towards the East River and Long Island City. Archer allowed himself a small sigh of relief and then turned his attention to the cop beside him.

'Yeah, I'm out of the 19th,' Archer said, in his best American accent. A benefit of coming here a lot as a kid meant he had developed an ear for it and he could pull one off pretty convincingly.

'Oh yeah? What you doing in Queens?'

'I live here. I was just headed to the city.'

The cop frowned. 'Why are you in uniform already? Didn't you leave it at the station?'

'Just got it dry cleaned,' Archer replied, thinking fast. The driver nodded.

'Oh. Gotcha.'

At that moment, a call came over the radio. It was a woman, from dispatch, wherever their base was in the area. She told the officer that the Long Island call was a false alarm. He picked up the receiver as he kept one hand on the wheel.

'Roger that,' he said, pushing the buttons on the receiver with his thumb and forefinger. '10-4.' He returned the receiver to its cradle and turned to Archer. 'Ah shit. Never mind. Tell you what man, I'll take you into the city to say thanks for coming along.'

Archer nodded, keeping his head slightly turned away. 'Thanks.'

They drove on in silence, approaching the Queensborough Bridge. Archer didn't say a word, but he sensed the guy next to him wanted to talk. He was friendly, and seemed professional. That however would change if he realised who the guy beside him in the car was and his current status with the NYPD.

'So you're the morning shift then?' the cop asked.

'Yeah.'

'You dodged a bullet not being on duty last night, man. It's been a long one, let me tell you,' he said. 'There was some heist at the Garden last night during the fight. Madison Square Garden, can you believe it? Guy and girl made off with almost a million bucks. Apparently the chick was an FBI agent. We've been scouring the city all night looking for them.'

'Really?' Archer asked, looking out the window.

'Yeah. The FBI is on the hunt as well. Two of their agents have gone missing and one of them was found dead in his apartment. They reckon the guy and girl did it. Real Bonnie and Clyde stuff, you know?'

'Yeah. Sounds like it,' Archer said as they moved over the Bridge.

There was a pause.

'So what's your name?' the guy asked.

Shit.

256

Archer didn't answer, his mind racing. He tried to remember the name on the tag.

'Griffin,' he said, eventually, trying to sound casual.

'I'm Willard. Good to meet you, man. You want me to drop you on your beat?'

'That would be great. I'm up around 90th.'

Willard nodded and pulled a right after they crossed the bridge, headed uptown. They moved up 1st Avenue, through the Upper East Side.

'I get off in thirty minutes. Can't wait. Cold beer and put my feet up. Let you boys take over and look for the gruesome twosome.'

Archer nodded. 'Hope we can find them. Right here's good.'

Willard frowned, looking at the street beside them.

'You sure? We're only on 81st?'

'Yeah. I'll stretch my legs.'

Willard shrugged and nodded then pulled to a halt. Archer grabbed the handle and pushing the door open, stepping out and closing it behind him.

'Thanks,' he said.

He walked around the car to the sidewalk and started walking off, feeling Willard's eyes on his back.

'Hey.'

Archer stopped, then turned.

From behind the wheel, Willard smiled and raised a hand.

'Nice to meet you man. Have a good one.'

Archer raised his own hand and the squad car moved off up the street.

At the lights, Willard turned left and headed down 81st towards 2nd Avenue, the car disappearing out of sight.

The moment he was gone, Archer sagged and sat on a bench, shaking his head, taking off the hat.

He'd thought he had problems before, but now he was on a whole new level.

He'd be at Flushing airport at 7:30 pm.

He'd have to be, to save the hostages.

On one side there would be Siletti.

And O'Hara.

Farrell.

Ortiz.

Regan.

And Tate.

On the other, there was one person.

Him.

He leaned back on the bench, sunlight shining down on him, the street around him quiet, and looked straight ahead, assessing his odds.

Six on one.

And knew it was going to take a damn miracle to stop them.

*

A hundred and twenty eight miles south from where Archer was sitting, the Atlantic City hotel room Tate was booked into under a fake name was plush and expensive. Tate always liked to skim a little off the top when he came down here. One night in the best suite normally cost close to five hundred bucks, but that was a drop in the ocean considering the amount of cash that was soon to be coming their way. It made the whole trip just that little more enjoyable, like a mini vacation. It was an executive suite for a business executive. Tate was down here on business, so technically he qualified.

He'd been here for thirty-six hours. He'd been in the casinos till three am last night and had cleaned the last of the stolen Chase cash, and had just taken an hour long bath. He'd drunk two beers and watched a Pay-Per-View replay of the welterweight title fight from the Garden last night. He walked out of the bathroom having towelled off and pulled on a white bathrobe, and strode barefoot across the padded white carpet.

Across the room, four zipped up bags sat in a line, neatly organised. Although this wasn't New York City, he still had to be careful when he came down here. He had a rule not to take more than $100k into any one casino at any one time. The FBI would take a great interest in what he'd been up to down here in the last year and he didn't want to leave a paper trail.

But he'd traded all the cash. The notes were clean, loaded up in the bags, a million and a half. He checked the time on the digital clock on the bed-side table. 11:54 am. Just before midday. He was planning on getting something to eat, then packing up the car downstairs and heading back to NYC for the extraction later tonight.

He grabbed a phone and dialled room service, asking for a steak, medium-rare, and a chocolate sundae. Once he'd eaten he'd pack up all his shit, get out of here and head back to help out the rest of the team.

Walking over the thick carpet to the bed, he examined the outfit he'd be wearing later tonight. He'd laid it out, making sure the stitching was tight, no loose fibres or chinks in the armour. He tapped it with his knuckle and it gave a dull *clunk*. There was enough Aramid and steel-plating under the cloth to stop fire from pistols, machine guns, shotguns, even semi-automatic rifles from a reasonable distance. Tate wouldn't be directly in the firing line, but he figured they'd be taking some heat before they got up in the air and it never hurt to be prepared. They'd come a hell of a long way as a team. He didn't fancy getting popped just as they were making their final getaway.

Suddenly, there was a knock on the door.

Room service. His food. Tate smiled. He reached for his pistol resting on a side cabinet, then thought better of it and tucked it under the sheet. He turned and walked forward towards the door, looking forward to his meal. Out of habit more than anything else, he stopped and peered into the spy-hole.

259

A man was standing there.

But there was some weird black shape obscuring Tate's view.

He looked closer.

And saw knuckles.

Wrapped around something metal and black, held up beside the spy-hole.

Tate froze.

And the guy in the corridor pulled the trigger to the pistol.

The weapon was silenced so the report was dulled, but there was a *thud* as the pistol fired a round. The bullet chewed through the wooden door in milliseconds with ease and entered Tate's forehead, the hollow-point separating and shredding into his brain. There was a spray of blood and brains from the back of his head as it blew apart, and he fell back, dead, the back of his head blown all over the white carpet.

The man in the corridor eased the key-card he'd taken from the dead hotel worker into the slot and shoved the door open. He stepped over the man in the bath robe and walked over towards four bags. He unzipped the first one and smiled with satisfaction. He checked the others.

They were the same.

He moved rapidly over to the bed and grabbing the helmet, balaclava, jacket and trousers, stuffed them quickly into a bag he pulled out from his jacket. He walked back over to the door, stepping over Tate's body and pulled the door closed behind him. Within ten minutes he was back. He went over to the four bags, looping the straps of two over each shoulder and grunted as he lifted the remaining two in his hands.

He walked to the door and stepped past Tate's body, blood and brains sprayed behind him on the carpet.

He moved out into the empty corridor and using a gloved hand, pulled the door shut behind him, and headed downstairs for the car park.

THIRTY TWO

As the sun slowly slid across the sky in its journey from dawn to dusk, Sunday lunchtime became Sunday afternoon and the time crawled on to four o'clock.

Archer was sitting in Central Park. The same bench in fact that he'd sat on a week ago in his suit, fresh from the funeral and his first meeting with Gerry. As it was then, the late summer weather was still beautiful, coming to the end of the season, fall fast approaching. Somewhere in the distance he could hear a saxophone, a jazz busker, the only other noise was the breeze blowing through the trees, the birds chirping and the sounds of people walking or cycling past. Amongst the wind and the birds, the perfect and fluid melody of the saxophone floating in the air, Archer closed his eyes.

So much beauty amongst so much pain.

They'd killed his father. They'd killed Gerry. They'd killed Parker, and Lock. They'd tried to kill him. They'd taken Katic, her daughter and Sanderson hostage and they would try and kill him again too.

Siletti wanted to meet at Flushing Airport, which meant he and O'Hara were in on Farrell's plans. Archer didn't know how. Maybe they had reconciled their differences, or struck up a deal. Maybe Siletti had promised Farrell Archer would be there later tonight so he could exact revenge. Maybe they'd all get in the helicopter with the cash and leave the city forever as a team.

He had no doubt that Siletti would try to kill him at the trade. The guy had all but promised it on the phone call earlier. Archer knew how it would play out. They'd have guns on Sanderson, Katic and her daughter and demand the cash or they pull the triggers. Archer would throw it over, along with any weapon.

Then they would open up on him. Maybe a shotgun to the back of the head, same as his father.

261

They'd order him to turn around and he'd hear the footsteps approaching.

Feel the cold barrel of the weapon nestle in the back of his head.

His life ended the exact same way as his father's by the same people who'd killed him less than two weeks ago. Then they'd waste the three hostages.

He opened his eyes and looked at all the greenery around him, the sun lighting up the place. Siletti and O'Hara knew that they didn't just have the winning hand, but the entire deck and there was only one man standing in their way. Once they took care of him, they'd get on that helicopter and fly away forever.

The perfect getaway.

Archer looked up and saw the sunlight filter through the brown trees and green leaves.

And he started to formulate a plan.

He sat there for another hour, working everything out in his mind, every possible scenario or outcome. He was still dressed as a cop, the hat over his head, so no one passing by in the Park would recognise him. At one point, he pulled the cell phone from his pocket and deliberated whether to call Cobb or not. He decided against it. Even if he could help, Archer only had three hours. Cobb was across the Atlantic Ocean. He couldn't do anything or get here in that time. And Archer had dragged Sanderson into this mess and it had got him taped up with a gun to his head. He was going to handle the rest of this himself. This was his problem and he was going to fix it.

He rose and started walking through the Park, headed north to the Upper East Side. The walk took him about twenty minutes. He exited the Park and crossed 1st Avenue and went straight to the parked police car on 92nd, pulling the keys from his pocket, unlocking it and climbed inside. In the front seat, he took off the police hat and started unbuttoning his shirt, changing back into his clothes quickly, getting out of the cop uniform. He pulled on his jeans, t-shirt, trainers and grabbed the navy blue overcoat. He checked the chamber on the Sig then tucked it into his coat.

He went to climb out to get the money from the back, but something made him stop.

There was something stowed between the two front seats.

A gun.

He reached over and pulled it from its home and held it in his hands.

It was an Ithaca 37, pump-action 12 gauge shotgun, the same weapon that Farrell and his team liked to use. In a compartment under the radio, Archer found ammunition for the weapon, twenty shells inside a small cardboard box.

And he had an idea.

*

Across the city in an FBI safe-house, Siletti checked the watch on his left wrist.

5:51 pm.

Not long to go.

He looked across the dark room at his three hostages. He'd duct taped and gagged all three of them and left them lying on the floor. O'Hara had blindfolded the kid, but neither Sanderson nor Katic were wearing one and the two of them glared up at Siletti, a mixture of rage and fear in their eyes.

Katic's hair had fallen over her face, hanging in strands over the grey-strip of duct-tape pulled across her mouth, and she was looking at him like she wanted to kill him. Sanderson had been a pain in the ass earlier, trying to fight them when they marched him downstairs to the Marriott parking lot, so Siletti had punched him three times in the face, breaking his nose.

263

Join the club, he thought as he saw the FBI Assistant Director sat against the wall, his eyes blazing with fury, blood staining the skin under his nose and the strip of grey duct-tape across his own mouth.

They were in an old storage place, a safe-house that only he and a select few other members of the FBI knew about. It was dusty and smelt of sawdust but it was quiet. No one was going to come in here. But just as the thought crossed his mind, a noise came from behind him and he turned, pistol in hand.

But it was only O'Hara. He was returning from a trip to get some food, two burgers and fries from McDonalds. They needed to fuel up before the evening's events. O'Hara walked over without saying a word and dumped the bag on an empty chair, passing Siletti a wrapped up burger who pulled back the plastic and took a bite, watching the three hostages.

The three of them would have to die. There was no question. All three had seen his and O'Hara's faces. Katic and the kid weren't a problem. He'd do them both, cut them up, then dump them in the sea, the pieces weighed down with bricks in individual bags. He'd do it down in Atlantic City, far away from here. No one would ever discover the bodies.

Sanderson was the only problem. He was an Assistant Director, which meant there was going to be a shitload of attention on what would happen if he disappeared. He also didn't know how he'd got down here and become involved. He figured the Bureau had sent him, but he'd come from the hotel where the Slavic bitch and the English asshole were staying and that was too coincidental for his liking. He needed to find out who'd set them up together.

He'd go to work on Sanderson later, and get him to talk.

But he had something else to attend to first. He took a bite on his burger and turned, looking over at O'Hara.

He was standing behind him, eating and looking down at the three captives, Katic in particular.

'Don't look at me like that,' he told Katic, who was glaring up at him. 'I blindfolded the kid for you. I can take it off.'

Siletti took another bite, then rose. He signalled O'Hara to follow him and he headed over to the bathroom, out of earshot. The other man followed him and they both stood inside the stall, the door open, the two hostages watching them, the girl blindfolded.

'What?' O'Hara asked him, inside the bathroom.

'I planned ahead,' Siletti told him. 'I brought us weapons and body armour for taking on Farrell.'

O'Hara's eyes widened.

'You did. Where is it?'

'I hid it behind those tiles,' he said, pointing behind O'Hara at the wall. 'Check it out.'

O'Hara turned. He reached over across the bathtub, reaching for the tiles.

In the same moment, Siletti's silenced HK USP pistol appeared in his right hand. He aimed the gun at the back of O'Hara's head and pulled the trigger.

The weapon gave a *thud*, like someone had stamped once hard on the floor. Blood, brains and skull sprayed into the air and spattered all over the wall as O'Hara collapsed over the bath. There was no shower curtain to shield Siletti from the gore, so he ended up wearing some of his former partner's brains and blood on his face and shirt.

Siletti walked back into the main room, not bothering to wipe himself down. Katic and Sanderson were staring at him, their eyes wide with horror. The girl was blindfolded, but she was shaking like the temperature was below freezing.

With blood and bits of brain all over his shirt and face, Siletti took a seat.

He grinned at them, taking another bite of the burger, and checked his watch.

Across the city, in a dark brick room below the Astoria Sports Complex, Farrell, Ortiz and Regan stood together, making final adjustments. They were all wearing the black reinforced body armour, black boots on their feet and the usual three layers of latex gloves on their hands. The stolen car they'd use was parked in a garage connected by doorway to the building, so they wouldn't have to go out on the street.

For this final job, they'd need a quicker rate of fire than the shotguns would offer. This time none of them gave a shit about ballistics. They'd be out of the country before anyone could make a match to the weapons they used.

Each of them lifted an M16 203 assault rifle from the desktop at the same time, slamming a full 32 round magazine into each base and pulling the slide, loading the three weapons. Each M16 was modified and also had a grenade launcher attached to the front, under the main barrel; there was a grenade already loaded inside, four more in special sewn-in compartments on their black uniforms.

They each checked the safety on the weapons, then laid them back down on the table, turning to look at each other.

'Final check,' Farrell said.

The three of them looked each other over, checking everything was in place, no gaps in their armour.

'Good,' Ortiz said.

'Good,' Regan said.

Farrell nodded. He took one last look at the room, where every job they had ever pulled had been planned. The last time he'd ever be inside this room.

This was it.

Showtime.

'Ready?' he asked.
His two companions nodded.
'OK,' he said. 'Let's do this.'

THIRTY THREE

The *Billie Jean King Tennis Center* was located in Flushing Meadows Corona Park, a 1200 acre area on the east side of Queens towards Long Island. Renowned as being one of the largest tennis venues in the world, the *Billie Jean King* was also the proud location for the U.S Open tennis tournament every year, one of the major highlights in the sport's annual calendar. The tournament was two weeks long, and the stands, even for preliminary matches, were always packed so the concessions stands, ATMs and businesses inside made an absolute killing in that fortnight. The main court, the *Arthur Ashe*, had the largest capacity for any tennis stadium in the world, 23,200 seats, and with other courts in the Center with many thousands of seats, every single person who sat in one was another potential customer.

Sunday was the end of the first week of the tournament, where most of the lower-seeded players had already been eliminated in the opening rounds and both the Men's and Women's draws were down to only eight players each. Unlike Wimbledon and the French Open at Roland Garros, the U.S. Open played matches at night, sometimes into the early hours the next morning if there was a prolonged fifth set. That early September Sunday evening, there was a big match on *Arthur Ashe* taking place as two of the top male seeds fought in the last sixteen for a place in the quarter-finals. The contest was being broadcast around the world and the stadium itself was packed to capacity.

Sunday was also the day that the first week's cash load would be escorted out of the Tennis Center and taken north up the I-495 to a secure location in Long Island. Door to door, the journey would take around eighty minutes and was usually a two man job.

268

But considering the wealth of the cargo in the back of the truck that evening, tonight the security was double loaded.

As the clock ticked to 7:01 pm and the last of the haul was being secured inside the vehicle, the crowd inside the *Arthur Ashe* cheered as a dramatic point ended. The cash was locked and secured in individual bags and bullet-proof cases, stowed in secure shelves inside the truck. As three stadium officials finished loading the money, four other men in black combat fatigues and boots stood on the tarmac behind the truck.

They were all tough, grim-faced men, military trained, and were heavily armed to say the least. Each man was equipped with an AR 15 assault rifle, a 9mm Berretta pistol on his hip and five spare magazines for each weapon in slots on their tactical gear. The weaponry was all authorised by the United States Federal Reserve, necessary back-up given the value of the cargo in their possession.

They'd be in the truck, protected by over two dozen tons of steel, but with ports either side so the men could fire out if they got ambushed or attacked. Unlike most armoured truck personnel who were retired cops, these guys were in their thirties and pulled straight from the military.

If someone was stupid enough to try and engage them when they were out there on the road, it would be the last mistake they ever made.

The security officials finished loading up the last of the cash into the truck as the four men stood there, watchful and alert. Once all the money was inside and secure, they climbed into the truck and pulled the heavy door closed behind them, sealing it shut and taking seats inside. A fifth man, the driver, walked around the side of the truck and climbed into the front seat, locking his door and then bolting it. They were all inside now. Secure.

The driver fired the engine, strapping on his seatbelt. He gave a thumbs up to the three stadium officials to his left and released the handbrake, setting off east through the 1200 acre park towards the eastern exit.

Eighty minutes, door-to-door, and counting.

As the driver headed down New York Avenue, through the Tennis Center and past the fans and spectators on the sidewalks either side of him, he used the time and slow movement to get a feel for the vehicle. He'd been with the armoured courier company for six years, but this was his first time driving this particular truck and his first time with so much wealth in the back. Despite its weight, the vehicle wasn't hard to manoeuvre. He kept his eyes on the road, and tried not to think about how much cash was in the back.

He pulled out of the Center, turning left, and then after twenty seconds or so, turned right. They were now moving down Perimeter Road, the long winding lane which ran all around the Park. They'd pass both a mini-golf and golf course on their right, then the swimming pool and Aquatics Center, then finally follow the road east then turn another right and head south on the Van Wyck Expressway, where they could transfer to the I-495 highway and get on their way to Long Island.

The truck moved on down the road. The place was pretty quiet. There was the occasional person walking in the park and a couple of groups sitting enjoying a picnic, but most of the activity in the area was back inside the Tennis Center, the action taking place on the courts.

They passed the golf course on the right. The driver glanced over at it and accidentally let the vehicle drift to the edge of the road. It dropped off suddenly, but he quickly re-corrected and pulled back onto the tarmac.

'What the hell was that?' called a voice from the back.

'Nothing,' the driver said.

Looking over, he realised there was a little ditch each side of the road. Nothing to worry about for someone driving a normal car, but a nightmare for something this big and heavy. If he drove too close to the edge, they could slip off the side and topple over like a turtle on its shell. Focusing on the road instead, he drove over a small bridge and the road started to curl to the right, towards the exit.

He glanced to his left and saw a black car parked on the grass with a couple of people sitting inside.

Suddenly, a third person stepped out from behind the car, also in all black, wearing what looked like a balaclava or a black helmet.

He saw the figure drop to one knee and lift something to their shoulder.

Aiming it directly at the truck.

He realised what it was a second too late.

The person in black recoiled as the rocket-launcher whooshed and in a split-second, the driver saw something zoom towards him.

Ortiz hit the truck first time. She was using a Stinger and it ploughed into the side of the vehicle perfectly. The rocket didn't penetrate the steel, as they knew it wouldn't, but the force of the blast smashed the truck over onto its side. It fell over with a giant crash and groan under a large fireball from the explosion and came to a shuddering halt on the grass, on its side. They knew there were four guys inside.

And now their gun ports were all but useless.

She dropped the rocket launcher to the ground immediately and grabbed her M16 203 that was resting on the grass beside her. While she did this, the car containing Farrell and Regan raced forward, coming to a halt by the upended truck. Across the grass, people on the grass and bystanders in the area started screaming and ran for cover as they reacted to the explosion and realised what was happening.

As Farrell screeched to a halt on the grass by the truck, Regan leapt out of the car. He had five long lengths of plastic explosive strips in his hands, the kind used for demolitions, the M16 slung over his shoulder. Laying the strips on the grass, he waited as Ortiz ran forward as fast as her body armour would allow. He had his back to the rear of the truck, and she didn't slow as she approached him, putting her boot on his hands and jumping as he hoisted her up onto the truck with a grunt from the extra weight of her armour.

He reached down and passed her up the demo strips one-by-one and she laid them in a hexagon on the side of the truck, carefully avoiding the gun ports.

That done, she jumped down and ran for cover behind the black car, joining Farrell and Regan who were already there.

The three of them crouched behind the car, covering their ears.

Farrell had a detonator in his hand.

He pushed it.

There was a loud crack, and a groan as the metal fractured from the shock of the explosion. Whoever was inside would have been incapacitated, like someone had tossed a flash-bang grenade inside. Ortiz and Regan ran forward. He pushed her up again, then used the wheel to clamber up himself, while Ortiz stamped on the damaged metal side of the vehicle. It fell away after the fourth stamp, and she dropped down inside.

The four guards were sprawled on the floor, their ears bleeding, rolling around in pain and agony, their assault rifles forgotten. Ortiz passed the AR 15s up one-by-one quickly, and Regan tossed them to the grass. She plasti-cuffed the four men, none of them putting up a fight, all four totally disorientated and in severe pain.

Outside on the grass, Farrell passed four black holdalls up to Regan. He took them and dropped them down to Ortiz, who started loading the money from the shelves

into them. The explosion had softened up any cages or
cases that were locked up and any that were still intact
needed just a hard kick to open them.

Outside on the grass, through the visor of his
bulletproof helmet, Farrell checked his watch.

'Thirty seconds!' he shouted.

Ortiz was just finishing zipping up the third bag. She
passed them up to Regan, who tossed them to the grass,
Farrell loading them into the car. Ortiz packed up the
fourth bag, pushing it up to Regan, who tossed it onto
the grass then reached down, pulling her up.

Ortiz dropped down to the ground, but on top of the
truck Regan looked ahead on Perimeter Road.

'Oh shit!'

An NYPD squad car, the lights flashing, was bearing
down on them, having pulled in fast from the east
entrance.

Without a second's hesitation, Regan lifted his M16
and fired, the weapon tight in his shoulder.

The fire-rate was set to automatic and he emptied the
magazine into the front of the car. The bullets shredded
through the windshield, stitching the two cops in the
front seats and killing them instantly, blood spattering all
over the windshield, the glass and headlights smashing
from the hail of bullets, the car slewing to a halt forty
yards away. The harsh sounds of machine gun fire
echoed around the park, breaking the silence.

As Regan reloaded his empty clip, Farrell stowed the
last bag in the car. Regan dropped down from the truck
and ran over to the getaway car, pulling open the door.
Just then, another NYPD squad car appeared, moving
fast, pulling off the road onto the grass to move around
the first car.

Still on the grass, Ortiz raised her M16. She emptied
the mag into the front of the police car, then moved to
the second attached weapon on the front of the M16
under the stock, the 203 grenade launcher. She aimed

and pulled the trigger and the grenade landed smack on the windshield. It exploded on impact and the shockwave reacted with the petrol in the fuel tank, exploding into a fireball and erupting with a force that made her look away and shield herself.

Moments later she ran over to the car, jumping into the front seat, Farrell behind the wheel, Regan in the back, the money in the trunk.

'*GO! GO!*' Ortiz shouted, pushing the catch on the M16 to let the old magazine drop and smacking a fresh one inside, doing the same with the grenade launcher.

Farrell put his foot down and the car sped forward. He moved off the road and onto the grass. Any witnesses and onlookers were already out of the way, screaming and running for cover so the path was clear.

'*Woo!*' Regan said, pumped up and excited from the back seat. '*Home stretch, baby!*'

Farrell sped along the grass, the Industry Pond approaching on their right. They needed to get out of the Park and head north on the Van Wyck, straight to the turn off for the abandoned Flushing Airport and their last ride out of here.

But suddenly, five more cars roared into view from the entrance, blocking their path, four NYPD squad cars and a black truck.

Farrell looked closer and swore.

There were three letters printed in white on the side of the black vehicle, three letters that alone meant nothing but together spelt a shitload of problems.

ESU.

THIRTY FOUR

Things just got a hell of a lot harder. They hadn't been expecting this. The NYPD standard-issue Beretta and Ithaca shotgun wouldn't get through their Aramid and steel plate body armour, but ESU was the NYPD's SWAT team. The officers inside the truck would be armed with sub-machine guns and assault rifles that stood a far greater chance of getting through their armour. Farrell shouted with frustration and braked hard, grabbing his weapon and climbing out. The other two joined him, and together, all the frustrations and anger of the failed Garden heist reappeared.

As one, they opened fire. The police cars and the ESU truck had pulled to a halt. They were forced to, as the three thieves just unleashed a lethal hail of bullets. The officers ducked for cover and rolled out the far doors, shielding themselves from the barrage of bullets, as the sound of automatic gunfire echoed around the Park.

Ortiz was fired up and angry. She walked forward, firing down on one of the squad cars. Two of the cops started firing back with their pistols and she drilled them both, emptying her magazine and shredding their car. Behind the other four cars, the other officers started leaning over the vehicle and firing down on her. They managed to hit her a few times, but each round pinged off her armour and helmet. She realised they were aiming for her legs. The North Hollywood duo had screwed up by not protecting their ankles and feet. Farrell's team had learnt from that and the three of them were covered in Aramid and plating all the way down to their boots.

Regan was shooting at the other cars, while Farrell was pinning down the ESU team. He emptied his mag, then fired three grenades one-by-one, firing and reloading. The task force was forced to huddle behind the truck, taking cover, as the grenades exploded against the front

275

of the truck. The ferocity of the assault had taken them all by surprise.

As Ortiz took over and fired down on all of them, Farrell rushed back to the car and climbed in.

'Let's go!' he shouted to Ortiz and Regan, who were still firing down at the ESU truck.

Ortiz gave them another grenade and moved back as she fired, then ducked into the car, pulling her door shut as Farrell sped to the left around the cop car and the two dead officers blocking their way. As Ortiz reloaded, Regan took over, keeping up continuous fire. The five vehicles had been shredded, most of the cops behind them injured, but Ortiz suddenly pulled three grenades tucked into the doorframe beside her, passing one to Regan while holding the other two herself. They were flash-bangs, not explosives, designed to stun and incapacitate.

Farrell saw what she was planning and slowed. She pulled the pins on both, the same time as Regan did on his. She passed them to Farrell, who threw the grenades rapidly out of the window towards the cop cars, one after the other, as Regan did the same.

The three of them leant to the side, covering their ears and shutting their eyes as bullets pinged off the car.

The three bangs were muffled, considering they had covered up and after three seconds, the three of them were back in action. Farrell pushed his foot down and the car sped off. As they drove away, Ortiz saw cops and members of the ESU team in black gear either grounded, writhing on the floor, or staggering, blinded and stunned. She had reloaded her M16 and fired as they sped forward, killing three of them as they stumbled around, trying to recover their senses.

Farrell roared through the gate and out onto the Van Wyck expressway, the I-678.

'C'mon!' he shouted, ecstatic. 'Everyone OK?'

Beside and behind him, Ortiz and Regan nodded, reloading their weapons. Their car was riddled with bullet holes, the windshields smashed, but the highway was pretty quiet as they sped up the expressway. The turn off to Flushing Airport was just a couple of miles away.

Farrell pushed his foot down as hard as he could, and glanced at a watch on his wrist.

7:23 pm.

In seven minutes, they were out of here.

Archer was in a car too, burning his way down the Grand Central Parkway, headed towards the airport. He'd unloaded all the cash from the cop car then locked up and headed back to the Marriott Hotel after making a quick stop at a store on the way. He'd gone up to the hotel room, pulling his Sig and dumping the bags in the corridor and eased the key into the lock. He burst inside, his pistol aimed, but there was no-one there. He grabbed Katic's car keys from the side, then left immediately with the bags and headed to the basement and the car park.

Traffic had been typically unpredictable and bad and he'd been held up, delayed on his way to the airport. He checked the time and swore.

7:24 pm.

He needed to be there in six minutes or the three hostages would die.

Suddenly, he heard a wailing siren from behind and an ambulance appeared in his rear-view mirror. He waited for it to pass, then immediately pulled in behind and followed it down the highway, moving fast.

7:24 pm.

Six minutes to go.

Farrell didn't slow as he turned off the highway and sped on towards the deserted Flushing Airport. The place was empty having been shut for almost thirty years, and the car hit the chain-link fence, breaking the lock and smashing it open, the vehicle speeding on into the abandoned airport.

The entire airfield was made up of old tarmac, empty hangars and overgrown concrete lined with weeds, but up ahead they saw a black helicopter waiting on the tarmac outside one of the hangars.

Farrell and Ortiz had come here on Thursday night and moved it out of the hangar. It was resting on wheeled supports either side and all they had to do was roll it outside gently, cover it with a giant tarpaulin, then lock the gate again and leave. No one ever came in here.

As they got closer, they saw Tate standing by the helicopter. He was in his full tactical gear, balaclava and helmet on, his car parked out of the way to the right. Farrell saw the side to the helicopter was open, the money from the previous heists already stashed inside. Tate stood there, his M16 in his hands and waited for them to pull up.

The car torched forward then screeched to a halt to the left of the helicopter. The three of them climbed out quickly. Farrell opened the trunk and the three of them each grabbed a bag and took it to the helicopter, packing the money away inside. Farrell ran back and got the fourth and brought it over. When that was inside with the rest, he jumped back out and pulled off his helmet and balaclava, taking a deep breath of air and running his gloved hand over his head.

'Holy shit! We did it, you assholes. We did it!' he said.

He walked over to Ortiz and Regan, who also pulled off their headgear and the three of them hugged, one at a time. They each turned and saw Tate standing there, watching them silently.

He still had his gear on, and he hadn't moved to join them.

'We did it, man,' Farrell said. 'We made it.'

Tate looked at him for a moment.

Didn't speak.

Suddenly, he raised his M16 and opened fire.

Tate used controlled, three-round bursts, all aimed at the head, the three of them unprotected without the helmets. Farrell, Ortiz and Regan took the rounds before they could react, blood and brains spraying on to the tarmac behind them as they all fell back, dead, each shot several times through the face.

Tate looked at the three corpses motionless for a moment. Then he went to turn back to the helicopter.

Suddenly, another car burst into view through the entrance, driving fast towards him. Tate squinted through the visor, pushing the release catch on his M16 and quickly reloading.

It was Archer.

THIRTY FIVE

Archer couldn't believe what he saw as he drove into the airfield.

Farrell, Ortiz and Regan were all dead. Shot by Tate. He'd screwed them. He saw the man lift his M16. Archer reacted fast and slid the car to a halt on its side, opening the driver's door and sliding out the side as a hail of bullets hit the side of the vehicle. He landed awkwardly on the tarmac, but pulled his father's Sig from his pocket as Tate continued to fire on the car. He heard a click and the firing stopped as Tate's magazine emptied.

Archer then rose up over the trunk of the car, his arm resting on the metal top, the Sig aimed dead straight at Tate's chest forty feet away. He fired relentlessly, one bullet after another, his aim straight from resting his arm on the car. Most of the bullets hit Tate in the chest and head, knocking him back slightly, but each one *pinged* and *dinged* off the body armour under his clothes. None of them were getting through.

As Tate dropped down to one knee to reload his M16, Archer saw another car pull into the lot from an entrance ahead and to the left, speeding over the weeded tarmac. Siletti was at the wheel. The car screeched to a stop beside Farrell and his team's getaway car and Siletti climbed out, a silenced pistol in his hand. Archer aimed and fired four more times at Tate, all four hitting him in the chest. None of them got even close to getting through the armour.

Siletti fired back, then took cover, running around the side of his car and popping the trunk. Archer saw him drag Jessie out, her hands duct-taped behind her, a grey strip over her mouth and passed her to Tate. Someone had pulled a blindfold over her eyes, and strands of hair hung over it, the girl shaking as she stood there.

'*Enough!*' Tate called, from under the helmet, grabbing the girl by the hair.

280

He threw his M16 to the ground and pulled a Glock pistol from a holster on his hip, putting the gun to the girl's head.

'Drop the gun or the girl dies!'

Behind the trunk of the car, Archer didn't move, his arm still gripping the pistol, aimed at Tate. He looked at Jessie, her body shaking and terrified. As long as the guy had the gun to her head, there was nothing he could do.

'Drop it!' Tate screamed.

Archer rose very slowly, then tossed the gun to the ground, still standing behind Katic's car.

Siletti had moved to the back seat of his car, pulling Sanderson out, dragging him towards Tate and pushing him to the ground. He was also duct-taped and bound. Lastly, Siletti walked back and dragged out Katic, pulling her by the hair to stand beside Tate, a silenced pistol in his hand, the harsh black barrel against Katic's soft features. The two sides stood there looking at each other, the helicopter behind Siletti and Tate, the dead bodies of Farrell, Ortiz and Regan between them. There was no sign of O'Hara.

'So what's the deal?' Archer called, at Tate, pointing at the corpses. 'You kill all your friends and walk away?'

Tate stood still for a moment, the gun still to the child's head.

He said nothing.

Then he let go of the girl, and reached up and lifted off his helmet. He had a balaclava on underneath, which he pulled off too.

Archer froze and stared.

He couldn't believe it.

He was looking at Supervisory Special Agent Todd Gerrard.

THIRTY SIX

'Gerry?'

'Don't move, Sam. Or the kid dies,' Gerrard said, grabbing Jessie again and putting the pistol to her head.

Archer stared at him.

He was stunned.

'Gerry, what the hell are you doing?'

'What does it look like I'm doing? The bags. Throw them over here.'

Archer didn't move.

Gerrard pulled back the hammer on his pistol.

'Don't make me kill her, kid. Throw over the bags.'

'Gerry, put the gun down.'

'*Bags!*' he screamed.

In his hand, Jessie started to cry, scared, her sobs muffled under the strip of duct-tape, her eyes shielded behind the blindfold.

Archer stayed still for a moment longer, then complied. He opened the trunk, grabbing the two bags by the handles, then threw them over towards him and Siletti, one at a time. They were about ten yards from each other and the bags landed ten feet from Gerrard. They landed with a thud, next to the corpses of Farrell, Ortiz and Regan and beside their getaway car. Archer still stared at Gerrard, in disbelief. He looked into his eyes.

But the man he'd known for so long wasn't there anymore.

'You played me, this whole time?'

Gerrard didn't reply. Beside him, Siletti grinned, ear to ear, like the Grinch.

'Yeah. We did,' he said.

'Where's O'Hara?'

'Dead. Same as you'll be soon enough,' Siletti said.

Archer looked at Gerrard, desperate for some kind of an explanation. His mind flashed back during the past week, through everything that had happened, like someone flipping through a stack of photographs.

And suddenly, it all made sense.

'So that's the deal,' Archer said, looking into Gerrard's eyes. 'You got sent here from D.C, broke and humiliated. Farrell and his team had just started pulling the jobs in the city. You were honest at first, but then everything finally just got to you. You met with Farrell, said you would make sure they never got rumbled so long as they gave you a slice. You did that for a while, but then they let you go. They decided they could do the rest without you. And you didn't have any evidence to convict them. You couldn't get within a mile of them. They knew you and every member of your team, and if you tried Farrell would shop you to people in D.C. You were stuck, in limbo. So you figured you could use me instead.'

Gerrard didn't reply.

'You knew I'd be wound up, not thinking straight because of what happened to Dad. You made it seem like I was helping you bring them down whereas all you wanted was to find out where they were keeping their cash. I told you Tate made the trips down to A.C, so you went down there and killed him. You didn't get called to D.C, did you?'

Gerrard didn't reply.

'But somewhere along the line, he got wise,' Archer said, pointing at Siletti. 'He confronted you about it. I'm guessing he demanded to be involved or else he'd start talking. O'Hara did the same. So you were working together, covering each other's backs. You thought Parker and Lock might have their suspicions, so you executed them. You know how to trick a crime-scene. You covered all your tracks. It ran like clock-work, right?'

283

Neither said a word. Katic looked up at him, tears in her eyes.

'But you screwed up. Because Sanderson is here. He's seen and knows everything you two are doing. How the hell are you going to explain his disappearance?'

'By leaving too,' Siletti said. 'We're out of here. We're never coming back. We've got enough money here to live on for three lifetimes.'

Archer saw silent tears streaming down Katic's face, her hair snatched in Siletti's grip. Gerrard turned to Siletti.

'Fire it up,' he said.

Siletti nodded with a grin. Turning, he dragged Katic with him to the cockpit and flicked some switches. The rotors started to move slowly, as the vessel warmed up. The engine made no sound yet though. Gerrard looked at Archer, who was staring right back at him, into his soul.

'I didn't want to kill your father, Sam,' he said. 'He brought it on himself.'

Archer stared at him.

'*You?*'

Silence.

'You were the one who killed him?'

'He shouldn't have come down here and messed with other people's affairs. He should have kept his nose out. He wanted to meet me in the parking lot. He wanted to confront me, to find out what the hell was going on, to tell me about Siletti and O'Hara. He figured I was still on the FBI side. But he had proof. And I couldn't let him do it. So I killed him when he turned his back. Shotgun. Just like Farrell and his team used.'

Pause.

'I didn't want to do it, Sam. But I had to. I made it quick.'

Archer blinked, fighting back emotion.

'You were his oldest friend,' he said, his voice shaky.

'Then what had he done for me lately?' Gerrard screamed. 'Did he help me out when I got canned? No. Did he even try? Did he care? No. He didn't give a shit. He abandoned me just like everyone else. He deserved it. He should have stayed in D.C. and left me the hell alone. Now he's dead because of it.'

There was a pause. Siletti had re-joined Gerrard, grinning wolfishly at Archer, holding Katic by the collar, the silenced pistol to her head.

Behind them the rotors to the helicopter were starting to spin, gathering speed, the blades whirring faster and faster.

'So what now?' Archer said. 'You two just pack up the money and fly away?'

'Exactly. But for you, it ends here,' Siletti said.

Archer saw the other man's eyes glance to Archer's pistol, on the ground.

He'd won and he knew it.

'Oh, I've been waiting for this,' Siletti continued. 'You'll be seeing your father real soon, you piece of shit. If you've got any prayers, say them now.'

He pushed Katic to the ground, throwing his silenced pistol to one side. He scooped up the M16 lying on the ground, and pulled the slide, a bullet flying out the ejection port.

'I'm going to give you every single bullet in this thing,' he said, the weapon clutched in his hands. 'Then the bitch, the kid and Sanderson die too. And there's nothing you can do to stop me.'

Archer looked over at Gerrard. He looked back, his eyes emotionless. Behind them, the helicopter was warmed up, the rotors spinning. The engine was slowly starting to whine.

'I'm sorry, Sam. I can't let you walk away,' Gerrard said.

He turned to Siletti.

'Time to go.'

Gerrard pulled on his helmet, fully protected in the body armour as Siletti grinned at Archer.

Archer didn't react. He just looked at Katic, who was looking at him desperately, tears in her eyes.

'Any last words, asshole?' Siletti called, raising the M16.

Archer looked at him, then at Gerrard. Saw them both standing there, near the back of the helicopter in the middle of the runway.

The rotors whirring.

He nodded, and looked down at Katic.

'Turtle.'

There was a pause. Siletti and Gerrard looked at him, confused.

Then Katic suddenly reached over and grabbed her daughter with her duct-taped hands, pulling her to the floor from Gerrard's grip and covering her in a flash.

It took Siletti and Gerrard by surprise, and for a split second they looked down at her.

At the same moment, Archer swept aside the right lapel of his coat, and grabbed something hanging from a strap looped around his shoulder.

It was a sawn-off Ithaca.

He grabbed the stock and the pistol grip and aimed the weapon, his hands steady as a rock, the weapon still and already loaded. He momentarily ignored Gerrard. He was wearing full body armour.

But Siletti wasn't.

Archer aimed the weapon straight at him and pulled the trigger. The weapon exploded, and the shell hit Siletti like a cannonball, throwing him back. Blood and bits of his torso and clothing sprayed in the air as the shell tore him in two.

He splayed back on the concrete, dead in an instant.

Gerrard looked to his right, seeing this happen, shocked. He quickly turned back to Archer and raised his Glock, safe behind his body armour.

Archer racked the pump on the Ithaca, crunching another round into the barrel. He aimed it straight at Gerrard's chest and fired. The weapon boomed, and there was a *clunk* as the round hit the steel body armour.

It didn't get through.

But the force of the blast knocked Gerrard back.

Archer fired again, and again, and again. None of the shells were getting through, but the force was pushing Gerrard backwards.

Towards the rear of the helicopter.

Towards the spinning rotors on the tail.

Archer fired twice more. Gerrard was thrown back, inches from the spinning blades. Archer paused, as Gerrard looked at him, his eyes wide through the visor of the helmet. He saw his eyes narrow and he recovered his balance. He thought he was safe. The Ithaca only carried seven shells. But Archer had also loaded one in the chamber.

Which made eight.

Archer racked the pump and pulled the trigger for the last time. The weapon exploded and the shell rocked Gerrard back into the rotors.

He screamed under the helmet as the spinning blades tore into him. They were spinning so fast, they shredded him into pieces, blood and flesh spraying into the air. What was left of him dropped to the floor, a severed and sliced mix of clothing, body armour and shredded flesh, bits of him scattered on the runway.

Katic pulled Jessie upright and hugged her, both of them crying. Behind them, there was a sudden clanging on the gate and Archer turned, seeing a fleet of NYPD squad cars and black vehicles from the FBI pouring into the empty airport.

He loosened the shotgun from the strap around his shoulder and lowered it to the ground, his hands in the air. As he dropped to his knees, he looked over at Gerrard's shredded body. His father's old friend. The man who betrayed and murdered him.

But now it was all over.

He'd fulfilled his promise.

THIRTY SEVEN

Once the NYPD and FBI arrived at the crime-scene, two things happened. Archer was arrested and taken back into Manhattan to Federal Plaza in handcuffs. The three hostages were freed and cleaned up and taken downtown as well. The officers who arrived were shocked, the same as the officers who'd arrived in Flushing Corona Park. Both crime-scenes were absolute bloodbaths. The total body-count in the half-hour was fourteen dead. Three of the most wanted bank robbers in the state, six NYPD cops, three SWAT team officers and two Federal agents.

Debriefing had taken another twenty four hours. Archer's story checked out, and every cent from the MSG heist was returned in the two black bags he'd brought to the airport. Sanderson and Katic had immaculate records with the Bureau and they backed up every word of Archer's story, each telling the interviewing detectives their version of events.

To strengthen the case, detectives at the scene also found a playing tape recorder inside one of the two money bags Archer had bought from a hardware store on the Upper East Side. They'd rewound the tape and heard confessions from both Siletti and Gerrard, admissions of guilt, before the noise of the helicopter drowned out their voices.

Archer admitted to killing the two Federal agents, but together, the pair of them had murdered four other Federal agents, including his father. Thankfully, the detective heading up the investigation was sympathetic; he also soon realised that without Archer's help they probably would have got away with it. He said it was unclear what had happened due to the noise on the tape. It seemed that Farrell and his team had been in a shoot-out with Gerrard and Siletti and the two sides had end up killing each other.

A call from Atlantic City PD reported that a man booked into the hotel under a false name had been found dead in his room, shot through the head. They checked out his ID and found his real name was Tate. The bags inside the helicopter were found to contain close to four million dollars with two more in the back of Tate's stolen car, almost every cent from the two Chase heists and the armoured truck at the Tennis Center. All the money was booked and returned, which pleased everyone, especially the insurance companies.

Archer and Katic were interrogated all night as Jessie was cleaned up, checked by a doctor and reassured by a female agent looking after her. She was scared and would need time to recover, but thankfully the blindfold had shielded her from seeing the carnage. Inside the interrogation rooms, Archer and Katic gave them every detail, from the very beginning, every angle. It was a long night.

Luckily however, once Sanderson cleaned himself up and got medical attention, he took over the investigation. Katic had an immaculate record as a Special Agent and the bruising on her face and body spoke for themselves, so her testimony checked out. And the taping Archer had recorded from inside the money bags confirmed everything they were saying.

With Sanderson's support and approval, they were home free. Not only had they taken down one of the worst bank robbing crews in the history of the city, they'd also removed two Federal agents who'd gone bad, men who'd killed four fellow agents. Needless to say, Archer was flavour of the month down at Federal Plaza. Seeing as he hadn't eaten all day, one of the agents even went down to Subway for him and got him some food.

As the clock ticked on towards Monday evening, one of the detectives seemed to be concerned about everything that Archer had seen. He was playing the hard cop, but Archer was too tired to even care.

'You know an awful lot. I trust we can expect total silence from you,' he said, sliding a prepared document over the table. 'You say a word to anyone about any of this, rest assured we won't be this nice. You're lucky we're even considering releasing you.'

'I'll sign it on one condition.'

'I'm not here to bargain.'

'I think you are. One of your agents murdered my father.'

Pause.

'What do you want?'

'Install Katic as head of the Bank Robbery Task Force. All that I ask. Make her the Supervisory Special Agent.'

The man looked at him, then nodded.

'That's it?'

'That's it.'

'OK. Deal.'

They shook on it, then Archer read through and signed the paper. The man swept it off the table.

'OK. You're free to go.'

Archer had left the interrogation room, gathered his coat and meagre belongings and headed outside into the main Plaza. Katic was standing out there waiting for him. No sign of her daughter.

It was just approaching dusk and the plaza was bathed in a golden glow as the sun set in the distance. She smiled as he approached her.

'Where's Jessie?' he asked.

'With her grandma. She came down from Chicago and is looking after her. You missed your flight,' she said.

He nodded.

'And your booking at the hotel ran out.'

He nodded.

'C'mon, you can stay with me.'

He didn't speak.

He just moved forward and kissed her.

And she kissed him back.

At Katic's apartment, an agent had left a message on Archer's phone. He said the Bureau had contacted British Airways and organised another flight home for him. Club Class again. This time, Archer had a feeling he was going to enjoy it a hell of a lot more.

With some spare cardboard covering the hole on the front door to her apartment and the holes in her bedroom door and with the place tidied up, Archer and Katic spent the rest of the day and night together. As they lay there together, Katic talked at length about her life since her husband died. Archer talked about his father, the time they had spent together before he'd left all those years ago and found that he felt strangely at peace with it now. That feeling of regret he'd carried with him all week was gone.

By the time morning came and they woke up, the two of them knew almost every detail about each other. But one thing that Archer didn't tell her was that she was being promoted. He figured it would be a pleasant surprise that would come best from the FBI.

Archer's flight wasn't until 6 pm, so they had the whole next day. They spent it wandering the streets, enjoying the end of the summer, Jessie back with them again, still shaken up but starting to recover with that inner resilience that kids have. They ended up in a playground in Tompkins Square Park, near Katic's apartment. Archer looked at the surroundings and realised this was where the photo had been taken of the three of them, Katic, her husband and Jessie.

As they sat there on a bench side-by-side, watching Jessie playing around with two other kids, Katic spoke.

'You know you're the first man I've been with since Ricky died,' she said.

He nodded. 'Don't feel guilty. He'd want you to move on.'

'I know. I feel that now.'

She looked at the trees, at her daughter going down the slide, playing with the other kids.

'God, it's beautiful here.'

He turned to say something, but he never got the chance. She kissed him hard, and he kissed her back. She withdrew and looked at him, her arms around his shoulders.

'Will you come back?' she asked.

He nodded. 'Of course.'

'I'll be here,' she said.

And he kissed her again.

When the sun started to set in the distance, the three of them jumped into a fresh Bureau car Katic had been given and headed through the city towards the Midtown Tunnel and Queens towards John F Kennedy airport. They could have gone through Brooklyn, which would have been quicker, but Archer wanted to make one last stop first.

He was standing back in that graveyard in Queens. Unlike the funeral the other day, the crowd of mourners were gone and he stood there all alone, looking at his father's headstone. The sun had started to move down the sky towards the horizon, and the place was lit up like gold in the late-afternoon light.

He stood there for ten minutes, alone with his father. Behind him Katic watched, leaning against the side of her car, Jessie beside her holding her hand, both of them looking on in silence.

In front of the grave, Archer took one last look at the headstone.

'Take care, Dad,' he whispered quietly. Then he smiled. *'And keep a look out for me. The way things have been going, I think I'm gonna need it.'*

He stood there for a few more moments.

Then he turned and headed over to Katic, who fired the engine and took him straight to the airport.

The plane crossed the Atlantic during the night and touched down in the UK at 7.30 am the next day, Wednesday. Archer once again missed the comforts of Club Class, sleeping the entire flight, but when they landed he felt good and ready to go. After disembarking and making his way through security he jumped on the Heathrow Express to Paddington, then took the Underground and headed straight home, grabbing a quick shower and changing his clothes. He took his car keys and locking up the apartment, moved outside to his car, firing the engine and heading straight to the ARU headquarters.

The drive took him about ten minutes and he saw the familiar building appear, moving into the car park and pulling into an empty space. Stepping out and locking the car, he walked into the building, signed in and headed straight upstairs for the briefing room.

He walked inside, and saw all his team-mates. Chalky and Porter, drinking coffee and talking. Fox and Deakins, arguing about something. And Mac, their sergeant, standing by the coffee stand, pouring himself a cup.

They all looked over as he entered.

'Hey, look who it is!' Deakins said. 'Welcome back.'

Archer grinned and nodded, moving to the drinks stand and pouring himself a cup of tea. Mac patted him on the shoulder as he stood next to him.

'Welcome back.'

Archer turned, cup in hand and walked over, taking a seat with the other officers on the team.

'I heard Cobb put you up on the Unit's budget. Lucky bastard,' Chalky said. 'Free trip to New York for a week.'

'How was it Arch?' Porter asked. 'You stay out of trouble?'

Archer looked over at him and smiled.

'Yeah. More or less.'

THE END

###

About the author:

Born in Sydney, Australia and raised in England and Brunei, Tom Barber has always had a passion for writing and story-telling. It took him to Nottingham University, England, where he graduated in 2009 with a 2:1 BA Hons in English Studies. Post-graduation, Tom moved to New York City and completed the 2 Year Meisner Acting training programme at The William Esper Studio, furthering his love of acting and screen-writing.

Upon his return to the UK in late 2011, Tom set to work on his debut novel, *Nine Lives*, which has since become a five-star rated Amazon UK Kindle hit. The following books in the series, *The Getaway, Blackout, Silent Night*, *One Way* and *Return Fire* have been equally successful, garnering five-star reviews in the US and the UK.

The Getaway is the second novel in the Sam Archer series.

Follow @TomBarberBooks.

Read an extract from

Blackout

By

Tom Barber

The third Sam Archer thriller.

*****

ONE

It was a few minutes to midnight on a spring night in London.

Inside a medium-sized office on the top floor of a three-storey building in West London, a man in his late-thirties was just finishing annotating the last page of eleven sequential A4 sheets of paper, his brow furrowed in concentration as he worked. He was a politician, but about as far removed from the stereotypical type as you could get.

Unlike a number of people in that career who so often sported the pasty complexion and soft, flabby physique that came with too much time sitting behind a desk, the man examining the papers had skin tanned and weathered by years in warmer climates. He was built like a professional rugby player, powerful arms and shoulders with not an ounce of excess body-fat on his midriff. He had a dark-featured chiselled face, a warm smile when he chose to use it and possessed a charisma that perfectly suited his chosen path as a politician. Collectively, these attributes had earned him a legion of admirers and supporters not just in his constituency but across the country. He'd entered politics on a sheer whim a couple of years ago, and no-one was more surprised than he at the meteoric success he'd enjoyed so far.

However, as humble as the man was, it wasn't a fluke that he'd done so well. Officially, the tabloids said it was due to his *inspiring and morale-boosting speeches* and his *refreshingly straightforward and honest approach.*

But as his campaign manager had told him, he ticked two very important boxes as a front-runner in the elections, two things that probably wouldn't make the bold print of the newspapers but nonetheless were qualities that none of his competition shared. Women wanted to sleep with him and men wanted to buy him a beer.

Handsome, eloquent and charismatic, he was very much a maverick in the Kennedy and Obama mould, someone the public could relate to and get behind, a surprise but sure-fire candidate for leader of the party in due course. *Show business for ugly people* was how politics was often described. The man working on the papers behind the desk in his office that evening was definitely an exception.

Changing one final word on the last sheet of the pile, the man dropped the pen on the page and stretched back in his seat, yawning, wearily rubbing his face. He'd been working on this speech for weeks, and tomorrow was the day he would finally deliver it. He knew its success would either make or break his campaign.

He was due to speak at 11 am to a worker's union across the city in Dalston, outlining his planned reforms and intentions for growth in the area if they chose to get behind him and help him get elected. Their support was crucial. He knew he had the middle-class vote in the bag. If he got the Dalston backing, it would be a clincher. Get them on his side, win the seat and who knew what could happen next. Given his recent run of success, he was sure as the night was dark that he could get to 10 Downing Street one day. He'd always been an ambitious man, and as everyone around him had started to realise, his confidence was infectious. Day by day, public belief in the man was growing, matching the same inner sureness that he'd always had in himself.

He stretched the tight muscles of his neck from side to side, rubbing the day's worth of stubble that had accumulated on his chin and cheeks. Blinking fatigue from his eyes, he checked the clock on the wall across the room. He caught it just as the long hand ticked forward, nestled side-by-side with the small hand. 11:59 pm. *Time to head home.* He needed to be on his best form tomorrow and that meant a solid night's sleep, or as good a one as he could get considering the importance of tomorrow's commitments.

He rose from his desk, reshuffling the series of papers carefully into numerical order, then slid them into a slender brown folder resting on the desktop. Closing it, he placed the folder inside his briefcase and clicked it shut, spinning the two three-digit dials with his thumbs.

He was wearing dark suit trousers with a light-blue shirt, and the sleeves were rolled up to reveal thick forearms and a series of faded tattoos. Working here at night alone was usually the only time that he could get away with revealing them, the only other place away from the privacy of his own home. At all other times, he had to keep the sleeves rolled down which was a bitch in hot weather. Personally, he liked the ink-work, but he wasn't a fool and knew the common stigmas that were frequently associated with tattoos. His campaign manager had emphasised some potential supporters still on the fence could perceive them in a less than positive way. He thought his manager was being over-cautious, but at this point every vote mattered and the politician with the tattoos couldn't afford to become complacent. Once he was elected, he could roll his sleeves up, literally. But for now, in public and with elections still on-going, the ink would remain covered.

He pulled on the jacket and tightened his tie, then checked the rest of his office. He had everything he needed. Across the room, the tall windows were shut and locked, long red curtains drawn in front of them. He would be back here in six hours, but that gave him more than sufficient time for a rest and was all he really needed. He used to manage on half or a third of that in his former life, hunkered down in foxholes, bunkers or military camps in dark corners around the world. Six hours was plenty.

Walking around his desk, the man moved to the door and stepped outside, then shut and locked it behind him, the briefcase in his right hand. He stood at the top of stairs, the building around him still and quiet, the only sound the faint ticking of a large grandfather clock downstairs in the reception hall. His offices were above a law firm and an up-and-coming showbusiness agency, so the silence in the building was a welcome contrast to the constant hustle and bustle of the day. He figured there might still be some people in the law offices below, unfortunate souls who were pulling an all-nighter, working hard on cases and scouring legal documents that couldn't wait until morning. He knew how they'd be feeling. He'd slept here a few times himself on a couch in his office.

Double-checking he had everything, the man turned and moved down the carpeted stairs towards the ground floor. To the right of the front door was a reception desk and to his surprise, despite the lateness of the hour, his receptionist was still sitting there, her head down, hard at work on something, distracted. She was a sweet girl called Jamie, just turned twenty five. She'd knocked on the front door at the beginning of the year asking if there was any work going in the building. She explained that she'd graduated last summer from a well-respected university with a good degree, but unfortunately, with the current state of the economy, such qualifications no longer guaranteed a job in the City, or in any city in fact. The man had liked her instantly, admiring her resourcefulness and after approval from the law firm and the showbiz agency he'd offered her a spot running the front desk. She'd proven adept at her role, working from morning to night without complaint, juggling the needs of the law firm, the agency and the up-and-coming politician's office. Altogether, she did a fine job.

Just as the grandfather clock in the hall struck midnight, she sensed him coming down the stairs. She looked up and smiled. There was a pause as both of them waited for the twelve chimes on the clock to pass so they could hear each other speak.

'Good evening, sir,' she said, once the building was quiet again, the last chime echoing in the hall.

'What are you still doing here, Jamie?' the man asked, stepping onto the marble floor and approaching the desk. 'It's late. You should be at home.'

'I've got some exams coming up for my law course. Here's a good a place to study as any.'

'When are the exams again?'

'In a couple of weeks.'

'Well, good luck. I'll see you tomorrow. Don't stay too late.'

'Yes, sir. Good night.'

He nodded and moved to the door.

'Oh, sir?' she added.

He turned. Jamie reached for something on her desk and held it towards him.

It was a letter.

'I almost forgot. This arrived for you about an hour ago. I didn't want to come up and disturb you, but it's addressed to you personally.'

He frowned and reached over, taking it and examining it in his hand, turning it over and checking both sides.

'Mail? At this time of night?'

She nodded.

'Did you see who delivered it?' he asked.

She shook her head.

'It just dropped through the letter box,' she said. 'As you say though, it seemed strange so I opened the door and checked outside. I couldn't see anyone. Whoever posted it had gone.'

He looked at it in his hands, then shrugged.

'OK. See you tomorrow,' he said, and pulling open the front door, he left.

Outside, the man walked down a couple of steps and passing through a small black metal gate, he crossed a cobbled road and headed towards his car, a black Volvo, parked across the street. Although it was midnight, the street-lights lining the pavements clearly illuminated either side of the road, breaking up the shadows and providing light for anyone out and about. Although the pavements were quiet, the man could hear soft and slightly muffled activity coming from a pub up the street on the corner. The street itself was still, with no traffic. Most of its daytime residents were already at home, but a faint glimmer of light was still visible from slits and cracks in curtains that weren't entirely closed, most likely workers pulling a late one or people who lived here.

Putting his briefcase down on the cobbled ground, the man took the keys to the Volvo from his pocket and clicked his car open. He pulled open the door and climbed inside, slamming the door shut behind him. He placed the briefcase on the passenger seat and tossed the letter on top of it, then slid the key into the ignition and prepared to twist it.

But then he thought for a moment and changed his mind, taking his hand off the keys.

He glanced down at the letter.

He was intrigued.

Who the hell would drop off mail this late at night?

Reaching over, he picked it up. He ripped open the envelope, then pulled out a letter.

He unfolded it and started to read, curious.

He read it from beginning to end, slowly.

He only read it once.

Then he found two photographs inside the envelope. He looked at them both, staring at each one slowly, examining every millimetre, every pixel of detail.

And for the next hour, he remained where he was.

He didn't move.

He barely even blinked.

He just stared straight ahead, the letter and pair of photographs resting on his lap.

Not long after he read the letter, Jamie stepped out of the building across the street and locked up, but she didn't notice him sitting there in the car. She headed off down the pavement, turning the corner and disappeared out of sight, as the man sat motionless in the Volvo, staring unseeingly through the front windscreen.

After just over an hour had passed, he made a decision and twisted the keys, firing the ignition. He drove straight home, on autopilot. The next thing he knew he was parked outside his front door, in a quiet neighbourhood in the west of the city. He got out of the car and shutting the door behind him, walked up to the front door and entered his home.

He moved into the house quietly, listening, waiting. There was nothing. The residence was silent and dark. He placed his keys gently on a table by the door, and then headed straight upstairs. After a few moments, he came back down again slowly, in a daze, walked to the kitchen and took a seat at the table in the dark, all alone, a still black figure silhouetted by the moonlight from the open curtains behind him.

He sat motionless for some time. Then he rose and walked into his den next door. Pulling open the top drawer of his desk, he retrieved two separate items and tucked one into each pocket.

Then he walked back into the hallway, grabbed his coat and left the house.

He sat on a bench on the South Bank until morning. He watched the sun rise on the horizon, bathing the London skyline in an orange glow, the air fresh, the smell of salt from the Thames in the air, the city waking up from a deep slumber in front of him. It was one of the most beautiful things he'd ever seen. He felt unaccustomed tears well in his eyes as he looked at the view, the sun slowly bringing light to the city and the start of a new day.

He checked his watch. Then he reached into the inside pocket of his suit jacket and pulled out the letter and the two photographs. He took a lighter from another pocket and sparked a flame. He set the paper and photos on fire, watching them curl and burn away between his fingers, eventually dropping the smoking edges of what was left on the ground by his foot, twisted, black and destroyed.

He then reached into his pocket again and pulled out something else.

It was an old revolver, six bullets inside, the second item he'd retrieved from the desk in his den.

He put it in his mouth and pulled back the hammer with his forefinger.

He took one last look at the city in front of him.

And he pulled the trigger.

8611928R00181

Printed in Great Britain
by Amazon.co.uk, Ltd.,
Marston Gate.